Books by Gloria Herrmann

Single in Seattle

Reeling in Love
Puppy Love

Reeling in Love

ISBN # 978-1-78686-130-6

©Copyright Gloria Herrmann 2017

Cover Art by Posh Gosh ©Copyright 2017

Interior text design by Claire Siemaszkiewicz

Totally Bound Publishing

Single in Seattle

REELING IN LOVE

GLORIA HERRMANN

Dedication

Friends are the family we get to choose for ourselves.
I want to thank Wendy Porter for being my sister from another mister — for sticking with me when others couldn't. This woman truly gets me and has helped to keep me sane through every book I have written since we became besties. She understands why I wanted to write this story and why it was so important for me to showcase the good, the bad, and the not so pretty sides of friendship. I know that, no matter what, she will always be right there with me, probably laughing at me but also taking part in my shenanigans. I love ya, Wendy, my sexy and crazy Scottish friend for life.

I have had many friends cross my path and appreciate every experience that came with those friendships. They all shaped my concept for this story in some way or another.
I need to thank my mom, Connie Terpening, for being my best friend and knowing and keeping all the secrets of my heart. She taught me many things, like how to be trustworthy, kind and how to be a good friend. My mom also showed me how to love hard, to fight and to survive this crazy thing called life. Sometimes thank you is just not enough for lessons like that. I love you, Mom.

Chapter One

"I think we got it," Molly said confidently to the almost naked man standing in the corner, wearing nothing but a stark white towel draped across his tan waist.

"You sure?"

Molly nodded as she scrutinized her work. "Yeah, the lighting was brilliant. I don't think we could have done any better."

"If you say so. You're the expert with that thing." The model pointed at the large camera Molly cradled in her hands, the screen displaying the digital shots from the day of working with him.

Molly loved her job as a professional photographer. Her friends were insanely jealous. What woman wouldn't be? She spent her days in her studio behind the lens of her trusty camera, capturing sexy images of some of the most gorgeous men from all over the world. Either she was paid to travel to them or they flew to Seattle to have her work her magic. Authors in the romance industry adored her photos. Her attention to detail had won her awards over the years, but what she loved the most was bringing the characters from books alive. Sure, it didn't hurt to look at well-defined muscles and sculpted abs that begged to be touched and to know what was hidden beneath the scrap of cloth that usually covered these men, but that wasn't how the business worked. Her friends would argue it was just because Molly didn't throw herself at these scantily clad men that she was missing out on these valuable opportunities.

If they only knew how nervous most of these men were, their fragile egos stripped down for her. It took Molly the first half of the shoot to calm them, easing them out of their shells, getting them just to loosen up enough for the right shot. It was more like babysitting rather than staring at a buffet, despite what her best friends thought. Not all the models lacked self-confidence, however. There were some who would stroll in, look directly into the camera and own it. But, for the most part, a lot of the guys were unsure and needed coaxing. Molly often felt more like a counselor than the world-famous photographer that she was.

Today, the Seattle sun was shielded behind soft, white clouds, filtering its rays into her studio that overlooked the Puget Sound. Her tall, glass windows provided the most stunning views of the shimmering water and the bustling city. Molly had worked hard for this view. It hadn't come easy or cheap — or without her busting her ass to make her name known in the photography industry. She had the scars — mostly emotional, but scars, nonetheless — to prove the struggles she'd endured, climbing to the top. Now she was one of the most sought-after photographers. Models from all over the globe wanted her to shoot them. *New York Times* and *USA Today* bestselling authors and publishers almost begged for her to shoot their covers. They wanted the best and…well, Molly was. Her skills proved that she had something special and everyone knew it.

Not bothering to sit down at her desk — bending over, instead — to focus on the images she was uploading to her laptop to edit, she almost forgot to say goodbye to the model she had just worked with. It wasn't until he was standing close to her, now fully dressed, that she realized he was still in her studio. Having him near her like that shifted the atmosphere in the room. His dominating presence was invading her space, creating nervous waves in her stomach. She inhaled his expensive aftershave, looked up from her screen and smiled.

Molly managed to say, "Great shoot today. Thanks again."
Remember to breathe, Molly.
"Yeah, it was amazing. You're amazing." The man

paused, running his fingers along his day-old beard, the perfect blend of refined and unkempt sexy. His voice was silky and oozed well-practiced enticement. Molly watched him stand still, contemplating his next move. She was tempted to grab her camera and snap another shot. The light was hitting him just right and his pose was thoughtful and natural. This man was gorgeous.

He turned his mesmerizing gaze toward her and asked, "Do you want to grab a drink?"

Molly swallowed. It wasn't the first time she had been asked out by a model after a shoot. Sometimes it was the result of having bonded over their frail vulnerabilities. Sometimes they figured she was as good a lay as any while they were in town — another stamp in their romantic passport, so to speak. Molly wasn't so sure about this one. He wasn't overly emotional or guarded about his body, nor did he seem to really desire her. *So, what is he after?* She watched him scan the large studio. There was her answer. This type of square footage didn't come cheap and he knew that.

"You know, maybe another time. I'm really excited to get this edited." Molly pointed at her sleek silver laptop, delivering a fake smile in hopes it would put him off.

He nodded and thanked her again as he saw himself out. *The nerve.* Molly rolled her eyes and released the air she had been holding in her lungs. While she was in mid sigh, her cell phone chirped.

"Hello," she answered, a little more gruffly than she'd intended.

"Wow, so what's with the 'tude, lady? Bad day?"

It was one of her best friends, Tiffany.

"Just got done working with a model."

"Well, then why do you sound all cranky? Was he awful? So good-looking that you couldn't handle it?" Tiffany teased, causing Molly to laugh and her mood to lighten.

"You know the type. He wanted to go out for drinks — "

Tiffany cut her off quickly. "And you said, yes, right?

7

Because if you didn't, you honestly need to have your head examined."

"I'd have to say he was more interested in my real estate than me." Molly frowned.

"Like real estate, as in the prime location between your legs? You know, it's all about location, location, location, baby."

"I wish." Molly huffed in frustration. "No, more like the prime location of my studio."

"That sucks."

"Tell me about it. He was gorgeous and he smelled divine. He was totally your type—tall, dark and devilishly handsome."

She heard Tiffany's disappointment through the phone. "Really? Oh, I just don't know how you do it, Molly. I have to give it to you. I would simply come undone working with those gorgeous men and not taking advantage of them every chance I got."

Tiffany always acted like she was some aggressive sex kitten, but they knew the truth. She was actually quite timid, which was a huge reason why she was single. All three of them were single and not dating anyone special. It didn't usually work that they were unattached all at the same time, but they were now. Their other best friend, Mackenzie, was the mother hen of the group. Well, more like the bossy one—completely overbearing, but with an absolute heart of gold. She, too, teased Molly about her line of work, but Mackenzie loved being a teacher, as it helped fill her maternal void. They had biological clocks that had gone haywire over the last couple of years, but everyone had warned them as they entered the dirty thirties that baby fever would hit soon after, and it had for Tiffany and Mackenzie. Every time they passed a stroller, neither could resist the temptation of peering in to catch a glimpse of some infant swaddled in fuzzy pink or blue blankets. Molly? She had her moments. They were brief and passed quickly when she heard the wail of a newborn or the shrill sound of a tantrum from a toddler. That didn't tempt her to want to rent out her womb for nine months.

She looked at her spotless, chic studio. Her smile went deep into her soul, masking the want for a baby. Her space sparkled and gleamed with the afternoon Seattle sunlight, illuminating sleek lines and utterly contemporary taste.

If she were being completely honest with herself, yes, she did indeed want a child, eventually. But Molly also realized she was missing a very important part of the equation—a man. She didn't want just a sperm donor, though she and her friends had discussed that over far too much wine and Chinese food one night, considering it as a last resort. That had left them laughing for hours. No, Molly wanted the real deal. They all did. They wanted a man—a sexy, successful and simply wonderful man. *Is that really asking for too much?*

Being single, especially in Seattle, came with its challenges. Molly thought the enormous Emerald City should be plentiful with eligible bachelors, but Molly assumed that, as with any place, being single was a mixture of bad luck and an overly detailed list of the personality traits she wanted in a boyfriend. As time passed, her list had grown a lot shorter. She'd crossed off quite a few of her must-haves and was looking to review her available options. Now she figured it was mainly the bad luck that was keeping her single. Molly had been unattached the longest out of her friends, who were more like her sisters. Tiffany had been on a dating spree recently, but Mackenzie and Molly had known that none of the guys were Mr. Right for their friend. Mackenzie also had a pretty extensive list of requirements for her ideal mate, and she was even more stubborn than Molly when it came to sacrificing the qualities she was willing to live with, so she dated very little.

"Well, since you didn't want drinks with that sexy model, how about meeting up with us?" Tiffany asked.

Molly smiled. Yes, a drink with her best pals she could do. "That sounds lovely, actually." She could use some cheering up. The best cure for her bruised ego was some quality time with her besties.

"Great. I'll pick up Mac and we'll swing by the studio and grab ya. Sound good?"

"Perfect. I have some edits I want to go through, so just buzz when you guys get here."

Molly said goodbye and hung up. She stared at the monitor in front of her, the images of the model in various poses looking back her.

* * * *

Lost in her work tweaking the images with an array of filters, Molly was so engrossed that she almost didn't hear the loud buzzing that echoed off the large studio walls. She got up quickly from her desk and jogged to the massive double doors to let her friends in.

"Jeesh, what were you doing? I have been ringing that dang buzzer for, like, *forever*," Tiffany complained as she slipped past Molly into the studio. Mackenzie frowned and hugged Molly.

"We've only been standing outside the door for a minute," Mackenzie assured her.

Tiffany walked over to one of the large windows facing the Puget Sound. The sun was setting, casting a tangerine hue over the haze of the city. "God, do you ever get tired of this magnificent view?"

Molly shook her head as she joined her, staring out at the glittery lights in the surrounding buildings that seemed to stretch up toward the sky. "Nope."

"Yeah, I didn't think so." Tiffany laughed as she faced Molly. Her dark hair was loose on her thin shoulders. Tiffany's large eyes were a soulful brown and she had the best cheekbones. Tiffany was gorgeous in a unique and completely unexpected way. Molly's brain acted as a camera, capturing shots of her friend's delicate features as the sunset cast a shadowy light on her face. Tiffany sensed what Molly was doing and threw her a pouty look.

Mackenzie stood next them. The willowy blonde towered over Molly, making her feel short and stubby. Mackenzie had the figure of a teenager, slim and athletic. Her sun-kissed hair was cut in a sleek bob, framing the sharp angles of her face. She was another beautiful woman. Molly couldn't help but snap mental pictures of Mackenzie, too. She searched Molly curiously with soft mocha eyes. They all had brown eyes in varied shades of the common color, but resembling their different tastes in coffee. Tiffany had the espresso, dark and bold. Mackenzie was more of an iced mocha with an extra shot. Molly's resembled the instant crap coffee variety that no one really liked. Molly hated her eyes. They were plain. Her friends had tried to convince her otherwise, but they both had spectacular depth and richness in theirs. Molly thought hers looked like a muddy puddle after a typical downpour in Seattle—watery, with a sad, muted tone. Nothing special.

"What's going on with you?" Mackenzie reached for Molly, concern swimming in her eyes and worry creasing her otherwise wrinkle-free face, the result of fabulous genetics.

Molly sighed. *Is there anything going on with me?* They usually accused her of being moody, but she was an artist. *Isn't that sort of the job description? Acting the part of the tortured soul?* They sure never let her play that role for very long.

Tiffany stared at her hard and added, "Yeah, you seemed cranky on the phone. So what's up?"

"I don't know. I mean…" Molly really couldn't explain how she felt. She had a blessed life. Granted, she had worked for it, but, regardless, she knew she was lucky. Happy? Well, that was a different ball of wax.

"Drinks. That's what we need." Tiffany perked up, her hand on her hip, taking a sassy stance. She reached for the oversized purse that was slung over her shoulder. A Louis Vuitton knock-off, but it looked as real as they came. It was their little secret. Tiffany dug around and retrieved a bottle of Prosecco, holding it up for them to all gaze at her prize.

"You were carrying that in there? Oh dear. Seriously, Tiffany," Mackenzie scolded.

Tiffany winked and answered with a wicked grin.

"I, for one, am thrilled our friend is lugging around a bottle. You never know when you may need it." Molly grinned happily at Tiffany. "It does make you look a little like a wino, but you're my favorite drunk."

"No, you have me mistaken. I'm fun, not a drunk." Tiffany defended as she moved toward a long table that was against the wall opposite the windows. "Besides, at least I bring the good stuff."

"I have an idea. Let's stay in. Want to order some food?" Mackenzie suggested.

"Yes, let's do that. Molly's got one of the best views in all of Seattle. Let's just hang out here," Tiffany replied while she peeled the label away to get to the cork.

"Chinese?" Mackenzie whipped out her cell phone and started to dial their favorite takeout.

"Hell, yes," Molly and Tiffany answered in unison.

These were her girls. It didn't matter if they stayed in or went out on the town. As long as they were together, they were guaranteed to have fun.

Shortly, they were seated around a large glass table that Molly normally used to lay out prints from shoots. They dined on their fill of chow mein, pork fried rice and more Kung Pao shrimp than any woman should ever eat. White cartons, soy sauce packets and chopsticks were littered around them as they chatted about everything—mostly about the lack of sex or romance in their lives. Biting into a crispy fortune cookie—her favorite—Molly surveyed her beautiful friends. She couldn't understand why any of them were single. Tiffany was gorgeous, sweet and sassy... What was there not to love about her? Mackenzie was stunning, witty and full of love... She had so much to offer. Then there was her. She knew she might not be the sexiest thing on the planet, but she was successful, caring and everyone constantly complimented her on how pleasant she was, even telling her she was sort of hot, especially when she wore her glasses. *So how is it that I haven't landed the perfect guy yet?* Cracking open another cookie, she read the thin slip of white paper. Bold red font stared back at her, reading, *'There is nothing truer than the company of friends.'* How right is that fortune?

More wine flowed and, to keep the mood light, Molly blasted the radio. She and her two best friends danced barefoot in the empty studio, singing their hearts out and putting on a drunken performance that could rival the best pop star's. Tiffany swayed her hips to the song. Mackenzie took a while to loosen up, but then started to bop to the beat. Molly busted out some goofy moves that reminded her of middle school dances, her favorite being the 'running man'. They laughed hard, clutching their sides when Tiffany took a spill on the slippery wood floor. In their feeble attempt at helping her up, they all ended up on the floor somehow, spread-eagled, staring up at the vaulted ceilings. Music continued to play, filling the wide and open space, but the mood had shifted. That was when the laughter died and the deep realness of their friendship was exposed.

"I love you, guys," Tiffany whispered, her dark tresses fanned out against the honey-colored bamboo floor.

"Me too," Mackenzie added softly.

Molly tried to swallow the lump that was forming in her throat, feeling tears starting to surface. "I love you both. Thank you for tonight."

They all stayed on the floor, listening to several more songs before Tiffany said, "God, this floor is killing my back. I feel old."

Mackenzie and Molly both laughed.

"And for the record, we *are* old," Mackenzie replied.

"I wanted to say the same thing, but figured I would tough it out until one of you cracked." Molly started to get up.

Mackenzie and Tiffany groaned as they eased themselves

off the floor. Working quietly as a team, they cleaned up the remnants of their dinner.

"I would totally live here, Molly," Mackenzie commented as she tossed several cartons into a waste basket.

Tiffany was wiping up some sticky Kung Pao sauce. "Seriously. This studio is so fabulous. You need to let me move in here."

"I do love this place." Molly looked around at her kingdom. An enormous clear-glass shelf that held her many awards was against one of the walls. Expensive frames that contained some of her best work were hung precisely in the perfect locations. Various shades, light fixtures and tons of other photography gear were set up in one corner. The room celebrated her. It showcased all of her efforts but, more importantly, it proudly displayed her passion for this form of art.

After every last morsel was cleaned and the work space was back to being immaculate, they made their way back to the window. The sun had long since disappeared, leaving the city lights to twinkle silently as the three of them stared out at the busy traffic below.

"Thank you again, guys. I really needed this tonight."

Mackenzie and Tiffany linked their arms through hers as she stood in the middle.

She would be lost without them. They knew all her secrets and her fears. They had supported her during her moments of crippling self-doubt. They'd loved her when she was at her worst. They'd dried her tears when critics had given her harsh reviews. They were her cheerleaders. They'd pushed her to continue to pursue her dream so many times when she'd just wanted to give up. They had been the first to celebrate when she finally did become successful and had told her countless times how much she deserved it.

These women were more than just friends. They were her tribe, her sisters. They were Molly's everything.

Chapter Two

Molly watched as a seagull snatched a dirty French fry from the asphalt. She sipped her to-go coffee. The cinnamon-infused latte was an early afternoon treat that Tiffany had insisted on, and it was simply delicious. The mere mention of caffeine had been enough to lure Molly away from her studio, and it was a brilliant opportunity to take her camera and maybe capture something cool. There were many perks to living in Seattle — great coffee, interesting people and places.

After setting her coffee back down on the weathered wooden bench they had been sitting on for the last thirty minutes or so, she twisted the plastic lens cap off her camera and peered through the tiny window to focus on the seagull that was attacking another fry.

"Those birds are gross," Tiffany stated as they both stared at the creature that was nearly bald on his left side, just under his soft white wings with their pale gray tips.

Molly came to his defense. "They kinda are, but they're just trying to survive. We all are." The gloomy weather matched her mood. She'd felt argumentative ever since she'd woken up. Her morning had started off pretty rough. Her coffee pot hadn't worked because she'd forgotten to set the timer the night before. When she'd showered, she'd reached for her conditioner, only to find the bottle completely empty — well, just about. She'd scraped what little conditioner was left on the sides of the bottle, getting her finger stuck once. No, the morning had been simply craptastic. Traffic on the way to her studio had been a nightmare, then, after locking herself inside her haven, she'd planned to work on some photos then found that they had just disappeared. Yeah, not a good day.

"Just look at that thing. He's missing a lot of feathers. Probably has rabies or something."

Molly zoomed in with her camera, seeing the patches of exposed pink skin on the bird. She snapped several pictures. "Poor thing probably has anxiety."

Tiffany kicked a stray French fry toward the bird, spooking it. The balding creature flew away in search of a safer place to dine on the tourists' scraps.

"So, no models today?" Tiffany asked as she combed her fingers through her long hair that the wind was quickly tangling. They sat there staring out at the dark and choppy water in front of them, the late afternoon sun partially hidden by growing storm clouds.

"Nope. I have a guy coming in later on this week for a shoot. He's supposed to be a really big deal."

"Really? Please let me know if he's single."

"Trust me. You don't want to date a model." Molly snapped a couple more pictures of some seagulls that caught her attention. They weren't bald like their buddy, who was still scavenging for rogue fries and popcorn left behind by people enjoying the waterfront.

"Well, let me find out the hard way. I'm so sick and tired of not finding anyone. I need a man, like...*badly*." Tiffany emphasized her feelings by throwing her arms up in the air suddenly.

Molly was unprepared for that and nearly dropped her camera.

"Look at all these people. Why can't I find one guy?"

"I get it and it sucks." A sudden wave of optimism washed over Molly. "But they say there's someone for everyone."

"Well, they're wrong. There are more women on the planet than men, so apparently *they* got their numbers all screwed up," Tiffany countered with a silly smirk.

"What about lesbians?"

Tiffany laughed and nodded. "Good point."

After finishing their coffees, they decided to walk along the pier. Molly would pause to capture shots of barnacle-covered boats that were anchored in the harbor. The pungent smell of the raw ocean was a scent that Molly loved. Something about the mix of the salty sea and the breeze made Molly feel better. Today had been crappy, but she was glad it might be finally turning around.

* * * *

The rest of the week was met with bouts of more awful rain, brief moments of sunshine and even a few seconds of hail. That was Seattle...the ever-unpredictable weather of the Emerald City. Molly was gazing out of her windows, rain splattering hard against the glass. She took in the sights of cars splashing through large, dirty puddles. She could hear the distant sounds of horns honking. No one was happy about this crummy weather. Molly peeked at her watch. Her model was late — not like fashionably late, more like several hours late. They had lost some unexpected sunshine that would have been perfect for shooting. Now she'd have to rely on artificial lighting. Molly grew more annoyed as time ticked on. *Where is this guy?* She'd already sent him a text message — no reply, of course. He'd better be worth the wait was all she could think when the buzzer chimed loudly.

She stomped to the doors to answer then opened them slowly. It was like opening a present, revealing whatever gorgeous thing that might be hidden behind them. And gorgeous it was. Standing at least six foot four and leaning against the door jamb was one of the most attractive men she'd ever seen. *So worth the wait.*

He flashed her a crooked grin and all was forgiven.

Oh, I'm in trouble with this one.

"I'm so terribly sorry. I meant to call, but my phone died." He waved a small black cell phone at her as some sort of proof.

"That's fine. It happens to the best of us. Come on in." Molly moved aside to let him pass.

"Wow, this space is incredible." He seemed to glide by her. His movements were graceful as he evaluated the studio.

"Thanks." Molly closed the doors and hurried to catch up with him. "As you can see, I normally get a ton of natural light, but the gods are frowning on us today."

"Or smiling on someone who's doing a rain dance," he said.

"We're in Seattle. No one is asking for rain." Molly felt herself grow nervous in his company. She watched as he ran his hand through his overgrown caramel-colored hair. It wasn't shaggy, but that perfect model-type hair, enough to manipulate for different looks. She envisioned what it would look like in the morning after he woke.

"So, what's the game plan?"

There was that crooked grin again. This time she noticed it was paired with green eyes that seemed to be sizing her up. Molly's core heated. *Oh, this man is good.* He knew the effect he had on women. It had been apparent the moment he winked at her and spun around to look out of her window.

"Killer view."

He can say that again. Molly couldn't take her eyes off him. This wasn't like her at all. She never responded this way. Well, that wasn't entirely true, but her body didn't usually have such an instant and wicked reaction to one of her models.

Standing next to him may not have been the brightest move on Molly's part. Being in that close a radius was driving her senses wild.

"So what kind of shots did you have in mind?"

Molly tried to keep her eyes trained on the traffic lights below, shining in all the puddles that had formed in the streets. But temptation got the best of her and she turned to meet his eyes. What she hadn't expected was him peeling off his shirt. As he removed it with such finesse, lifting the cotton garment that only moments earlier had stretched tightly across his well-sculpted chest, he revealed some of the most defined abs she'd ever encountered, which in her case were a lot. They were her weakness, her complete and utter undoing. The wonderful shape of the V... Not every guy had it, but when they did, it made her brain do silly things. His seemed to point into his jeans that were riding low on his hips. Her mouth suddenly grew dry and she swallowed to compose herself. He followed her eyes, his grin widened and he winked once more.

Molly prided herself on being able to stay professional. Temptation presented itself often, this being one of those times. She had worked too damn hard to soil her reputation. Granted, getting tangled up in the sheets with a guy that looked like the one standing before her would probably be incredible. But what would happen after that? He sure didn't look like the settling down, white-picket-fence type. She had to tear her eyes away from his colorfully inked arms. The muscles seem to flex all on their own. Her camera was about to have a field day with how hot this guy was, that she would be able to capture just the right angles for the author who had requested the use of this model for their cover. That was the easy part. The problem was his allure. He oozed sex appeal. He knew how good he looked. That was the annoying part of dealing with guys like him. Add in that when they were slightly interested, they thought they could turn on the charm by winking and smiling their way into her pants. *Yeah, not likely.* They didn't realize Molly had worked too damn hard, earned too much respect, to give all that up just for a night in bed.

"You ready to do this?" The model shot her a perfect set of stark white teeth that were cradled in luscious lips.

Molly blinked and tried to gather any professional fiber left in her being. "Absolutely."

Stay strong, Molly.

* * * *

"Pour me another, too," Molly whined. The buzz was settling in nicely. Her brain was fuzzy and everything was making her giggle.

"Oh, but of course." Tiffany grabbed the bottle and poured more wine into Molly's glass, then moved to fill Mackenzie's as well. She grabbed her own glass and shook out the last precious drops.

"So, what's the plan for tonight?" Mackenzie asked.

"To finish another bottle." Tiffany held up the now-bone-dry one and walked into the adjoining kitchen to retrieve another.

It was Friday night and, like every single Friday for as long as Molly could remember, they got together. They called it *Friendship Friday*. They would laugh all night, drink far too much, then cap it off by passing out in front of a rented movie. It was like a grown-up slumber party. They would rock pajamas, messy buns and no makeup. Usually, they would pick out a cheesy romantic comedy, a couple of bottles of wine to wash down the high calorie snacks they would scarf and stay up until the wee hours of the morning. Most of the Friday nights were awesome, but they had spent their share crying and drowning their broken hearts after break-ups, terrible losses or just the frustrations of adult life. There had been nights when they'd shared their dreams and hopes for the future, but what had always remained the same was that they'd spent Friday together, and the plan was in place to always do this.

"What movie did you get, Molly?" Mackenzie had hung her long legs over the arm of one of Tiffany's couches and she turned to face Molly, who was seated on the opposite couch with her legs tucked under her.

Tonight they were at Tiffany's. The rotation of hosting their *Friendship Friday* night kept things interesting. One of them would host, providing an ample buffet of all the most carb-infused goodness possible, another would bring the drinks and the other was responsible for finding something to entertain them. It was a simple plan and it worked.

Tiffany's apartment screamed shabby chic in the best way possible. Her style was eclectic, funky and it matched her personality to a T. It had a comfortable feel. She kept bright and colorful throw pillows everywhere that had the most incredible patterns. Velvety soft throws were lying on the mismatched furniture in the living room. It was warm and cozy, and Molly loved hanging out there. Tiffany lived in the newly redeveloped Fremont area. It had seen its share of not-so-good times, but now it was quickly being flipped into a trendy neighborhood inhabited by artists and hipsters. Cute shops and eateries were moving in and making it the cool place to be. Plus, it was home to the Fremont Troll, an enormous concrete sculpture that was under a bridge and becoming a growing attraction for tourists.

Shoving a throw pillow to her side, Molly got up to grab the rental she'd picked up on her way over. "Gosh, I can't remember." She felt a little wobbly as she fetched her purse and pulled out the clear plastic case. "Oh, it's that new one, with what's-his-face…"

"Um, can't think of his name, but I know which one you are talking about." Mackenzie looked up toward the ceiling as if the answer were written there.

"You know, that one guy… He was in the last thing we saw," Molly explained as she tossed the DVD case onto Mackenzie's flat tummy. The alcohol was not helping her memory at all.

Tiffany smiled. "No, it's not that guy. It's that other one. We watched his movie like two weeks ago, remember? I suggested this one because I knew it was coming out soon."

"Well, if you can remember all that, then how come you don't know his name?"

Tiffany lifted her drink. The red liquid sloshed inside the half-filled glass. "Because I have had too many of these."

"Point taken." Molly plopped back down next to Tiffany.

"God, what a week it has been." Molly groaned.

"How can you even complain?" Tiffany quickly replied. "Working with all those gorgeous men just has to be *so* difficult and wearing," Mackenzie teased and eyed Molly over the rim of her wine glass.

"It is. Trust me."

"Oh please. I'd kill to do what you do." Tiffany patted Molly's leg. "That model you shot yesterday was so hot. When you sent me a picture of him, I almost died."

"He was okay." Molly felt the lie slip off her tongue.

Tiffany's mouth gaped open. "Um, just okay? Did you not see those abs? Oh God…and those arms."

"Tiff is right. He was fine, Moll. I pretty much drooled all day over those pictures. You're mean, by the way, teasing your poor friends like that. You should have invited us to help with the shoot." Mackenzie giggled.

"Also, didn't you say something about wanting to do laundry on his washboard abs?" Tiffany added, smirking behind her wine glass.

"I said you could do laundry on them. Besides…been there, done that," Molly replied with a shrug.

"Well, damn, I hate you even more now. I want to be able to say that." Tiffany rolled her eyes.

"You know, Molly is right, too. Being with guys like that has to be difficult. They are constantly trying to maintain that level of perfection. I don't think I could ever feel comfortable being their girlfriend. Like, what if they were always comparing me to other better-looking or fitter women? I'd hate that." Mackenzie paused, looked at them thoughtfully. "I just want a guy that looks good and thinks I look just as good."

Mackenzie, Tiffany and Molly all raised their glasses. *Cheers to that.*

* * * *

"Okay, let me have you move to the left just a little." Molly was bent at an awkward angle, trying to capture the shot of the model in front of her. "No, too much. Right there. Hold it." *Snap. Snap.* Molly released the breath she had been holding in and so did the model.

"Thank God. I was worried I was going to pass out," the model said.

"Well, put in some more hours at the gym and you won't have to suck it in," Molly teased. She watched as he rubbed his very well-defined abs and saw the concern grow in his chocolate-colored eyes. *Oh dear*. This was a model she had worked with a number of times, and they were doing a brand new shoot for an up-and-coming author. She adored him and actually considered him a friend. "I'm just kidding, Peter. You're all sorts of delicious, babe."

She saw the relief flood him. The tension that had been in his face and eyes vanished.

"Seriously?" he asked.

These guys—most of them, anyway—were so worried that they weren't hot enough, and Molly couldn't help but wonder why they had even gone into modeling in the first place. They had to have realized at some point how incredibly gorgeous they were. But she supposed that everyone was insecure about something. If she even looked half as good as some of these models, she knew she wouldn't be insecure about that.

"Yes, these shots are fab." Molly examined the images on the small screen of her camera. They were good shots. He'd posed well and the lighting couldn't have been better. "You want to see?" Molly held up her camera for proof, daring him to peek at the remarkable images she had just viewed.

The model pulled a plain, white cotton T-shirt over his head, covering his tan and perfect torso. "Awesome." He looked at the small screen and sighed. "Hey, you wanna grab something to eat?"

Molly laughed, which wasn't her intention, but she just couldn't help it. "Weren't you just complaining about your body…like a minute ago?"

"Yeah, but you reassured me that I'm all kinds of delicious. I'll just hit the gym twice tomorrow."

"True." Molly's stomach growled at the mention of food.

"Sure. You got anything special in mind?"

"Yeah, I was thinking we could head on down to Pike Place. I'm kind of in the mood for some chowder."

"That sounds really good, actually." Even though the noon-day sun was burning brightly outside, the temperature had been chilly since the start of the day. It was spring, after all. The sun would often give a false sense of warmth, but she was thankful it had even made an appearance. Most of the week had delivered a torrent of rain to the city, flooding streets and making just getting around miserable. The leftover dampness had caused the air to feel downright cold when she'd woken up that morning.

Molly grabbed her coat and they left her studio in search of some food. The unexpected warmth was welcomed as they ventured out into the crowded streets. Chatting about nothing in particular, they edged toward their destination, the legendary sign clearly visible a few blocks away. The salty ocean breeze floated delicately around them. The pungent scent of raw fish tickled her nose as they approached the world-famous Pike Place Fish Market. Spectators were gathered as the afternoon's catch was thrown into the open area. Molly and Peter paused to watch as the men with their galoshes and rubber aprons flung the enormous fish through the air, catching every single one. Smiles and gaped-open mouths were plastered on the people, who were mesmerized by this act that had been a long-standing tradition, ever since Molly could remember. When she had been a little girl, her parents had taken her down to Pike Place. While her mother bought flowers and browsed the produce, her father would stand with her and watch in awe as the men brought in the day's catch in the most fun and exciting way.

"Look out!"

She heard the words, felt something hard hit her, then ringing echoed in her ears. Everything went black momentarily.

"Are you okay?"

Molly looked up to see stormy-gray eyes looking at her with concern.

Her hand was wet and her butt hurt. *What the hell happened?* She looked around and saw all the people staring at her, hands covering their mouths in shock. Peter, her model buddy, had grown pale and worry was etched on his perfect face. Molly tried to remove herself from the cold puddle she found herself in, thanks to the leftover rain.

"Oh, no. You just sit for a minute," Gray Eyes ordered.

Molly admitted defeat and remained seated. She tried wiping her hands on her jeans. Her butt was still cold, and now the embarrassment was settling in. "What happened?"

Peter crouched down next to her, smoothing her dark tresses that she had worn loose. As he gently moved the hair, she felt a soreness near the side of her head. She was confused and not quite certain of anything. She looked around, trying to make sense of everything. Then she realized where she was and what must have happened as she tried to rub the dull ache that was growing more uncomfortable. She wanted to die, to crawl under a rock or hide somehow. God, she'd gotten hit with a fish.

Kill me now.

As panic hit her, Molly tried to scurry away, but large, firm hands gripped her tightly.

"Ma'am, let's give it a few minutes, okay?"

Ma'am? Despite being utterly embarrassed and all out of sorts, being called 'ma'am' made her cringe. She could only nod. There was no point in resisting, plus those eyes and that sexy voice had a soothing effect on her. Since she wasn't getting up any time soon, she might as well take in the scenery. The man in front of her was gorgeous, in a completely different way from her model buddy, who was still in a state of shock.

"Molly, you went down like a ton of bricks. It all happened so fast." Peter sounded like he was about to cry. She couldn't help but think he was overreacting a tad. But she could admit that her ego and dignity were just as bruised as the side of her head. Heck, maybe even more so.

"Molly…so that's your name." Those gray eyes twinkled and a half-smile appeared.

Was it terrible that she was memorizing every fine line and wrinkle? The dark shadow of stubble covered his strong jaw line and the faint crow's feet gathered into feathery creases by his incredible eyes. She had decided they were her favorite feature of his. They reminded her of clouds when a storm was rolling in, varied shades of light and dark, mixed in a brilliant way that she couldn't stop staring at. If only she had brought her camera. She'd love a shot of him. She could picture it now — a black and white. His nose was slightly large but added character. His lips were full, and Molly absentmindedly licked hers. His wavy black hair had sneaky gray hairs by his temple. *Damn.* He was sexy all the way around.

"Well, Molly, you got in the way of one of my fish." When he spoke again, that pretty much sealed the deal for her.

Got in the way of his fish? She crinkled her brow and scowled at him. "Um, excuse me?"

The gray eyes laughed, right along with his sensual mouth — a full deep laugh. He was laughing at her and she didn't like it one bit. In fact, she found herself growing angry and annoyed. It was his stupid fault that she'd gotten hit. Now she was upset that she felt attracted to him. It was probably from being assaulted by his dumb fish. Molly rose a little too quickly from the damp cement floor. Her head throbbed and she was instantly caught by surprise with a wave of dizziness that washed over her. Molly's balance was off kilter, but somehow she managed to not hit the ground.

"Whoa. I told you not to get up yet, babe," he said, as he cradled Molly securely in his arms.

"I'm fine, really," Molly argued, but she couldn't help but enjoy being held.

"Yeah, I can see that," he fired back, amusement dancing in his sea of gray.

Peter moved to her side. "Molly, maybe we should go to a hospital or something?"

"I'll be okay," she promised. Anything to prolong being held, because it felt absolutely wonderful, despite the growing number of people that were watching.

"She'll be okay. It would've helped if she'd just listened to me, but somehow I don't think she's the listening type." He looked down at her longer than necessary, as if trying to solve a puzzle. "I have a feeling this was fate."

Chapter Three

Molly had been doing her own thing, happily minding her own business, until life had intervened. It had delivered an awful headache, and the butt of her jeans was still damp, not to mention her bottom still hurt a little. Molly still couldn't quite conceive how in the heck she'd managed to get knocked out by a fish, but, then again, that was sort of her luck. Her friends were kind enough to point out that she should avoid black cats crossing her path, walking under ladders and should lock herself up when Friday the thirteenth rolled around every so often. Bad luck or simply clumsiness was just naturally Molly. It was who she was. It was surprising that she wasn't superstitious — maybe she should be.

"Oh my God, are you serious, Molly?" Tiffany asked, her entire body vibrating with hysterical laughter. "This has to be the strangest thing I have ever heard."

Molly nodded. "It was so mortifying." It killed her having to relive the tale.

"I bet. Did they at least offer you a free fish? You know, for your trouble?" Mackenzie looked upset. Her scowl told Molly she was not pleased in the least.

"Yeah, maybe even the fish that clobbered you?" Tiffany suggested. She continued to amuse herself at Molly's expense.

Molly huffed. "No, I was not given anything." She rubbed her head. It was still sore from the very humiliating experience.

"You want more ice, babe?" Mackenzie, always the mother hen, was already getting up to grab ice and probably some aspirin or something. If anything, Molly knew she was having the best care if Mackenzie was around.

They were huddled around in the living room of her apartment in the Belltown district, a very upscale and gorgeous area of Seattle. Her place was small and cramped, and she hardly spent any time there. She preferred the light and vastness of her studio. It was her true haven.

"I'm okay, really. I promise, guys." Molly felt a little dizzy as she tried to get up from her couch. It was an odd eggplant hue and far too large for the tiny space, but she had been drawn to the color and couldn't resist it. It was also the most comfortable couch she'd ever lounged on. It was great for naps, and that was how she determined if a couch was awesome or not. She could use a short one right now and she wished her friends would leave. She appreciated their concern, but Molly was exhausted and sleep sounded divine.

"I want to know more about Mr. Gray Eyes." Tiffany lit up with curiosity as she inched closer to Molly on the shared couch. "Peter said he was fine as hell. We want details, Moll."

What was there really to say? Molly had only been home for a few hours. The girls had raced over the second Peter had gotten her home and semi-settled. She felt like everyone was making a far bigger deal about this ridiculous incident than necessary. Granted, if it had been either Tiffany or Mackenzie, she'd be there in a heartbeat, too. That was how it was — one for all and all that jazz.

"You need to just stay put and let us take care of you," Mackenzie ordered as she brought a dish-towel-covered plastic bag, filled with ice. "Here. Put this on it."

The ice stung against the swollen knot that had formed since the incident. *Ouch*. She dabbed the ice again, wincing each time it made contact.

"So, tell us about your hero? Peter said he was annoyingly good-looking," Mackenzie commented.

Oh, Peter. She'd be scolding him the next time she saw

the model. Nothing like being tossed to the wolves. Molly sighed and admitted, "Well, he does have quite lovely eyes." She didn't feel the need to elaborate on how they'd transported her into a raging sea of emotions. That could be the slight brain injury talking, so best to wait before announcing it.

"Just lovely, huh?" Tiffany pressed further, patting Molly's leg. "Yeah, I'm sure that's all they were."

"Shouldn't you guys leave so I can rest?"

Mackenzie shook her head and made her case. "Nope. In fact, we aren't going anywhere at all. You can't be left alone."

"What? Why?"

"Concussion," Mackenzie stated clearly, as she sat back down in the wingback chair that was diagonal to the couch. "So, no, you will not be left. Sorry, dear."

Molly looked to Tiffany for a little back-up. Tiffany gave her a frown and shrugged her shoulders. "You know how Mac is. She's bossy, and I'm scared of her." Tiffany pretended to cower, causing Mackenzie to laugh and throw a decorative pillow at her.

"As you should be," Mackenzie said, shaking her finger at them. "You both should be."

"Oh, please. You might be bossy, but you couldn't hurt a fly," Molly argued. Her sore spot was growing numb with the ice.

"You wanna find out?" Mackenzie teased as she balled up her fists. "I'll have you know I'm pretty tough."

Tiffany and Molly burst into laughter, causing Molly's head to zing with pain, but it was worth it.

* * * *

Several days later, Molly found herself no longer hurt or bruised from her incident with the flying fish. She was kicking back in a chair in her studio, her feet elevated on her table, perusing several edits in front of her. But her focus just wasn't there today. Distracted and craving something to eat, Molly decided to head down to Pike. She knew why she really wanted to go back, if she could only be honest. Molly had been arguing with herself most of the morning, wondering if going back to the scene of her humiliation was really a bright idea. Then again, Molly knew full well she wasn't exactly known for making the best decisions. After grabbing her camera, she left her studio.

The city smelled of sunshine and remnants of rain as Molly stepped outside. The sky was a soft blue with strands of wispy clouds feathered across it. The day was simply gorgeous. Unable to resist, Molly snapped a couple of pictures. She documented life with this camera – the good, the bad, the ugly…and the quite beautiful, such as today. She couldn't dismiss the happy spring in her step as she headed toward the public market. Mr. Gray Eyes probably wasn't even there. It was a little late in the day, so the day's catch had already been brought in – more like thrown in. Molly winced at the memory of that heavy fish clobbering her.

As Molly approached, she saw tons of people – no surprise. When the weather was even half as fabulous as this, people took advantage of it. Suddenly she felt a nervous storm thrashing around in the pit of her stomach. *Okay, maybe coming down here isn't exactly a good idea.* Weaving her way through the thick crowd, she emerged at the fish market. She spied to see if any fish were being thrown. She'd be extra cautious from now on. Lesson learned. Customers were browsing the ample variety of fresh seafood, some of Seattle's best and most world-renowned. Molly kept her distance, hanging back just far enough to get the lay of the land. It wasn't like she wasn't familiar with it. She'd been there lots of times. Taking out her camera, she became a spectator, hidden and safe behind the lens as she looked out onto the busy world before her. *Snap. Snap.* The shots she'd just captured were of a mother leaning in to speak to her small child, pointing at some lobsters and giant halibut. The mother and her son each wore happy smiles as they made this memory together. *Click. Click.* A couple laughed in unison, the man bending down at just the right moment to kiss the woman. That perfect moment was now tucked inside Molly's camera. She took some shots of a few signs, peeking from behind her camera, squinting to see if the angle that she saw in her mind translated onto the screen. Then she caught sight of the smiling face with the most incredible gray eyes. Within an instant, he turned and they connected in a magnetic stare. *Crap.* Molly turned her glance away as quickly as she could, keeping trained on her camera and pretending that maybe he hadn't seen her.

Deep breaths. Molly kept repeating it in her mind as she tried to swallow. Her throat was parched, those nervous waves crashing unpleasantly inside her.

"So, you're back," he called out to her.

Molly looked up to the voice she vaguely remembered, but the eyes? She could never forget them. She had tried, but every time she closed hers, there they were, looking at her with concern and amusement.

She offered him a weak smile. "Not planning on hitting me again, are you?"

Several customers raised their eyebrows and pretended to mind their own business, but she could sense their curiosity at her remark.

"She means with a fish," Mr. Gray Eyes assured the tourists. He sent her an annoyed glare. "Thanks," he muttered as he leaned against the counter and glass cabinet that separated them.

"I'm sorry. I didn't mean…"

He waved his hand. "Not a big deal. How are you feeling, by the way?"

Molly lifted her hand to head, her fingers grazing the slightly sore spot. "I'm much better. Thanks. Yeah, that was one helluva blow to the old noggin."

"In all the years I've worked here, I have never seen that happen. You must be something special." He winked and gave her a half-grin that made her skin prickle.

The effect this man had on her was crazy. Had she really lost all sense and reason when she'd gotten whacked on the head? That was the only logical excuse she could come up with.

He stared at her quietly for a moment. She shifted her weight and timidly kicked her sneaker-covered toe at the pavement.

"You know...I never got your number. I wanted to know how you were doing. You've been on my mind."

"Yeah, I'm so sorry, I, uh...well." Molly stopped speaking. She felt like she was stuttering over her thoughts. She had been only partially conscious, and exchanging numbers really hadn't crossed her mind the last time they had been together.

"It's okay. You're here now, aren't you? So either I made some kind of impression or you're a glutton for punishment."

A bit sure of himself, isn't he? Molly thought. "What if I'm here to buy some seafood?"

"Oh, I'm sure that's why, because what better revenge than to eat the fish that attacked you? Sorry, babe, but it got donated that very afternoon," he explained as he shrugged his shoulders.

"Donated?" Molly was confused. *Who donates fish? Apparently, Mr. Sexy Gray Eyes.* She needed to find out his name.

"Yeah, there's a cat rescue up the road. This awesome lady takes in all the strays, and we like to help her out. That whopper of a fish you got nailed by? Well, that probably fed most of her cats that night."

"Happy to help." Molly laughed. She found herself drawn to the rough sound of his voice. Her eyes absorbed every feature on his face, memorizing the fine details. "I'm so sorry. I really should be thanking you. That's sort of why I'm here. I appreciate you helping me the way you did afterward," she admitted shyly.

Granted, when she had left her studio not thirty minutes earlier, that hadn't been her true intention, but now that she was standing right in front of him with a blur of activity surrounding them, she couldn't think of anything more she wanted to do. Well, that wasn't exactly true, either.

"I appreciate it, but they say things happen for a reason. Don't ya agree?"

"Yeah, I suppose so. Just passing out in front of everyone and stumbling around like a fool really isn't exactly my idea of a great way to meet."

"Let's fix that. I'm Owen, by the way." He wiped his hand and extended it to her.

She hesitated briefly before accepting. "Molly."

"I know." There was that sexy grin again.

She felt awkward and all out of sorts. This man was proving to be a little more of a challenge than she'd been prepared for.

"Well, Owen, thank you again. I'll let you go." Molly went to leave. She wasn't quite sure what else to say and she was feeling all flustered in his company.

Owen held up his hand. His gray eyes and sexy grin just seemed to grow brighter. *How is that even possible?*

"Oh no. I don't think so. I have waited several days for you to show up back here. I'm not letting you run off again without getting your number." He grabbed a piece of receipt paper and a pen from his apron pocket. "Okay, shoot."

Molly rattled off her cell phone number. What would she do if he actually called her? Knowing how most men were, it was about collecting the prized digits. The actual calling hardly ever happened. It was just a game.

"Great. So, when are you free?"

"Um, like for a...?" she stammered.

"Yes, a date. You know... It's what people do when they ask for a number and want to get to know someone a little better over drinks and dinner, sometimes coffee — whatever the other person is willing to go for." Owen laughed then cocked his head to the side, examining her carefully. "You thought I just wanted your number and wasn't going to call? Nope, I'm calling, sweetheart. You can bet that gorgeous little face of yours."

Well, she hadn't expected that. In fact, Molly wasn't so sure what to expect from Owen, but she knew one thing. She was going to be surprised at every turn.

* * * *

"Finally!" Tiffany squealed as she stirred the bubbling pot in front of her.

"I know. I should be happy, right?" Molly asked as she minced up garlic for the Italian dinner they were preparing together at Mackenzie's home.

Mackenzie lived in the Queen Anne district of Seattle, just north of downtown. The neighborhood offered the most adorable Craftsman-style homes. Mackenzie's was quaint and charming, and it was located near the school where she taught kindergartners. Her kitchen was the envy of both Tiffany and Molly. Not that any of them did a whole lot of real cooking, but, when they suddenly felt the need to be all womanly and domestic, her kitchen was the best to play Betty Crocker in. She had counters galore, which provided tons of elbow room for them all to pretend they knew what they were doing.

"I think it's sweet that he wants to go out, but just be careful. I mean, what do we really know about this guy?" Mackenzie was pouring them each some wine. "He might be the nicest guy to have ever walked the planet. He might even be your *one,* but he could also be the next Green River Killer or Ted Bundy."

"Gosh, Mackenzie, must you always be so doom and gloom about everything?" Tiffany flipped Mackenzie an annoyed look. "It's not like any of us are getting asked out. We need to sort of jump on the offers we do get, because, I hate to say it, but not one of us is getting any younger."

Molly watched pink anger flash across Mackenzie's pale neck, a sure sign that she didn't like what Tiffany was saying. Intervening now would be best. "Speaking of which, one of us has a birthday coming up."

"Ugh, must *you* be so doom and gloom?" Mackenzie quickly replied, throwing Tiffany and Molly an irritated look.

"Birthdays should be celebrated." Tiffany pointed out, turning her attention back to the pot in front of her.

"You just want a reason to celebrate something," Mackenzie shot back.

"Oh, come off it. We all love celebrating," Molly said as she lifted her nearly empty wine glass.

Tiffany and Mackenzie laughed, nodding in agreement.

"You have a point there. I just like a good party, is all." Tiffany reached for her own glass.

"I agree. I'm all for a good party." Mackenzie added more wine to all of their glasses.

"Then it's settled. Instead of celebrating a certain cranky someone's birthday, let's just throw a party. You can bring Owen," Tiffany tried to suggest, casually.

"Uh, no one said anything about bringing dates," Molly said.

"I just did." Tiffany gave her a purely evil smile.

Molly huffed. She hadn't even been out with Owen yet. He had called her a couple of times already. She'd ignored the first call because her nerves had gotten the best of her. Then he'd tried again, and, for the effort, Molly felt she owed him. It wasn't that she didn't want to go out with him. It was just she was a little afraid of the wild feelings that would erupt inside her when she was around him, which—as of now—had only been twice. She wasn't so sure what would happen if they actually spent a decent amount of time together.

"What are you scared of"—Mackenzie leaned in closer to Molly, wrapping her arm protectively around Molly's shoulders—"besides him possibly being a psychopath?

36

That, I can totally understand."

"It's not that, Mackenzie. It's sort of hard to explain, actually." Molly couldn't form the exact words needed to relate to her best friends what it was that she felt when she was around Owen—some weird cosmic connection that she hardly understood and that she was trying to make sense of herself.

"Well, out with it. Come on," Mackenzie ordered, squeezing Molly again and giving her an encouraging smile.

"Yeah, what's up?" Tiffany turned the knob on the stove and met them at their side of the old-fashioned green-tiled counter. "It's not like you to clam up like this. You're usually the first one to spill her guts. Maybe that fish did more damage than we realized."

"Shut it, Tiffany." Molly took another sip of her wine, savoring the rich flavor, letting it bounce and splash against her palate. They'd watched plenty of shows and attended enough wine tastings that they were all masters — or at least they believed they looked the part. "Like I said, it's difficult to put into words."

"Try to explain it to us," Mackenzie said as she studied Molly. "I can't imagine it's anything too wild. You've only seen him twice, and the first time you were half knocked out, so that doesn't really count."

"Mackenzie has a point, Moll. Is it like a love-at-first-sight thing?" asked Tiffany, her eyes twinkling with amusement.

"You know, I'm not too sure, but there's some kind of connection I can't quite explain or really understand," Molly relayed, hoping they could decipher her ramblings.

"It really does make sense. Some things are funny like that. Look at how weird the circumstance is to begin with. I have never seen anyone get hit with a fish there, like *ever*." Tiffany went back to the stove, using the wooden spoon to stir the sauce they were attempting to create. "Can I have that garlic, please?"

"I wonder if we should have cooked it first?" Molly

questioned out loud.

"Too late. It's going in now," Tiffany commanded, motioning for Molly to give her the strongly scented garlic cloves that they had minced.

"Back to this Owen thing. Let's not get distracted here," Mackenzie said as she grabbed a salad she had prepared earlier out of the fridge. "Tiffany is right, as much as I hate those words even coming out of my mouth," Mackenzie teased and Tiffany playfully stuck her tongue out.

Her two friends were incredibly close, but it hadn't always been that way. Each had been a friend to Molly first, and it had been Molly who'd decided to bring them together. In some ways it was still a work in progress. In others, it was as though they had all been friends their entire lives.

"Very mature, Tiffany," Mackenzie stated as she continued on, giving Molly her full attention. "Anyway, it is kind of astronomical, the odds that you would get this fish thrown at you by men that do this all day long without ever injuring someone? Then, to have an incredibly great-looking guy come to your rescue and for him to want to go out with you, too? It could be fate, right?"

"And an amazing story to tell your grandchildren. Just imagine the looks on their little faces as you explain that their grandpa nearly killed their grandma with a fish. I mean, who does that? But then, for him to rescue you... It's all kinds of romantic." Tiffany looked over from the pot, sampling a dab of sauce off the spoon. "This tastes awesome. Just putting that out there for you ladies."

Molly let out a laugh. "Yeah, I guess it does have all the makings of one of our cheesy movies."

"You should totally go out with him." Tiffany pointed at Molly with the spoon.

Molly looked over to Mackenzie, who was serving salad in little bowls that matched the small stack of plates that were on the counter waiting for the rest of the meal.

"Mac, what should I do?"

"Tiffany is right. You should probably go out with him

and at least give it a shot. But you'd better not pull some kind of stunt like you did with that model, Jax. Got it?" Mackenzie said firmly.

"Got it, Mom."

"Hey, I'm just looking out for you," Mackenzie defended herself as she started to hand Molly the plates to set the table. "I would literally lose my shit if something happened to you, Molly."

"I'm with Mac on that one. Who else would go on afternoon latte runs with me? Mackenzie lives too far north," Tiffany whined and jutted out her red lipstick-stained bottom lip.

"But what if the sex is super incredible? You want me to just pass that up?" Molly asked playfully, raising her voice a few octaves to sound innocent.

"Well—" Tiffany started to say.

Mackenzie whirled around, her blonde hair swishing against her chin as she quickly responded, "Yes. Even if it's Jax-worthy type of sex. I don't want that kind of headache again. You don't even know how terribly worried I was."

Yeah, he wasn't my best choice for male attention, Molly thought.

"I have a feeling that sex with Owen might be a whole lot hotter than with that model, just by how weird Molly is acting." Tiffany raised her perfectly plucked eyebrows and smirked.

Molly had screwed up. It had not been one of her finer moments, and even though it had been such a long time ago, Mackenzie was never going to let her forget it. But there was one consolation. The sex had been mind-blowing. Molly never mixed business with pleasure—only that one time—and she'd learned very quickly to never do that again.

"Okay, just never mind, you two. Dinner ready yet? I'm in need of carbs like...yesterday." Molly motioned toward the colander of freshly cooked noodles that sat on the stove. "Carbs make everything better." After Mackenzie's nod, she began filling her plate.

"I thought that was wine?" Tiffany asked, falling in behind Molly and faking a puzzled expression as Mackenzie carried the bottle to the table.

"Yeah, I think you're right. It's wine, for sure." Molly sat down, grabbed her glass then swallowed a mouthful of the bold drink. "Wine and carbs... Who says it can't be both?"

"Might as well throw chocolate in there. I can't live without that, either," Mackenzie added as she took her seat, the last to have served herself.

Tiffany sat across from Molly, Mackenzie at the head of the rectangular table, all with their plates overflowing with spaghetti.

Mackenzie raised her glass in a toast. "To my girls... May we never know the absence of carbs, chocolate and wine."

"Or men," Tiffany added happily.

Molly rolled her eyes, giggling she said, "Or friendship."

As they clinked their glasses, Molly thought it was nights like this that meant so much to her — to be surrounded by the people who understood her best. She silently prayed that whatever this thing was with Owen — fate or some kind of disaster waiting to happen — she just wanted her girls to always be there, preferably with carbs, chocolate and lots of wine.

Chapter Four

Molly's cell phone vibrated against the glass table, causing the loud buzzing to echo in the studio. "Sorry about that," she apologized to the model, who was uninterested in being there.

It had been a long shoot with this blond god. He was golden from head to toe and was quite aware of just how incredible he looked. He also had the attention span of a goldfish, maybe even less. Speaking of fish, she peered down and saw that Owen had sent her a text message, just one of several. He had been hounding her all day to call him. She scrolled through the new message, the same as the others. It was a simple plea for her to contact him. Molly felt herself grow a little agitated, and dealing with this annoying model wasn't helping matters.

She just stared at the message, contemplating her next move—answer the text or play hard to get?

Last night Mackenzie and Tiffany had convinced her—after a little too much wine—that maybe just having coffee—somewhere public to limit the chances of her being kidnapped and murdered—would be fine by them. Molly didn't think Owen was the murdering sort, but then again, most murderers probably didn't seem like the type, either. She shooed away the thoughts of doubt and suspicion that she knew were pointless and ridiculous.

"Are you almost ready?" The model whined as he ran his fingers through his shaggy hair, making it even more perfect. *How is that even possible?* Molly shrugged and put her phone down.

"Yes. Let's do this." She put on her most fake and animated

smile. Molly saw the model was in no mood for her niceness. Heck, her high-pitched and sugary-sweet reply annoyed her too. She inhaled deeply. She would grin and bear it to get through this session. The author using this royal pain in the ass was paying a lot of money for the custom shoot, so she reminded herself of that a couple of times while she gripped her camera tightly and bit her tongue.

She just needed several more poses, ordering him to give her his best 'pouty, yet sought-after bad boy look', then they could wrap up. Molly wasn't sure how much more she could take of this guy. His overall aura sucked, making her want to hurry through the shots. The way she figured it, he was gorgeous, no question, so the pictures were going to be fabulous — no need to overthink it.

What Molly needed was Tiffany to rescue her and either bring her a coffee or lure her out of her cave to go grab one. Caffeine seem to flow constantly in her bloodstream. It was part of her DNA, and there was no question she was an addict. Molly had even attempted to kick the habit, but after a brief stint in decaf rehab, she was right back at it, the need even stronger than before. There was no going back. She would always have her torrid love affair with coffee, so the people who judged her caffeine consumption could just shut it.

Just a couple more snaps. *I've got this!* Molly reminded herself over and over again. She had been working with a string of difficult models lately. Peter was a pain, but she loved his gay ass, and they had worked together enough times that it was okay for them to annoy each other. Right now, even with all Peter's constant whining, she'd much rather suffer through working with him than spend another second with this guy.

He wasn't even speaking to her. He didn't need to. His coolness spoke volumes. *Two can play this game.* Well, okay, maybe not. Molly wasn't really any good at the whole 'silent treatment' nonsense. Rudeness, however, wasn't something she could stand and so she bottled up her normally super-positive attitude and tried to keep quiet. She wasn't sure who was really being punished, him or her. She should start blabbing nonstop. It would serve him right. *Snap. Snap. Done. Thank God.*

After the model gathered his backpack, he slipped out of the studio without another word. What a joy it had been to work with him—not. At least his pictures were going to be fabulous, so it hadn't been a complete loss.

She felt worn out. Her body desperately craved more coffee. As she yawned, tiring her eyes from looking at the bright monitor in front of her, Molly mentally tried to will coffee to magically appear. No luck. Well, the coffee wasn't going to get itself, but as Molly fetched her purse and keys, the buzzer to her studio made her nearly jump out of her skin. Maybe the model had forgotten something—like his manners—but, then again, he hadn't brought them in the first place. Molly laughed out loud at her own sarcastic thought. She used what little energy she had stored and answered the door. What she didn't expect was to see Mr. Gray Eyes aka Owen standing there, holding a cardboard drink holder with two coffees and a small paper sack that had something delicious and sugary protruding from it.

"Owen." Distracted by the coffee and his gorgeous smile, Molly was a little slow to react.

"Molly," he playfully shot back. After mocking her, Owen quickly recovered with a sly and sexy grin then held up the coffee as a peace offering.

Her caffeine habit struck again, taking her prisoner, as usual, and here was Owen—unbeknownst to him—feeding her addiction. Bringing coffee earned him some major brownie points, but Molly was curious how exactly it was that he'd found her studio.

"Sorry for coming by like this. No, wait… I'm not sorry." Owen laughed, causing a happy light to dance in his already-beautiful eyes. Molly sighed.

"How did you find my studio?"

"You know, the usual creepy stalker way. I followed your

every move," he answered nonchalantly.

Molly raised her eyebrows and Owen laughed again.

"I just looked you up. You are listed, by the way. Sorry, but your secret hideout isn't so secret."

He had a point there. She hadn't thought about that. "Well, since you are bearing gifts of coffee, you can come inside." Molly moved away from the door and welcomed him in.

"So I did good, then?" He raised the cardboard tray.

Molly nodded and Owen slid past her.

"Wow, this is some place you've got here."

She closed the door and watched him as he gazed up at the ceiling, his mouth slightly open in surprise. "Thanks. I love it here," Molly said as she headed over to her large table, waving for him to join her.

"I can see why."

"Come on. Bring those cups over here. God, you have no idea how much I needed a coffee." Molly yawned and took a good long look at her salvation.

He hurried over to her. She noticed again that he was fairly tall, but everyone was tall compared to her. Despite her headache from caffeine deprivation that was nagging at her from behind her eyes, she noticed how his legs looked long and muscular in the dark-wash jeans he was wearing. The cream-colored cable knit sweater only enhanced his golden, sunbathed skin and the darkness of his hair. But Owen's eyes? They were bright and captivating, and they were almost enough to distract her from the much-needed contents of those cups.

"Thank you for bringing these." Molly accepted the one that was offered to her as Owen sat next to her.

"Who doesn't love coffee?" Owen asked, raising one eyebrow. "Especially in Seattle."

Molly nodded in agreement and anxiously took a sip, not caring if it burned her mouth. She could tell almost right away that something was off. She glanced up at him, taking another swallow. She waited for it—the buzz. It never came. "Owen?"

"Yeah?" he answered, sipping his and eyeing her curiously.

"Please, for the love of all that is right and holy in this world, tell me that this isn't — "

"Decaf?" Smiling, he nodded. "No one needs caffeine this late into the day."

Molly blinked hard for a moment before stuttering, "W-What?"

Owen's face lost its smile once he realized that Molly wasn't happy. "Well, it's just that I can't sleep if I drink coffee in the afternoons. I actually cut off any kind of caffeine right around noon. I have to be up early to be out on the water to fish," Owen explained.

Molly couldn't care less about fishing or anything that was not caffeinated at the moment, and she pushed her cup away from her. "I can't even." She was annoyed and the persistent throbbing was now growing fiercer.

"I'm sorry. I really didn't know if you even drank coffee," Owen defended himself as he took another sip.

The cup stood there in front of her, beckoning and teasing her with its false promises. She reached for it again. She was already missing the taste of the fine roasted blend of beans. Too bad it was decaf and served no real purpose. Molly sighed. His heart had been in the right place. She'd give him that.

"Let me make it up to you. How about dinner?" His eyes searched hers, and she could see the worry behind them. "I don't think I can screw that up."

Should I take the leap and go for it? Molly wasn't sure what to do. After weighing it all out in her mind, she decided that the man had brought her coffee, after all, even if it had been decaf. That would have normally been a deal breaker, but looking into his eyes, she felt herself melt. His lips were pressed tight. She could read the doubt and anticipation on his face, as hints of his aftershave wafted over to her.

"Yes." Molly was suddenly very hungry, but dinner was

the last thing on her mind. Was it bad that she wanted to jump his bones? She didn't even know this guy. This was another reason why Mackenzie felt the need to mother Molly. She wasn't exactly the best at making decisions and her impulsive nature quite often got her in trouble. Molly mentally flicked off the angel that was on her shoulder, advising her to behave and not to have such lustful thoughts. *Um, does that dumb angel see how hot Owen is?* She could almost see a tiny devil grin with delight as it sat perched on her other side. Maybe she should suggest takeout and make this a bedroom dinner date?

* * * *

"This is amazing, Owen," Molly moaned. Succulent and golden, not quite as gorgeous as Owen, but some of the best fish she had ever eaten.

"It was caught this morning by yours truly," he said with pride.

Molly watched him as he ran his thick fingers across his lips — slowly, effortlessly — and it drove her wild. She wanted those fingers to be touching her. Who would have thought eating fish 'n' chips by the waterfront as the Seattle evening sun slipped into the water would be so arousing?

Owen eyed her curiously. "You okay?" But the sexy smirk on his face told her that he knew very well she was more than okay.

She tried to gather her wits and scolded herself for getting caught staring at him. "Yep, all good."

"Want to take a walk, then?" Owen offered.

She could tell that he didn't want this night to end any more than she did. "That sounds great."

Owen gathered their trash and quickly shoved it inside a large garbage can. He held out his hand to her and Molly hesitated for a moment. This felt too easy, too comfortable and very much like the start of something. Was that really what she wanted? It had nothing to do with Owen and *everything* to do with her. The ship of 'what ifs' began to sail inside her mind, bobbing all around her thoughts. This was what Molly did, what she was famous for—besides her photos—her self-doubt and self-sabotaging ways. Why couldn't she just be normal and grab his hand? Something warm and strong gripped hers. Owen had made the choice for her.

* * * *

Friendship Friday was in full swing at Mackenzie's house. They all had their pajamas on and were seated on the floor. Beer and pizza was tonight's choice—a full-on carb party, no questions asked. Well, there were questions, but they were all centered on Molly's impromptu dinner date with Owen.

Molly leaned back against the couch, stretching out her short legs that were covered in pink flannel with tiny green frogs. The pajamas were playful, silly, comfy and had been a gift from her young niece. Molly loved them. She grabbed her beer bottle, letting the bitter taste splash in her mouth before swallowing it down.

Mackenzie had on navy blue silk pajama bottoms with a matching top and she was lying on the champagne-colored carpet. She tucked a throw pillow under her head and stared up at the ceiling when she spoke. "I still think it's odd that he went to your studio." There was a coolness in her tone that confused Molly, but she brushed it off. Mackenzie could come off as overbearing or moody at times, but she always had the best of intentions.

Tiffany was sitting crossed-legged, wearing black yoga pants and an over-sized Seattle Seahawks T-shirt, her long hair in an untidy ponytail, strands of hair still loose around her face. "I don't. I mean, he's been trying to get Molly to agree to have coffee. He brought coffee," Tiffany argued as she nibbled on the large slice of gooey cheese pizza from her paper plate.

"So you don't think it's kinda creepy that he just showed up unannounced?" Mackenzie shot back. Molly could feel some tension starting to move in like a storm front, and it worried her. Mackenzie and Tiffany had been known to disagree quite a bit, and it was usually over the most ridiculous things. Molly feared this might quickly become one of those tiffs if she didn't intervene.

"Hey, it worked out. Yes, it was a little surprising that he just showed up, but it led to me going out to dinner with him. Let's not forget that."

And it had been unexpectedly lovely. She hadn't laughed that hard with someone of the opposite sex in ages, nor had she fought the tangle of butterflies that seemed to take flight inside her. There was just something about Owen that messed with her chemistry. It was like his body had sent off little waves of attraction, and there was no use in fighting it. She and her body were completely ready to surrender to him. Molly had lost the thread of the conversation, thinking about all the ways she found Owen hot, when she heard Mackenzie raise her voice slightly.

"Yeah, it worked out this time." Mackenzie shot icy daggers at Tiffany before she peered over at her. "Moll, you need to be more careful. Anything could have happened. You were alone in that studio and no one would even have known you were in trouble." Mackenzie sat up, looking at Molly with more concern than anger.

"Molly is a grown-ass woman, Mackenzie," Tiffany countered back, crossing her arms like an upset child. She huffed.

"You guys, it's okay. Owen's a good guy, or… Well, at least he didn't kidnap or kill me," Molly joked. She wanted this to stop before it got out of hand, but she worried it might be too late.

Tiffany rolled her eyes and frowned. "Seriously, not everyone is a psychopath. I hate that Mackenzie acts this way any time either of us want to date anyone."

"Excuse me? I act like *what*?" Mackenzie's eyes were

burning with anger. Her voice boomed, and Molly knew she was too late to stop the blow up.

"Mackenzie, just calm the hell down. You always make such a big deal out of stuff."

Molly swallowed another gulp of beer. It hit her nervous stomach as she watched her two friends prepare to battle. This was not going to be pretty.

"I don't make a big deal, but I also don't wander around like a bumbling idiot, either."

"Are you saying that either me or Molly is the idiot in question? Because you better check yourself, like right now," Tiffany shot back, her volume rising slightly.

"Oh, come on. You know exactly what I mean. Don't twist my words, Tiffany. You always try to pull that crap, and it gets old."

"Yeah, but you always act like we're the foolish ones and have no clue how to live — and *you* have all the answers. You have it all together and we are just running around stupidly."

"Well, you have had *your* moments, Tiffany. I'll give you that." Mackenzie stared at Tiffany, not backing down. Molly was growing more uncomfortable as the tension in the living room was building, thick and nasty.

"Mackenzie, you are far from perfect, so it's kind of like the pot calling the kettle black, isn't it?" Tiffany stood up. Mackenzie jumped off the carpeted floor.

Molly wasn't sure where to go or what to do. *God, I hate it when they fight.*

"Oh, please. I have my shit much more together than you, sweetheart."

"Really? Because I don't see you all happily married and living the dream, now do I?" Tiffany asked with her hands on her hips.

Crap. Tiffany had gone there. Molly closed her eyes, willing this all to stop.

Mackenzie's shoulders slumped, and her whole face went blank. "I think you should probably go home now."

"Fine by me. But just remember, you need to quit trying to mother us. Molly is allowed to do what she pleases. She doesn't need to check in with you."

"Sorry that I was being a good friend and caring about her safety."

Tiffany started to grab her purse and jacket. "A good friend wouldn't make her friends feel like they were complete morons all the time. She would support and encourage them. Just sayin'." Tiffany ran out of the door, slamming it hard as she left.

Damn. Mackenzie remained standing and Molly felt trapped as she awkwardly remained on the floor. She should probably go. Molly hated being caught in the middle, being tugged by both Mackenzie and Tiffany to see their side. It was not something Molly liked one bit.

"Can you friggin' believe her?" Mackenzie was staring out at the door, her arms crossed, hugging herself.

"Mac, I don't really want to…" Molly's voice trailed off.

"Yeah, I know. You never do. That's because you always take her side." Mackenzie looked down at Molly.

"No, I don't. That's not fair, Mac." Molly rose from off the floor.

The night was ruined — no more beer, no more junk food and definitely no getting to watch the movie Tiffany had brought over. Molly had looked forward to this night all week.

"You're right. It's not fair, but it's true. You are always so afraid to say something against her. It's like you feel this need to protect her at all costs." Mackenzie stared at Molly, making her feel like she had just been punched in the gut with guilt. "What about me, Molly?"

"Oh dear. Mac, I'm sorry —" She tried to apologize but was met with Mackenzie raising her hand for Molly to stop.

"Don't bother. This is something that will never change. It's always been this way, and it always will be." Mackenzie walked over to the coffee table that they had pushed out of the way from where they had all been sitting just minutes ago, and she grabbed the plastic case that held the DVD. "Can you please give this to her?"

Molly nodded and accepted the case. "I really am sorry."

"Yeah, me too." Mackenzie flopped down on her couch, covering herself with a fleece throw. "I'll call you tomorrow, okay?"

Molly frowned and started to grab her bag. "Night, Mac," she said quietly as she left.

Fights happened, she knew that, but this one hurt a little more than the other arguments in the past. This one felt like the cuts were deeper and she knew without question that this wound would take a while to heal.

* * * *

"No, I'm not going to call her. Molly, quit trying to fix this," Tiffany warned her.

It had been nearly a week since the fight on Friday and neither of her two best friends were speaking. Molly knew that this was going to take a while for them to get over, but she'd been hopeful that she could talk some reason into her.

"I know, but, Tiff, you guys are friends. It's all so dumb, if you think about it. Mackenzie was just being—"

"Yeah, I know. She was only being *Mac*, and, quite honestly, I'm sick of it." Tiffany grabbed her coffee and put it to her mouth, looking away briefly from Molly. Molly followed her eyes. They were wet and focused on the busy street just outside their favorite coffee shop. "Gosh, you always defend her, Molly."

Her too? She kept being accused of taking the other's side, when, in reality, she didn't want to take either, but being in the middle meant being a part of their tug-o-war game.

"She says the same exact thing. See? You guys are more alike than you realize." Molly attempted to point out.

"No, we aren't. We couldn't be more different."

"That's not true. I disagree."

"Well, we'll just agree to disagree," Tiffany replied coolly then switched gears. "So, are you seeing Owen tonight?"

Owen. He'd been starting to really grow on her. She'd give him that. He wasn't at all what she'd expected, even after having dinner with him once last week. Getting hit by that fish may very well have been a good thing. She and Owen had been chatting on the phone daily. He'd made it a practice to stop by her studio with one decaf and one regular coffee around the same time each day. And he made her laugh, a lot.

"I kind of like him," Molly said as she picked at the last remaining crumbs of the banana nut muffin in front of her. "Like a *lot*, Tiff."

"Don't tell Mac that. She might freak out. Mackenzie's probably convinced he has some sort of evil plan to get you to fall for him, then he'll end up hurting you. She doesn't really trust men. You know?"

Molly nodded but wished that Tiffany wasn't so hard on Mackenzie. "Come on," Molly begged. "Eat your scone or I'm stealing it."

"I'm not hungry." Tiffany shoved it toward Molly.

Tiffany wasn't acting like herself at all, and Molly was worried. Maybe this argument had had much more of an impact than she'd even realized. There had always been a little surface tension. They were constantly fighting over Molly, to some degree. But considering that they had been friends for years, she'd hoped that they had their own bond by now. It had seemed like it at times, but maybe Molly was wrong.

"You know...I'd better go." Tiffany got up from her seat and gathered her large bag and sweater. "Have fun tonight, and let me know all about it, okay?"

"What about Friday?" Molly asked hopefully.

Tiffany shook her head. "Let's not discuss it right now."

"Can't you guys just get over this?"

Tiffany bunched up her long dark tresses as she swung her imitation Louis Vuitton bag over her shoulder. "Molly, don't push. Okay?"

Molly sat there, defeated, when Tiffany left. She watched as her friend looked both ways then crossed the busy street that was just outside the shop. She loved Tiffany and Mackenzie both. They were the sisters that she'd never had. Of course, she loved her brother, but a sister was something she had always hoped and prayed for — another female that she could share secrets with, someone that would know her inside and out. She'd found that when she'd met her two best friends, that thirst for sisterhood had finally been quenched. It tore her up knowing there was a chance they may not recover from this fight.

* * * *

Her stomach was a nasty bundle of nerves, and what for? Because this was a real date, not just coffee or grabbing some fish 'n' chips. No, this was like a shaved legs and cute panties and bra type of date, not that she actually had any intention of sleeping with Owen. It just made her feel sexier, which would then give her a boost of confidence.

Okay, who was she kidding? Hell yes, she wanted to screw his brains out. The man exuded a kind of confidence that Molly found herself almost envying, but she was drawn to it. She felt the heat grow low in her belly whenever she heard his voice, and she swore her nipples tightened when she saw him...smelled his musky aroma. She'd had to use her trusty vibrator to take the edge off a couple of times after he'd left her studio in the afternoons. She couldn't imagine what being with him through an entire date would do to her.

She fussed with her outfit, looking at the full-length mirror that was mounted behind her bedroom door. Molly wasn't sure if she liked what she was seeing — a black top that was loose and had a plunging neckline. The tight dark-wash jeans made her butt look good. The downside was that they made her legs look stubby. There was just no winning sometimes. *Oh well.* She wore large silver hoop earrings. Her brown hair was in relaxed waves and her makeup wasn't half bad. The pink lip gloss did wonders for her thin lips, making them look lush and full. She'd paid good money for that stuff because it worked wonders. There was a knock at the door. *This is it.*

Inhaling as deeply as she could, Molly held her breath as she opened her front door. There Owen stood, looking confident and incredibly handsome, dressed in a light blue polo shirt and khakis that clung to his body. She could see hard muscles straining against the fabric of his clothes, muscles that weren't bought in a gym like so many of the models she worked with. No, these were developed and earned through hard labor—manly work. Her mind had an active imagination that had just gone full throttle, and her body's reaction? *God help me.*

"Wow, you look amazing, Molly," Owen eyed her up and down. A pleased look danced across his face.

Suddenly she felt self-conscious as she let him inside her apartment. "Thanks. You look great too." She watched him walk by and snuck a peek at his assets. Her brain went into overdrive, picturing him without all those pesky clothes on. *Nice ass...*

"Your place is so..."

"Small. I know." She was able to push the naughty thoughts away, for now.

He stood there in the tiny living room, surveying the space. "Well, yeah, I guess so. But it's nice."

"But it's not my studio, right?" Molly stood next to him, suddenly aware that he'd been holding flowers, a lovely bouquet of sunflowers—strong and sturdy stems with bright yellow heads. They were gorgeous and one of her favorite flowers.

"Your studio is awesome. That view you have there—" Owen stopped when he realized he was still holding the flowers. "Oh, gosh, I'm sorry. These are for you. I wasn't sure which kind you liked."

Now she saw the nerves. That confidence seemed to

disappear as he fumbled with the flowers, handing them to her in an awkward motion.

"These are beautiful and I love them." Molly paused. She had almost stepped in to kiss him. *Too soon.* Yet she couldn't deny the hot flash of attraction she felt for him.

Owen's gray eyes twinkled and he flashed a boyish grin. "I'm glad you like them. When I saw them, they reminded me of you. They are bright and made me smile, just like you do."

"So I don't come off as an orchid or a tulip or a rose?" she teased as she wandered toward the kitchen in search of a vase.

"I guess not."

"I always pegged myself for a lily."

Owen's face grew confused. "Really? I should have—"

Molly laughed as she filled up a tall glass vase that she'd retrieved from under the sink. "No. Gosh, I don't consider myself any kind of a flower at all—maybe an ugly old weed, but definitely not a flower."

Owen moved in close behind her and whispered, "Oh, but you are. You're a gorgeous flower, rare and vibrant, and you smell incredible."

Molly tensed up, her body becoming immediately aware of his. He towered over her. She felt sheltered and she found herself growing warm. She stood there, waiting for him to make some kind of move, willing him to do something, but he never did. He backed away, leaving her smoldering.

"Hungry?" Owen asked innocently.

He has no idea.

* * * *

"God, you're funny." Owen was wiping tears from the corners of his eyes.

"It's not funny. I swear it really happened to me. You, of all people, should know. I don't exactly have the best luck," Molly pointed out playfully.

They were seated across from each other. A small candle flickered in a clear glass jar in the center of the table. Owen couldn't have picked a more romantic place. Soft music floated in the air that also carried a heady scent of garlic. Italian food was a favorite of Molly's and the atmosphere of this little hole-in-the-wall restaurant was perfect. She felt happy. That was the only way to describe it. But having dinner with Owen anywhere would probably have had the same effect on her.

"That's true. You know, I'm glad that you were in the way that day." He stared at her, claiming her with his eyes.

"In the way? Oh no, you got it wrong, buddy. I was standing there, minding my own business, not in the way at all. It was *your* fault."

Owen pulled back. His face scrunched up in confusion as he replied, "What? Oh, babe, you got hit a little harder than I realized." An arrogant smirk was on his face, causing Molly to feel an unexpected bubble of irritation erupt inside of her. Owen pointed at her and explained, "No, you were standing right in the line of fire. You were too busy either talking to that model buddy of yours or just not paying attention, but I can assure you that I'm not the one at fault. It was you, doll."

Molly raised her eyebrows, surprised that he refused to believe he'd had any part in her being hit by that stupid fish. Maybe throwing fish in a public place wasn't such a great idea. Couldn't they just bring in the catch on a cart or something? She huffed. Things had been going so well until he'd brought up that fish incident, but perhaps she was being oversensitive. What did she know?

Dating was not her thing. She'd avoided it like the plague. She never knew where she stood with the guy. The whole awkwardness of getting to know someone was almost just too brutal to endure, especially in public. Then there was eating in front of some complete stranger while trying to decide if he was marriage material or just someone she might want to practice indoor sports with. Then there was Owen. He sat across from her, his features slightly shadowed in the low-lit restaurant, but the smug look on his face could be read clearly.

Only moments ago, Molly had been convinced that Owen might be, at the very least, worth considering for boyfriend material. She'd absolutely wanted to play in the sheets with him, but now she wasn't so sure. Something about Owen was making her reconsider her dislike of dating. He'd made her feel comfortable. It wasn't every day that she met someone with gorgeous eyes, the most kissable lips and who had the ability to make her melt. Sure, their meeting had been the most unlikely of circumstances, but he'd made her laugh and she'd made him laugh. But she wasn't laughing now. Right now she would much rather be in her studio or tucked away in her bed.

Molly let out a long sigh, hating herself a little as she digested all these rambling thoughts, allowing them to make her filled with self-doubt. *Why do I have to do this every time I find myself out on a date? Overthinking, wanting to creep back into my shell to hide and overwhelmed by anxiety… God, I suck at dating.* Molly actually started to feel bad for Owen. The poor guy had no idea what kind of nut job he had reeled in. She just wanted this to end. *Check, please!*

Chapter Five

Molly watched the rain splatter against the tall windows in her studio. The room was dark from the missing sun that had been kidnapped by yet another rainstorm, but it suited Molly's mood just fine — gloomy and wet. Wiping away a rogue tear — oh, there had been plenty earlier — Molly had locked herself inside her tower. She'd tried working on various edits, but her mind and heart weren't invested in doing anything productive today.

It was also Friday. Tiffany and Mackenzie still weren't speaking, and she was pretty sure that they wouldn't be hanging out basking in their amazing friendship. The more Molly thought about it, the more she realized that neither had really talked to her over the last couple of days.

She took her cell phone out of her back jeans pocket then peeked down at the screen. She frowned. No word from Owen, either. Their date had been a couple of nights ago and she couldn't help but feel like it might very well have been their last. Was she surprised that she'd screwed it up? Nope. This was her pattern and why she was in her thirties and single. She was romantically challenged and she had no idea why. Her parents were still married, so she couldn't use the whole broken home excuse. Her brother, who was only a few years younger, was happily married with a couple of adorable offspring. Most of her other friends were all starting to create their own perfect nuclear families with two point five kids. Not Molly, Tiffany or Mackenzie. Mackenzie had been the closest. She had actually been engaged.

Molly closed her eyes, remembering the pained expression

in her friend's dark eyes as Tiffany had brought up the ugliness that they'd all worked so hard to forget. Being left by the love of her life only days before her wedding day was something Mackenzie might never quite get over. Why had Tiffany needed to go there? Because she had felt backed into a corner and she'd lashed out with the only ammunition she had. Was it fair? No, but Molly understood…sort of. She wouldn't have even dared to bring up that nasty little piece of history they'd all barely survived. Molly knew Tiffany would not have normally thrown that at Mackenzie, but she'd reached her limit. People said stuff when they were angry, but the question Molly had kept pondering all week was, why had things gotten so blown out of proportion? The fight had escalated so quickly. The more Molly thought about it, the more confused she was. Couldn't have this whole thing been avoided? It just didn't make any sense to her and she wasn't sure it ever would.

So what was the game plan for tonight? A lonely Friday. Maybe she should order takeout and try to get some work done, or retreat back to her tiny apartment and hide under her covers. Today sucked. More tears sprang from her eyes. How much water could one person cry out? She felt like a hormonal mess, which only made her more upset. That sensation of not having any control over her emotions — not truly having a valid reason for crying — only pissed her off more. Gently swiping away more tears, Molly stared out of the window, letting her forehead press against the cold glass. Seattle seemed to sparkle with the rainfall. The dismal gray that hovered over the city was ignored as life continued to move at a hurried pace below. She was lost in her blank thoughts when she heard the distant sound of her door buzzer. Molly sighed. She was in no mood to deal with people.

Cursing under her breath, she opened the door and there he was — Owen, with a sturdy cardboard container balanced in his hand and a white paper sack that she knew was filled with scrumptious treats. But it was the delicious half-curved smile on his face that made her realize how much she had missed him.

"I promise it's not decaf," he joked while Molly tried to catch her breath.

"It had better not be."

"Can I come in?"

Molly knew there was no point in turning him away. The man had brought coffee, after all. Besides, he looked all sorts of handsome, which wasn't hard for him to do.

"If I said no?" Molly placed her hand on her hip, taking a firm step closer into the large metal door jamb. *Might as well play the game.*

Owen grinned. Light danced in his stormy eyes. He stepped closer, eliminating the empty space between them. "I'd ask again until you caved."

"Why? I haven't heard from you in days."

"Two. Only two days." He held up two fingers and slowly let them rest on her lips. The unexpected warmth of his touch sent a quiet tremor through her. Owen looked down hungrily at her. "You needed time to cool off."

When she took a step back, he lifted his fingers from her lips and she instantly missed them. "Me? You started it. You don't know what I need." Molly knew exactly what she needed, but her temper tantrum and stubborn ass made having that virtually impossible.

"Oh, babe, let's not do this. Trust me. I know what you need." He raised the coffee again. *Why does he have to bribe me with my addiction?* The man was the devil. He was good, she'd give him that.

She braced herself against the door jamb, not entirely sure what to say. She decided to keep her mouth closed and hoped that it would speak volumes to him. She didn't want to battle him, especially as her nose had begun to pick up delicious scents, but she wanted to make a point that she couldn't be bought by some fancy coffee. Who was she kidding? Of course she could. This was coffee she was talking about.

"Owen, I just don't know…"

He moved in again. His lips brushed her forehead. "Molly, couples fight."

Couples? Molly was not expecting that word to escape his mouth, but that was nothing compared to feeling the soft pressure of his lips suddenly crushing down onto hers. Her mind became a whirlpool of thoughts, confusion and desire, all spinning. The warmth spread through her body. Her body had forgiven him, regardless of what her mind thought.

"And couples make up," he added when the kiss ended.

* * * *

She was still wrapping her mind around the events that had taken place that afternoon. Molly had been home for a little while, immediately seeking refuge in the warm nest of her bed, surrounded by a mountain of pillows, safe from the damp world outside and alone to process her thoughts. It was as though her brain had taken stills—silent shots of what had transpired in her studio after Owen had shown up. Replaying the slide show over and over again, she still wasn't certain about what exactly had happened. Molly could see it in her mind. She even felt the slight numbness on her lips as she licked them, remembering the kissing after she'd let Owen inside. He had been careful to set the coffee down—that much she remembered—but then a tornado of pent-up frustration and need had swept them both up in a wild make-out storm. She had never been kissed like that. It was as though she were water for a man dying of thirst, him stealing every drop until he was quenched. He had been rough and gentle, a perfect balance that still had her body buzzing and craving more. She'd felt the hardness of his arousal and, though size wasn't supposed to matter, Molly knew better. The enormous bulge she'd felt had made promises that she hoped it could keep. She couldn't help but imagine how magnificent he must be at making love, judging by the way he kissed. The man had skills she had been unaware existed until they'd made out. Owen had teased her, bringing Molly to a frustrating edge by nipping at her lip or kissing her neck. She had quickly discovered how much power he had over her just with his mouth. Molly had never felt her desire begin to boil so quickly and that worried her.

Wanting him was only part of the problem. She'd also freaked out mid make-out. Molly still wasn't sure what had come over her. One moment she had been thoroughly enjoying locking lips with the delicious Owen to the point where she was wet with desire and nearly mad with the need to rip his shirt off so she could touch the warmth of his skin, then the next she'd panicked. It had crashed over her hard and taken them both by surprise. She'd been borderline psycho. Molly closed her eyes, desperately trying to erase the memory. She could still hear the echoes of Owen's apologies.

She wanted to call to Tiffany and Mackenzie, to beg them to quit fighting so they could comfort her. Ice cream sounded good right about now. She missed them and prayed that they could somehow get over this bullshit. Didn't they value their friendship the way she did? Molly had felt lost the whole week, as though her entire world was off balance. Mackenzie and Tiffany made walking the tightrope of life bearable and possible. God, how she wished they were hanging out tonight. It was *Friendship Friday* and here she was, all alone. Wiping away tears that had suddenly surfaced for the umpteenth time that day, Molly threw her comforter over her head. *Can Friday just end already?*

* * * *

The next morning it was still drizzling, the dark gray hue finding its way inside her home. The rainwater was streaking the windows of Molly's apartment. She didn't mind the lack of light that the day was providing since she wasn't exactly feeling all sunshine and rainbows herself. Molly sat at her dining table, clutching a jumbo mug of coffee. It was her third cup of the day, and her stomach was beginning to ache. She needed to eat something, to counteract the wicked amount of caffeine that was sloshing inside her empty belly. Unshowered and still in her pajamas, even though it was close to noon, she couldn't care less that she looked like a hot mess. She'd already witnessed just how awful she appeared when she'd visited her bathroom just moments ago. Her scary reflection had revealed crusty mascara clinging to her eyelashes, smudged eyeliner giving her horrible raccoon eyes, the skin near them puffy from all the crying. She looked like absolute hell.

Her oversized smartphone was in front of her and she was scrolling through her newsfeed on her favorite social media page, noticing several new 'likes' for a fresh edit she'd posted yesterday before her encounter with Owen. It made her smile. At least something was going well. The phone started to vibrate against the wooden table. Tiffany's face appeared. It was one of Molly's favorite pictures. Tiffany had her tongue out, looking every bit a spoiled child, but adorable as hell. Typical Tiffany. Molly recalled when they'd snapped it. They'd been drinking — no surprise there. It had been the end of summer, and the lighting had been perfect. They had so many good memories. Her heart started to ache. It had only been a little over a week since everything had gotten flipped upside down, but it felt like an eternity. She wasn't sure how much more she could take.

"Hello," Molly answered. She swallowed another sip of coffee, instantly regretting it as the liquid soured her stomach.

"Hey, what are you up to?" Tiffany asked, as though nothing were wrong.

"Um, nothing much. You?"

"I want to go out tonight."

Molly loved it when they would meet up at one of their

homes and pre-drink while getting ready to hit the town for a night full of dancing and ogling men. The three of them would fight over a section of the bathroom mirror and help fix each other's hair, all while a boom box blasted out tunes from their childhood and they sang along to their favorite eighties songs. Molly had taken mental snapshots, scrapbooking these special memories. She had also taken her fair share of actual pictures. After all, that was what she did. Photographs helped Molly catalog and treasure those happy and silly moments. She held on to them, those precious glimpses of their friendship frozen in time, forever, on film. She couldn't escape the sudden urge to grab her photo albums and reminisce.

"Molly?" Tiffany said a little louder, grabbing Molly's attention.

"Huh?" Molly had been lost in the past, a pleasant escape.

"Well?"

"Hell yeah, let's go out." She felt like she was trying to grab hold of the tail of a comet, wanting to snatch that excitement that she'd always had when the girls went out. "Want me to call Mackenzie?"

"Um, I was thinking, maybe just me and you?" Tiffany's voice dropped to an almost inaudible volume.

"Come on. How much longer are you guys going to keep up this nonsense?"

Tiffany released a long, exaggerated sigh. "I don't know, Molly. She hasn't called me to apologize yet."

"Well, you haven't called her, either." Molly tried to carefully point out.

"I sent her a text and she didn't even bother to respond. What more can I do?"

"When did you send a text?" Molly was shocked that neither Mackenzie nor Tiffany had mentioned this until now. She'd assumed there had been literally not one bit of communication.

Tiffany answered, annoyance obvious in her response, "After I had coffee with you. I felt awful, so I reached out."

Molly could hear Tiffany take a deep breath. "Look. I don't want to fight with her or you. I love you guys. But I think it's a little rude that she couldn't even text me back, don't you?"

"Yeah, you're right. She should have, especially if you had extended the olive branch."

"So can we please just go out and have a good time?"

"Without Mac?"

"Yes, please."

Molly couldn't help but feel as though she were going behind Mackenzie's back. Not that she wasn't allowed to live her own life or do something without Mackenzie in attendance, but, in an odd way, it felt dishonest and wrong. This was something they should be doing together, the three of them. There was no point in forcing the issue with Tiffany. She wasn't happy about it, but Molly relented. "Fine."

"Awesome. I'll meet you at your place at seven. Cool?"

"Okay, sounds good." It would sound tremendously better if Mackenzie were joining them. Maybe over some dancing and drinks, she could convince Tiffany to try to mend things with Mackenzie again. Or, at the very least, perhaps Molly could get a sneak peek at the text that Tiffany claimed to have sent. Molly couldn't deny she had some doubts about that. She still didn't know why Tiffany hadn't mentioned it until now.

After finally getting herself up and accomplishing some things around the apartment, it was time to get ready to go out. She spent a long time under the hot water in her shower. After scrubbing her face, ridding it of the old make-up, Molly just let the water cascade over her. She could feel her stress escape with the steam that had formed into a thick fog in the tiny bathroom. The soft floral scents from her shampoo and body wash had also relaxed her. With her spirit renewed, she was actually looking forward to dressing up and hitting the town. It would do her good to get out.

She lathered conditioner into her hair and, for some reason, an image of Owen appeared behind her eyelids. The kiss, the freak-out... They stood front and center in her mind. *Can't I just have a moment of peace without that man invading my thoughts?* She would make sure that tonight she would forget about him. Vodka had a lovely way of making her forget a lot of things.

Molly was humming as she towel-dried her hair. Wearing only a fuzzy aqua-colored robe, she stared at her closet. Now this could prove to be a challenge. She was sorting through her rack of tops when she heard her phone ring.

An image of Mackenzie appeared on her cell phone. *Crap.*

"Hey, Mac," she answered. Should she mention that she was going out with Tiffany? *Ugh.* She hated that Tiffany didn't want Mackenzie to go.

"Hey," Mackenzie replied, her voice soft. "I haven't heard from you, so I'm just checking in."

"Oh, thanks. No, I'm good here," she said a little too quickly, instantly feeling guilty.

"You okay? You sound a little strange."

"Totally fine."

There was a brief pause before Mackenzie spoke. "Good. You want to grab dinner or something?"

Oh no. The fork in the road. Should I be honest and just tell Mackenzie or lie to avoid hurting my friend? She could strangle Tiffany for putting her in this position.

"You know —" she started to explain.

"Let me guess...Owen?" Mackenzie asked.

Well, there was that option. She could totally use him as a scapegoat, but was that really fair to him or to Mackenzie? It would still be lying.

"No, actually, Tiffany just asked me to hang out with her." There. She had been honest, but, as she waited for Mackenzie to respond, somehow being truthful didn't feel all that great. Would she have felt better if she'd kept the truth from Mackenzie? *Hell, maybe.*

"I see. Well, you two have fun. I'll catch you later."

Mackenzie hung up before Molly could answer.

So much for honesty being the best policy. Molly knew one thing for sure. She was going to be drinking quite a bit tonight. She was tired of thinking and worrying. Molly needed to drown her sorrows, let her brain soak up some alcohol and maybe then it would just hush up for a while.

* * * *

The music was blaring. Thick and heavy beats emitted from the live band as they belted out songs Molly had never heard. It wasn't the first time she'd been to see a band and had no idea who they were, but that was how bands got discovered in Seattle — in dark and sweaty venues. Tonight, though, the exchange of body heat was making Molly feel kind of gross. She slurped down another drink in a feeble attempt to feel better. The fluorescent-pink straw siphoned the last remaining drops. Molly was starting to get a slight buzz, but her feet were beginning to ache from standing and dancing in the crowded club. She definitely was not as young as she used to be.

"How much fun is this?" Tiffany was still bopping along to the music as she nursed her own drink.

Fun wasn't exactly how Molly would describe it. The band was mediocre, at best. The drinks were more expensive than she remembered and she couldn't escape the guilt she felt that Mackenzie wasn't there with them. She should be suffering too.

"You want another?" Tiffany asked, her own glass now dry and empty.

"Sure," Molly answered. *Why not? Maybe the booze will make the night better.*

Molly noticed two bar stools had become free and she made a beeline for them. After she mounted one of them, her feet instantly thanked her. *Much better. Note to self... Three-inch heels are now only for occasions that permit a great deal of sitting, regardless of how tall or cute they make me look.*

"You don't want to dance anymore?" Tiffany had to scream over the thumping bass.

"I'm good. I can't believe how old I feel. When was the last time we went out to see a band or go dancing?" Molly shouted back.

Tiffany shrugged, the sequins on her top glittering with her every movement. Molly frowned slightly. She'd thought this would've been a good time. It had started off that way, but as the night had worn on, the excitement had lost all its charm and dazzle, and, as Molly yawned, she realized she was more than ready to call it in.

Tiffany playfully slapped Molly's thigh. "Quit that yawning. It's still early."

Molly was ready to complain when she noticed two men starting to approach in their direction. She signaled to Tiffany, who smiled widely. They probably just wanted to order a drink at the bar. *They can't be remotely interested in two old maids.* Molly was wrong.

The taller of the two spoke first. "Can we buy you lovely ladies a drink?"

They were working as a pack, a team, trying to take down their prey together. The wingman nodded to Molly, but his eyes drifted over to Tiffany with obvious interest. The one that stood in front of Molly was good-looking, and, under normal circumstances, she'd be happy to accept a drink from him, but he was all wrong. Was it the dark-blond hair that his hand had just run through or the deep cocoa-brown eyes that were waiting anxiously? The more she stared at him, the more realized there wasn't anything wrong with him at all. He just wasn't Owen.

"I'm good, thanks," Molly replied politely and held up the drink that Tiffany had just gotten her. She could feel Tiffany's questioning eyes. Molly was surprised at herself too. Any normal woman with half a brain would be willing to entertain this guy's offer. But Molly was anything but normal, and, God knew, she wasn't working with a full brain.

"Are you sure? You two seem a little lonely, and we'd love to keep you company." His voice was slick. He was the smooth one.

Then, without warning, her brain misfired the way it always did, and she could hear Owen's voice. '*Couples fight and couples make up.*'

Molly straightened her posture and quipped, "Our boyfriends might be back soon."

He raised his hands and apologized, "Our mistake. You both have a lovely evening." The tall and smooth operator and his wingman retreated quickly, moving on to stalk another set of prey.

"What the hell was that about? Boyfriends?" Tiffany asked after the two men were out of earshot. "They were kind of hot, and last time I checked, I didn't have a boyfriend and neither did you."

"I know, right?" She stared after the guys. They had started talking to two other women. *That was fast.* But that was how the whole dating world worked. It was a meat market, and they had to be quick. If someone wasn't interested, they moved on to the next possibility. Time was of the essence and couldn't be wasted on someone if they didn't jump at the chance. No one wanted expired meat.

"Oh, I see. Owen?" Tiffany wiggled her eyebrows and started to sip her cocktail.

Molly nodded.

"You really should call him tomorrow, you know, seeing how he's your boyfriend and all," Tiffany teased, as she let her bright-green straw rest between her teeth.

"Oh, stop. I had to think fast. It's hard, Tiff. I'm just shit when it comes to relationships. I don't know how to read men or what to do," Molly rambled. It was easy to admit that she was a complete failure at relationships, especially to Tiffany, who honestly wasn't all that much better than Molly.

"Nothing worth having is ever easy, is it?"

"I wouldn't know. I haven't had anything worth having

or anything close to it." They both laughed and returned to their cocktails. "You ready to go home?" Molly asked, hoping that Tiffany was ready to call it a night.

"Come dance with me, then we can go," Tiffany begged, her speech a little slurred. Her large eyes were shiny from a mixture of being slightly intoxicated and the lights inside the club.

"Okay, but only for a couple minutes." The second Molly slid off the stool her feet reminded her just how badly she wanted to go home, but the smile on Tiffany's face was worth suffering for a bit longer. "Deal?"

"Deal."

Chapter Six

Molly clutched her phone in the palm of her hand. She desperately wanted to take Tiffany's advice and call Owen. *So what's stopping me?* She sat near one of the windows of her studio, basking in the bright sun. There was not a cloud in the sky and the remarkable view of the surrounding skyscrapers and the waterfront reminded her why the price tag on her studio was so high. She would be able to enjoy the view a little more if she didn't have this whole thing weighing on her—to call or not to call? Trying to talk herself out of dialing his number, she reasoned that it was the weekend and maybe he had plans. She caught a glimpse of the time on her phone. It was a little after one. Deep down, she knew he was probably waiting to hear from her. Inhaling then releasing the air slowly, Molly prepared to dial when her buzzer chimed loudly. Saved by the bell, literally.

Thankful for the distraction, she hopped out of her seat with a little too much enthusiasm. When she opened one of the large doors, it was Mackenzie who smiled at her.

"Hey," Molly said softly. The guilt she felt for going out last night tightened in her gut.

"I was in the neighborhood and figured you'd probably be here."

They entered the studio and Mackenzie gravitated toward the window where Molly had just been sitting.

"I'm glad you stopped by."

"Are you?" Mackenzie threw her a knowing look.

"Well…yes, I am." Molly decided she had been a little unsure, but she needed to see if she could try to talk some sense into Mackenzie.

Molly grabbed another chair and brought it next to hers. "Sit," she ordered.

"Yes, ma'am," Mackenzie laughed nervously as she sat and stared out of the window. "I think you have one of the best views in all of Seattle."

"Well, it's not cheap. On days like this, though, it's so worth it."

Mackenzie cleared her throat, "So, how was last night?"

"In all honesty, not very awesome. When did I get old?" Molly joked, hoping it would melt the obvious tension.

"Around the same time I did."

"Well, I felt it last night. We went to go dancing and have a couple drinks. It wasn't long before my feet were killing me. The music was too loud, and I was surrounded by kids."

"Kids?" Mackenzie eyed her curiously.

"Yeah, twenty-something-year-old brats. I felt like a darn chaperone. But two guys did come up to Tiffany and me." Molly pointed out with a smirk.

"Really? Like they were looking for a cougar?"

"No. These guys were probably our age," Molly tried to explain.

"So...scavengers, then?"

"What the hell?"

"You know... Guys that are looking for the leftovers." Mackenzie winked.

"You're so mean." Molly playfully slapped Mackenzie's thigh.

"So what happened with the guys?"

Molly huffed. "I blew it for us. So, no free drinks."

"Uh oh." Molly didn't say anything as Mackenzie searched her eyes, then a smile appeared on her face. "This is about Owen, isn't it?"

Gosh, am I that obvious?

"What's going on with you and him anyway? Details, woman," Mackenzie demanded.

"I'm not even sure I know what's going on. We went out to dinner last week and we kind of got into a little argument," Molly started to explain.

"Oh boy, Molly, why?"

"To be honest, I don't know. Me, mostly, being oversensitive and moody, per usual."

Mackenzie rubbed Molly's arm and said, "You can't always be so down on yourself. Maybe he was to blame. It's not always you."

"Yeah, right. Trust me. It is." Molly felt her eyes starting to burn at the hint of tears and tried to blink them away. "So he gave me a couple days to cool off then showed up here."

Mackenzie cocked her head to the side and asked, "Why? To say he was sorry?"

"He brought coffee and he sort of apologized. He explained it like this — that couples fight and couples make up."

"Ah, so he brought a peace offering and used the word *couple,* which freaked you out, right?"

"Kind of. I mean, I wasn't aware that we were even stepping foot in that direction yet."

"That's because you always drag your feet. So, what else happened? Obviously something," Mackenzie pressed, still stroking Molly's arm soothingly.

Molly let out a long sigh. She could almost taste Owen on her lips as she relived that primal kissing and remembered how turned on she'd been. "We made out."

Mackenzie shook her head. "And this is bad how?"

"It's not. Like I said, it's me that is the problem."

"So you're making out with this supposedly great guy that has thrown a fish at you and brings coffee regularly, so now that I'm up to speed, then what?"

"I panicked and sort of made him leave." Molly cringed at the memory.

"Have you heard from him?"

Molly shook her head and said, "Nope. I think I may have screwed everything up. I hate me sometimes."

"Oh, babes, don't be like that. He obviously sees what we see if he keeps trying to come around and wants to put up with you." They both laughed and Mackenzie hugged Molly, whispering, "You are so worth putting up with, and he'd be a fool to give up."

After Mackenzie let her go, Molly decided to shift the conversation toward a matter that was really weighing heavy on her heart — Tiffany.

"So, are you going to call her soon?"

Molly watched as Mackenzie's back stiffened.

"Why should I call her?"

"Because she's one of your best friends, and this has gone on long enough."

"I know. It's just that it's a little different with her and me. It's not like us."

"We have all been friends for a long time. I love both of you, and I know you guys love each other, too." Molly knew deep down — heck, really, just right below the surface — they did love each other. Did they get on each other's nerves? Absolutely, but they were like sisters, weren't they? And getting on each other's nerves was what sisters did. Molly assumed anyway... She had a brother, and he got on her nerves all the time, but she still loved him with all her heart. She adored her friends equally, and they weren't even related.

"Molly, can we talk about something else? Anything else? Like maybe about how you should be calling Owen *right now*?"

She had her work cut out for her, but she wanted to get Mackenzie and Tiffany back together soon. She couldn't bear the thought of not spending another Friday with both of them — well, unless maybe she spent it with Owen. Molly was surprised when that thought slipped so easily into her mind. She really needed to reach out to him, to fix things.

* * * *

Monday was filled with more radiant sunshine and gloriously warm weather. Molly had tried to call Owen, but it had gone straight to voicemail. After having a couple of good nights' sleep and feeling the energy from the sun's brilliant rays, she felt perky and ready to conquer the world — well, the immediate Seattle area, at least. What Molly also had was a solid game plan. After stopping at her favorite coffee shop that was only a little way from the fish market, she decided to go to him, armed with one regular and one decaf coffee. She'd even bought an assortment of cookies that no one in their right mind could say no to, and she was hopeful that bribery worked on Owen as easily as it did on her.

As she came up to the scene of the crime from only a few weeks ago, where she had been clobbered by a fish that would change her fate and where she'd gazed into the sexiest eyes she'd ever seen, Molly balanced the coffees and started to search for Owen. When she finally caught sight of him, he was wearing a black rubber apron and an enormous smile as he spoke to another guy. Molly froze. Suddenly her nerves and ridiculous self-doubt took hold of her, clouding her sunny disposition. It was too late to turn tail and scurry away. Owen was staring at her now with a mixture of confusion and amusement. He said something to the guy next to him then slipped from behind the counter. She watched as he removed the apron and slowly made his way through the small crowd toward her with a sexy grin that made her unsteady. The effect this man had on her was unreal.

When Owen was suddenly in front of her, he didn't speak. He didn't need to. His eyes said it all. He bent down, kissed her on the head then pulled her toward him, completely circling her with his arms. "You brought coffee," he finally said.

"Decaf — and some cookies." Molly smiled up at him. The sea of nerves finally calmed as she gazed into his eyes. The weight of his arms around her made her feel secure and the reaction of her body to his reminded her how much she wanted this nearness.

"Let's go sit somewhere." He led her outside the market and away from the tourists and shoppers. He located a bench that gave a slight view of the water and took the coffee from her.

They sat and started to nibble on their cookies in silence – not awkward, but comfortable.

Molly spoke first. "I'm just not good at this, you know." She pointed at the two of them, not making eye contact as she continued, "I just wanted to say I'm sorry, Owen, for how I acted on Friday."

He held his cup to his mouth and said, "No need to apologize."

"But I feel like I need to."

"Why? You're here now. That says it all to me, babe."

Is it really that simple? Why did she always have to overanalyze and look for problems that probably weren't even there? She needed to learn how to just go with it. If he said they were good, then why challenge it?

Owen reached over and took her hand in his.

Just go with it, Molly.

With that decision made, she relaxed and enjoyed their time together until it was time to get back to her work. After she returned to her studio, she was humming as she clicked on a photo to edit. Molly felt at ease and happy. Spending that small amount of time with Owen had been enough to repair whatever damage she'd thought she'd done. They were good – beyond good, even. Owen had asked her to meet him for dinner later and Molly hadn't even hesitated or tried to come up with some sad excuse. She'd just gone with it. She was immeasurably proud of herself, and, if she could just stay out of her mind, Molly knew she'd have a halfway decent shot at making this relationship work. She now had a goal – not to overthink and just to go with the flow. She deserved a chance at happiness and, bad luck be damned, Molly was sure as heck going to give it a try.

* * * *

Owen was sexy, and he was also punctual. Molly? Not so much. She was still trying to shove her legs into skinny jeans that made her look anything but skinny when Owen buzzed the door to her apartment. *Crap.*

"Be right there," she shouted from her bedroom as she slid her feet into sparkly black flats. Molly paused in front of her full-length mirror for a moment. *Not too shabby.* The purple blouse that she wore hung loose. The dark-wash blue jeans clung to her legs, and her shoes were cute. Molly scrunched her hair in a feeble attempt to revive her sad excuse for curls. The dark waves were still pretty, but the bouncy spiral curls that she'd tried to create had already fallen flat.

Her doorbell rang out again and she hurried to the door. She inhaled before opening it. There stood Owen in a plaid shirt with an array of slate blues and white that did wonders for his steely-gray eyes. He wore relaxed jeans and his hair was still damp from a shower. Molly breathed in again and was welcomed with the scent of aftershave and soap, all masculine and driving Molly's senses into overdrive.

Calm yourself, girl. The night hasn't even started.

"Hi." Molly winced at how breathy her voice came out. And, besides that, she could feel her nipples tightening and that tell-tale dampness starting in her jeans.

"Hi, yourself." Owen moved in slowly. He knew exactly what he was doing. He could probably hear her heart beating against her chest like a wild bird trapped in a cage. Owen smiled at her, almost as if he was getting a kick out of watching her become flustered.

"Um, want to come in for a minute or are you ready to go?" Molly asked nervously.

"You may want to put these in some water," he advised as he handed her a bouquet of Gerber daisies that were a vibrant orange. How had she missed those? Had they been behind his back the whole time?

"Those are beautiful. Thank you. Well, come in for a bit while I find a vase." Molly accepted the flowers as Owen trailed after her into the apartment. "So what's the game plan for tonight?"

"I was thinking maybe we could keep it simple—drinks or dinner, maybe a movie. What are you in the mood for? Lady's choice." Owen shrugged. He seemed so large in her tiny space.

After finding a vase under her sink that could hold the flowers, Molly stood and thought about where they could go. A movie after dinner might be nice. It had been a while since she had seen one in a theater. The thought of popcorn and maybe some licorice was holding a lot of appeal, but could her skinny jeans handle that kind of junk food consumption? Not likely.

"Do you want to go out? You seem to be having some trouble trying to decide what you want to do," Owen asked.

"No, I do. I'm just trying to think where to go. You're the guy. Shouldn't you have had this all squared away and decided?" Molly tossed the ball back into his court.

"Good point." Owen nodded then his eyes lit up. "I've got it. Let's go."

And she had to admit that it was exciting not to know where they were headed, but it was even more fun when she realized what he'd chosen.

It was loud. Fun, but loud. No matter which one you went to, they were all the same. A bowling alley was a bowling alley—cheap beer, that weird funky smell from rented shoes, the hard, curved plastic seats and the obnoxious competitive spirit it brought out in everyone. Dinner turned out to be a greasy hamburger and fries, but Owen couldn't have picked anything more fun to do that night.

"You are so getting your butt handed to you," Molly said playfully as she grabbed the lime-green ball. Owen sat with his hand wrapped around a dark beer bottle as he nodded encouragingly at her, practically daring her.

She inched up to the slick and gleaming wood floor and

looked down the lane at the pins. She could do this. *Think strike*. And after sending the ball down the lane with all her might, Molly watched her ball roll into the gutter. It hadn't even made it halfway.

"Now what was that about handing my butt to me?" Owen asked as Molly returned to grab her ball again. "Need me to blow on it for luck, since you seem to be having so much trouble?"

"You know, that might not be such a bad idea." Molly raised her ball to him.

"Seriously?" Owen laughed. "Anything for my Molly." He blew on the ball and Molly quickly turned around to see if it had worked its magic.

Strike. Just like that, the ball had sailed smoothly down the lane, straight for the pins, knocking them all over with almost expert precision.

"Oh my God, did you see that?" Molly squealed. She ran to Owen, who had a happy but shocked look on his face. Molly wrapped her arms around his waist. He circled his arms around her. "I think you might be my good luck charm."

"Think? Babe, there's no other way you would have gotten that strike."

Molly slapped his chest. "You're so mean to me."

"Am not. How many strikes did you get before that?" Owen raised his eyebrow at her.

Molly bit her lip. He had a point there. "You know...they really should give some kind of extra points for the most gutter balls."

"They do." Owen bent down and kissed Molly softly. Her belly pooled up with warmth. Her lips zinged with electricity when they connected with his.

"I like gutter balls." Molly giggled.

Owen looked at her. "I like you."

Chapter Seven

She was focusing on the color saturation of the image in front of her when the chirp of Molly's cell phone interrupted her concentration.

She noticed it was Mackenzie and she answered, not hiding her giddiness. "Hey, lady, what's up?"

"Oh God, Molly."

The sound of Makenzie's voice through phone alarmed her. It was filled with strangled emotion. Something was very wrong. "Mac, what's going on?"

"My sister's been in an accident. Oh God, Molly." Her voice trailed off and was replaced with hard sobbing.

"Are you at the hospital? Is she okay?" Molly knew that if her sister was all right, Mackenzie wouldn't be calling like this. Her gut bottomed out. This was bad, very bad.

"Can you come to the hospital please?" Mackenzie managed.

"I'll be right over."

"Molly...are you there?"

"Yeah, I'm still here." Molly waited for Mackenzie to speak. The brief pause worried her even more.

"Can you call Tiffany and bring her with you?"

"Yes, I'll call her right now, okay? I'll call you when we get there." Molly hung up. As sick as she felt with distress, she couldn't deny her happiness at the silver lining and possible end to a senseless war. Mackenzie wanted Tiffany.

She dialed Tiffany's number and waited as it rang a couple of times.

"Hey, you," Tiffany answered, her voice cheerful and bubbly.

"Tiffany, Mackenzie just called. Her sister's been in an accident," Molly started to explain.

"Oh, no. Is she okay?" The cheeriness was now replaced with genuine concern.

"I don't think so. Mackenzie asked me to call you and for us to come to the hospital."

"Um, okay, no problem. Do you just want me to meet you there or do you want to pick me up? I'm still at work," Tiffany said.

"I'll swing by and grab you."

"Yeah, that works. Gosh, I hope her sister is going to be all right. How was Mac?"

"Like…barely able to speak, so I think we need to prepare ourselves. It might be kind of rough when we get there."

"I'm glad she asked for me to come too."

"Tiffany, you guys are best friends. We all are. She needs us right now, so of course she'd want you there."

"And I want to be. I love Mackenzie. She just makes me mad sometimes. But I have her back anytime she needs me."

"Well, she needs us now." Molly sighed. They had been through serious stuff before, but from the way Mackenzie had sounded, this was going to be rough, and she needed their support. "I'm leaving now. I'll see you in ten minutes or so."

"Okay. I'll be outside."

Molly hung up and gathered her purse. She prayed out loud. It wasn't something she did often, and she always felt a tad guilty. But right now, she knew that Mackenzie needed all the prayers she could get.

* * * *

Hospitals were all the same — that sick, sterile disinfectant smell, the neutral-painted hallways, bright overhead lights and glossy floors. Molly hated hospitals. She knew Mackenzie was not a fan, either. She had already lost both her parents before she'd met Molly, and her sister was her only relative left. Molly's heart ached for Mackenzie and the fear she must be feeling. The thought made Molly quicken her pace to the front desk, Tiffany keeping up with her, a stoic expression on her face. She had been quiet the entire ride over. Molly hadn't bothered with chit-chat and had focused on weaving her way through the heavy mid-afternoon traffic to just get them there as quickly and safely as possible.

When they reached the information desk, a petite woman wearing colorful scrubs smiled at them. Molly rattled off her request for help and the woman quickly gave her the information on where to locate Mackenzie. She was in the ICU. This was definitely not good.

Stepping into an elevator, Molly started to grow emotional. She told herself to pull it together, to be brave for Mackenzie and be the rock that she knew Mackenzie would need.

"Shit, the ICU?" Tiffany finally said after Molly pressed the button to the correct floor.

"I know." It was all she could manage.

The elevator dinged and the doors opened. Relief flooded Molly as she bounded out. They hadn't needed to walk far when Molly caught sight of Mackenzie. She was standing in a small waiting room off to the side of the elevators. Her head was down. Her blonde hair hanging around her face was a little tangled, not in its usual perfect style. She was looking at her phone intently, probably wondering where the heck they were. Mackenzie looked out of place and completely oblivious to her surroundings.

"Mackenzie," Tiffany called out, surprising Molly.

Mackenzie looked up. Her eyes were puffy red circles and her pale skin was blotchy. She looked like hell — completely fragile — and it broke Molly's heart. She wanted nothing more than to scoop her up and hold her tightly. The woman standing in front of her was not the strong and confident woman who always claimed to have all the answers. The person before her was utterly destroyed. It only killed Molly more when Mackenzie burst into ugly and uncontrollable sobbing. Tiffany raced past Molly and grabbed Mackenzie, pulling her into an embrace. Molly joined them, creating a tight circle, just as it should be, the three of them. She could feel the vibrations move through her as Mackenzie was racked with harsh crying and slight moaning. Molly couldn't quite make out what it was that Mackenzie was saying. Apparently neither could Tiffany, who looked at Molly for help.

They pulled apart—Tiffany on one side of Mackenzie, Molly on the other, each holding onto their piece of her.

"Mac, how is she?" Molly asked softly.

"She's gone, Molly. She's gone." More tears flowed from Mackenzie as she gulped at the air, swallowing as she tried to speak. "They want to know if I want to donate her organs." The soul-shattering cries returned.

Tiffany and Molly moved in unison. Together they cradled Mackenzie as she collapsed into a heap, a tall blonde rag doll leaning on them for support. They didn't need to know the details. Those would come later. This was about them riding this wave of grief with their friend and helping her survive the storm.

Mackenzie had no one but them—no parents to make the call as to whether or not to donate the precious organs. She was on her own to make this decision. Even they couldn't truly advise her.

Her sister was younger and unmarried, no children. She had just been a kid, really. She'd just graduated college the spring before. Now she was gone. Her short life had been snuffed out far too soon. If they'd ever needed a reminder of how quickly life could be changed, planned paths altered in an instant, they had just been given one. The three of them stood there—out in the open, clinging to one another—all weeping loudly and not caring who heard them. They were surfing in the tidal wave of loss, an undertow of pain and an unfair ocean trying to drown one of them, but they were stronger when they were together. Molly was thankful that at least one of her prayers had been heard.

* * * *

Hospital coffee sucked, even in Seattle's hospitals. Molly was trying to doctor a cup that would be suitable enough for Mackenzie to drink, not that Mackenzie would probably even touch it. She was in a state of shock, something neither Tiffany nor Molly had ever seen before.

They had been there for a few hours. Molly assumed that the glorious sunshine from earlier was now gone. The day had started out so beautiful and full of promise. And in the blink of an eye, a sister had lost her only sister, turning this day into a horrible nightmare. Life was a constant balancing act. One moment everything could be rainbows and butterflies, the next unexplained, gutting tragedy. The universe was funny like that, always making sure to remind you not to get too comfortable. Without darkness, you would never know light, and without pain, you would never know joy, but, God, why did it have to hurt so much to learn these lessons?

Mackenzie stayed with her sister for a while. The hospital staff was caring but urging her to make the donation soon, as there was limited time in order to harvest the organs.

Tiffany and Molly had waited in a small private room that usually held families awaiting terrible news or having to make the most difficult decisions of their lives. It was decorated in muted and quiet colors, which didn't seem to soothe at all. Molly had checked on Mackenzie at one point, and it was the most heart-wrenching thing she'd ever witnessed. Mackenzie had climbed into the hospital bed with her sister, a younger and shorter version of her. Her sister's blonde hair was stained and crusty with red. Her eyes were closed, and she looked like she was only sleeping. An array of wires was coming out every which way. They were all hooked up to machines, but there were no beeping sounds, no monitors indicating numbers that no one really understood. It had been eerily silent, except the sound of air being pushed into her body, feeding oxygen to her organs.

It had been too much to take. Molly had retreated back to the waiting room, loving Mackenzie even that much more for her strength and bravery. Molly and Tiffany had sat, holding hands and waiting as Mackenzie gave the permission then said goodbye before she joined them.

Shaking away the images that would forever be imprinted on her brain and heart, Molly finished stirring in a little more powdered creamer. She brought the swill to Mackenzie, who reached out to accept the white Styrofoam cup, but she only held it. They were all quiet as they tried to navigate this new-found grief. Tiffany rubbed Mackenzie's shoulders and she looked up at Molly. They didn't know what else to do or say. They could only give so much comfort, but there was no way they could ever take away the sting of what she was experiencing. And it killed Molly.

They all knew what was happening at that very moment. Each time a nurse walked by and offered them a sympathetic, tight-lipped smile, they were reminded that it was being done. They also knew this was just the beginning of what was going to be a very hard road for Mackenzie — that the reality hadn't quite sunk in yet, and when it did, it was going to be brutal.

"We probably should go home now, Mac," Molly whispered, with Mackenzie leaning on her shoulder.

"Yeah, Molly's right. How about we go home with you?" Tiffany offered as she ran her hand up and down Mackenzie's arm.

They remained huddled there together. No one made the move to disband. Molly was more than ready to leave the room with the muted colors and felt that it was time to take Mackenzie away. They would help her make arrangements, but right now Mackenzie needed to go home and rest. This had taken its toll on her.

"Come on," Molly said, peeling Mackenzie off her, her

friend's blonde hair flat against the sides of her face, damp from all the tears she'd shed.

Mackenzie nodded but remained in her seat, even after Molly and Tiffany rose. They looked over at each other. They'd never seen Mackenzie like this. She was the strong one, the mother hen and the one that led their pack. Now they had to step up and take care of her.

Molly and Tiffany each took hold of one of Mackenzie's arms and tugged her out of the chair.

"I don't want to leave her," Mackenzie cried. "She's my baby sister, you guys."

"Mackenzie, she's gone, love," Tiffany said while Mackenzie buried her face in her hands, muffling the cries.

"She'll always be with you." Molly tried to reassure her.

"Molly, you have no idea how hard this is. Your brother is alive. Your parents are still alive. I have no one. They are all gone, so no, they aren't with me. They are all gone," Mackenzie said angrily, shocking Molly with the vile sound of her voice.

"She was just trying to help, Mackenzie," Tiffany explained.

"I appreciate you both being here, but, Tiffany, please, just don't start in on me right now." Mackenzie covered her face once more.

It was simply heart-wrenching to watch her friend be tortured by this grief. Molly shouldn't take anything personally. As difficult as it would be, Molly knew there would be more tongue lashings ahead because Mackenzie was hurting so badly. No, she couldn't relate. The only thing she could offer was to be there for her friend.

They were finally able to get Mackenzie out of the hospital. It wasn't easy, but they managed to get her inside Molly's car. Tiffany drove Mackenzie's small sedan, and they made the trek to Mackenzie's home.

The car ride was quiet. Molly was scared to utter a single word. She turned the radio on low and let music fill the void where conversation should be. When they arrived,

Mackenzie ordered them to leave, but they fought her on that, refusing to budge. They knew it was important to be there, just in case she needed anything. Mackenzie was not happy about it at all and ended up stomping away to her bedroom, slamming the door hard and causing Molly to jump.

"What do we do?" Tiffany asked as she plopped down on one of Mackenzie's couches.

Molly joined her and sighed. She didn't have the answers. That was Mackenzie's department. "I'm not sure. Just be here for her, I guess."

"Gosh, but she doesn't even want us here, Moll."

"I know, but we can't even begin to imagine how she feels. We can't take it personally."

"God, how screwed up is this? I mean, why do things like this happen?" Tiffany started to pick at imaginary lint on her pants. "It's unfair."

"Hard to say, but it sucks."

Tiffany shook her head and said, "Let's talk about something else. I can't even deal with any more negative stuff or my brain will explode."

"I hear ya. Today has been such a weird frigging day. Everything was so wonderful earlier, then I got the call from Mackenzie. It's crazy how quickly things can change in an instant." Molly snapped her fingers.

Tiffany agreed and changed the subject. "Tell me what's up with you and Owen."

Molly couldn't help but smile. "Well, I took your advice and Mackenzie's. I tried calling him. He didn't answer."

"Oh no, but I have a feeling it all worked out somehow." Tiffany cocked her head to the side, grinning at Molly.

"I went to him. I figured...what did I have to lose, really? You know?"

"Good for you. And?"

"It went well. We went bowling, of all things."

"I'm glad that you did that. I'm proud of you. Lil' go-getter, you. But bowling? Seriously?"

Molly swatted her and rolled her eyes. "I'm sort of proud of myself, too. You know I'm awful at relationships. I just hope I don't screw this up." Molly bit her bottom lip as she spoke.

"You won't. I don't think Owen will let you."

"Probably not. That poor guy seems to handle my bat-shit craziness with a little too much ease."

"Yeah, bless his heart."

Tiffany and Molly both laughed, which felt wonderful, and it reminded Molly that life did carry on.

* * * *

The next few days had been rough. Molly was sitting in Mackenzie's bed. Chocolate wrappers and balled-up tissues were scattered around them. She was trying everything to cheer Mackenzie up. Molly had decided to stay with her. Tiffany had to get back to work, but she always stopped by afterward, usually bringing dinner with her. Molly had spent the last half an hour trying to convince Mackenzie to go shower. She had spent most of the day curled up in a ball, begging Molly to let her sleep. But at least things were getting a little better every day, though. Today they'd watched a movie, eaten chocolate and cried. Yesterday, they had watched a movie and cried. The day before, they'd just cried.

"Mackenzie, you look like hell. You will feel so much better if you shower."

Opening another chocolate, Mackenzie acted as if she hadn't heard her. Molly huffed and hopped off the king-size bed that was far too large for the bedroom. She started to gather the tissues and wrappers.

They'd already barely survived a visit to the mortuary, and Molly had been walking on eggshells ever since. Enough was enough. It was time to get a handle on things. Like pulling off a bandage, she needed to do it quickly.

"Come on, girl. You gotta snap out of this," Molly said

firmly. "It's time to get yourself together."

"I know."

"Then go shower," Molly ordered, grabbing more tissues and throwing them away in a little waste basket that was tucked beside one of the nightstands.

"Ugh, do I have to?"

"Um, yeah. You're sort of gross." Molly pinched her nose closed to prove her point.

Mackenzie sniffed herself and ran her fingers through her tangled mess of blonde hair. "I suppose you're right."

Well, damn. Molly surely hadn't expected that. That was progress.

"Maybe we can go for a walk later?" Molly suggested.

"Don't push it." Mackenzie moved slowly off the bed.

"Just saying that a little sunshine might do us both some good."

"Baby steps, Molly."

"Oh please, don't give me that crud."

Mackenzie rolled her eyes and said, "You don't have to keep sticking around here. I know you have stuff to do."

"That's the beauty of my job. I can schedule it whenever I want. It's awesome being the boss."

"But I'm sure you had clients lined up, boss lady," Mackenzie argued.

"That's none of your concern." Molly shook a finger at her playfully.

"Fine. What about Owen?"

"What about Owen?" Molly rolled her eyes.

Mackenzie's voice softened. "You should go out with him. He's probably dying from not seeing you. You don't need to be locked up in here with me. I'll be okay. I promise."

"Well, I'm glad that you think that, but I'm not going anywhere yet. Just let me be here with you, okay?"

Mackenzie smiled and said quietly, "I will be okay, Molly. I appreciate you looking after me, but I think I can manage now."

"Um, this coming from the lady who has refused to

shower for a couple of days. Yeah, you're managing just fine."

Mackenzie laughed. "Okay, you have a point there. But I'm headed to the shower now. That should count for something."

Molly raised her eyebrows at Mackenzie. "Yeah, now that you finally caught a whiff of yourself."

"You are so mean, but, God, I love ya," Mackenzie said as she stomped off to the bathroom.

"Love ya too, stinky." Molly started pulling the linens off the bed. The pale floral pattern on the sheets matched the comforter. The design reflected Mackenzie perfectly. It was classic, ultra-feminine and beautiful.

After hauling the bundle of dirty bedding into the laundry room, Molly poured the detergent into the washing machine. Its clean scent was pleasant and hung in the air for a moment. Maybe Mackenzie was right. Perhaps it was time just to let her be for a while. Mackenzie was made of some strong stuff, and if anyone of the three of them could survive something as terrible as this, it was Mackenzie. Molly was torn. Part of her was anxious to get back to her studio, yet she was glad she'd spent this time with Mackenzie. They hadn't laughed or had fun, of course, but just being with her in this tough time — being there for her — had been enough.

But before she would abandon her buddy, Molly decided to make some grilled cheese sandwiches. Carbs seemed like an appropriate send-off.

* * * *

The city lights were twinkling off the water. Seattle could be so gorgeous and full of romance. Owen held Molly's hand in his as they strolled along the waterfront after dinner.

"How's Mackenzie holding up?" Owen asked cautiously. They had danced around the elephant in the room all evening. She'd been expecting him to ask all night, but she knew he'd also wanted to do everything to keep her mind off the sad subject.

"She's a tough chick. I have to hand it to her. I don't think I could cope as well as she is," Molly answered as Owen led them to a bench with a remarkable view of the harbor as the sun lowered into horizon. Smaller boats bobbed silently in the water. There were hardly any tourists walking about, and it was peaceful being in Owen's company.

"So what's next, a funeral or service of some kind?"

Molly was slow to answer. "Actually, I think her sister's ashes will be ready tomorrow." She wasn't really prepared for how that was going to go, but they would be there for Mackenzie.

"Just a thought—it's not my place or anything—but if Mackenzie wants to scatter her sister's ashes out in the ocean, I'm happy to help."

"That's sweet of you and a wonderful offer. We haven't discussed anything yet. It's been a lot of crying and just trying to hold it all together, you know?"

"I can imagine. You know, when I lost my uncle, it tore me up. It's hard to lose family. I was incredibly close to him. He was the one that got me into fishing." Owen's voice went quiet and Molly reached for his hand.

"I'm so sorry, Owen," Molly whispered.

"It was a couple of years ago. He had a stroke and it was quick. We weren't prepared for it, but we got through it." Owen's eyes grew shiny with held-back tears.

"To be honest, I haven't lost anyone since my grandmother passed away when I was a kid. I dread the day when one of my parents dies." Molly could feel her heart slice with fear and sadness. Owen wrapped his arms around her and sheltered her.

"Well, it happens, but life carries on." Owen smiled at her and kissed her gingerly on her forehead. "My uncle would've liked you a lot."

"Really? Why?" Molly asked as she smiled up at him.

"Because I like you a lot." He lowered his lips to hers. The velvety softness and warmth of his kiss sent tingles through her. After pulling back, he looked at her with those gray eyes, the lights of the city reflecting in them. "You need to meet my parents someday."

Molly swallowed, her insecurities invading her brain. "What if they don't like me?"

"Don't look so worried. They'll love you."

"Owen, we've hardly been seeing each other. Isn't it a little soon?"

Pulling her close to him, securing her to his chest, Owen said, "The way I see it, when you know, you know. And, babe, trust me. I know." He planted another kiss on Molly, this time on her nose.

* * * *

Mackenzie had called them both to meet her at the funeral home to pick up her sister's ashes. It had only been a few days since Molly had quit staying over. Mackenzie was coping, but just barely. That much was obvious to both Tiffany and Molly. She had dark shadows around her eyes, a rumpled and messy look to her outfit and she even seemed thinner.

Molly knew that today was going to be awful and she had been dreading it all morning. Standing next to her as Mackenzie received the cremains from the mortuary receptionist made it final somehow. Seeing Mackenzie hold that small wooden box containing all that was left of her sister broke Molly's heart into a million and one pieces. Molly blinked away the tears she'd been desperately holding back. She looked over at Tiffany, who was carefully wiping away her own. Mackenzie wasn't crying at all. Her expression was soft, and she looked to Molly and said, "Can she come with me to *Friendship Friday*?"

Molly had not expected that to come out of Mackenzie's mouth. It was almost Friday and she wasn't certain that they would be hanging out, considering everything. It wasn't as though this was some sort of *Weekend at Bernie's* type of thing. They were dealing with ashes, so the request wasn't all that strange. A little morbid maybe, but after all was said and done, did it really matter? As long as it made Mackenzie happy, Molly would do anything to help.

With Molly's new mantra tattooed on her brain—'just go with it'—she said, "She never really was much of drinker, but as long as she brings snacks, it's totally cool. But I get to pick the movie."

Mackenzie laughed. So did Tiffany. The heaviness of the situation was forgotten, even if for just a brief moment.

Chapter Eight

Molly ran her fingers along her lips. They were numb. Owen sat back with a smug and satisfied expression locked onto his face.

Molly had made the enormous mistake of trying to convince Owen that she was the better kisser. He had proved her wrong. *Damn him.*

"I told you I was better."

Molly glared at him. He *thought* he'd won. She still had a few tricks up her sleeve. They were cuddling on a small love seat in her studio. The lighting was dim and the nearby city lights tried sneaking in through the large windows. Molly had to think for a moment, which was difficult. Her body was not quite satisfied with just kissing. Desire spread like a raging wildfire, quick and fast, burning hot as it teased Molly. Lust pooled in her belly and it clenched with need. She hoped that Owen was suffering like she was. It would only be fair.

The love seat, as contemporary and chic as it was, was proving to be a bit small. That could turn out badly. In her mind, Molly saw herself slithering over him, straddling his lap, hopefully feeling his hardness pressing against her then showing him who was truly the better kisser — and maybe getting more than a kiss. Much more.

But when she tried her maneuver, she wound up on the floor. It didn't really surprise her. This was her, after all.

"Oh my God, Molly, are you okay?" Owen quickly jumped up.

Molly was laughing hard. Of course she'd fallen, because she was anything but graceful. She was a clumsy goofball who really had no business attempting to be sexy, even when she felt sexy. It had seemed like a fairly rock-solid plan in her head that unfortunately hadn't quite translated when she'd attempted it. And it sure had been a mood killer.

"Molly, seriously, are you okay?" Owen asked again as he hovered over her.

"Yes," Molly was finally able to answer between the hysterical laughs escaping her.

Owen lowered himself next to her on the floor. The look he gave her was not what she expected. It was smoldering, quiet and twisted with concern. It made her nervous for a moment. Those pesky butterflies were tangled inside her.

"You have no idea how beautiful you are, do you?" His fingers began to play in her hair that was fanned out on floor.

Molly looked up at him. "Um, I think you have mistaken me for someone else. I'm a complete klutz."

He had his mouth on hers in mere seconds. He roamed his hands over her body and she desperately wanted to feel him against her. She tasted the lust in his kiss, the hunger. Her body quaked with sudden need for him—a need she'd known she had, but the depth of it now shocked her.

"God, I want you, Owen," Molly whispered in his ear as he broke the kiss then trailed his lips to her neck. She wove her fingers through his hair, pulling him closer to her, instinctively spreading her legs to invite him there. She cursed the jeans she'd opted to wear. A skirt would have gotten her where she wanted to go a whole lot faster. She ground against him and moaned as he returned the motion, letting her feel his hardness. *God, he's huge.* She writhed wildly, grasping and rubbing, wanting more contact. This dry humping was not cutting it. She needed to feel him inside her.

"Please," she whimpered, as the need between her legs grew heavy.

He shifted his weight and returned his mouth to hers,

hushing her. Molly flicked her tongue against his and nipped at his bottom lip, praying that it would send him over the edge. They continued the teasing dance with their tongues dueling, deep and wet, hot and needy. Her whole body was tingling and demanding to be touched. Her breasts were heavy, her nipples taut. She felt like she was going to die if they kept this up. She wanted more. She wanted release. She wanted to come — with Owen.

"For Pete's sake, Owen, you're killing me."

Owen pulled away briefly. "I told you I was a better kisser."

"Okay, you win. Can we please…?" Molly whined as she reached down to the waist of his pants.

"Nope."

Her hand stilled. "What the hell? Are you kidding me?"

Owen answered with a sly smile. "Not here and not like this."

"Ugh, I hate you right now." Molly shoved Owen off her. She was trembling with need and had just let him know how much she wanted him. She could tell how much he wanted her. She could see the tenting in his jeans. *How can he do this to me? Why is he doing this to us?*

"Trust me. I will make it up to you," he offered as he got up from the floor and reached to help her up.

Molly swatted his hand away. "Might as well leave me here. I'm all hot and bothered. At least the floor is cold."

"Yeah — and hard. We aren't kids anymore," Owen joked. "I'm more about making love in a bed at this stage in my life."

"Where's the spontaneity in that?" Molly threw her arms up. Owen seized the opportunity and forced her off the floor.

"Are you always this cranky when you're horny?"

"No, just when someone won't comply," Molly replied hastily, taking deep breaths to lower the lust that still clawed at her belly.

Owen tugged her to him and kissed her gently on her

forehead. "I didn't even realize I was that good a kisser."

Molly stuck out her tongue at him. *He is, and I need a cold, cold shower.*

* * * *

"Can you pour me some more?" Tiffany asked, lifting her glass in the air as Molly held the nearly empty bottle of Moscato.

"Mac?" Molly shook the bottle in her direction.

"Yes, please," she answered.

It had been a long day, but they were all seated around Mackenzie's kitchen table. Her sister's ashes were in a small wooden box on the chair next to her. *Friendship Friday* was back — all of them lounging around in comfy pajamas, no makeup and lots of wine.

They had kept their snack choice simple for the night. There was a platter with a variety of cheeses, crackers and fruit, and it all went great with the wine.

Nibbling on a cracker, Tiffany sighed with a deep contentment.

"What was that for?" Molly smiled when she took her seat next to Tiffany.

"Nothing. Just glad that we're all here tonight."

"Me too," Molly added before she sipped from her wine glass and looked over to Mackenzie, who wore a thoughtful expression.

"It's funny how horrible stuff can bring people back together, isn't it?" Mackenzie said as she grabbed a square slice of cheddar cheese and popped it into her mouth.

Tiffany shifted nervously in her seat. They'd never discussed the fight. It had been swept away, but they all knew it was hanging around.

Mackenzie continued to speak after she sipped her wine. "I mean, if my sister hadn't gotten into that wreck and died, I probably wouldn't be sitting here with you guys."

Tiffany looked down. Her shoulders dropped and Molly

knew it had to hurt. That was a low blow and Molly decided to quickly squash this before it got out of hand.

"No, you're wrong, Mackenzie. We would be, because eventually you and Tiffany would have gotten over that stupid bullshit fight and realized how important your friendship is." Molly paused, letting the words sink in before she started again. "It's terrible that it took your sister's death to realize that you needed your friends there with you. You asked for her to come to the hospital with me, Mackenzie. You needed Tiffany."

Tiffany didn't speak and Mackenzie looked a little taken aback. *Too bad, it needed to be said.*

Mackenzie inhaled deeply, her eyes trained on the ceiling. "I guess you're right."

Tiffany rose from her seat and went to Mackenzie, wrapping her arms tightly around her. "I'm sorry for being an asshole."

"Me, too," Mackenzie responded, letting her head rest on Tiffany's arms.

"Should I grab my camera and snap this little Hallmark moment?" Molly asked, then put her drink to her lips.

"Oh, you shut it. So tell us what's new with you and Owen?" Mackenzie tossed Molly a playful, annoyed look.

She had to think about that for a moment. What was new? Oh yeah, that she was beyond sexually frustrated. That she was pretty much convinced that Owen was trying to see how far he could push her until she snapped and finally tied him to her bed.

"Um, things are good, I guess," Molly answered.

Mackenzie eyed her suspiciously. "Hmm..."

Tiffany came right out with it. "What Mac is trying to ask is, have you guys boned yet?" There was no beating around the bush with her, brash and direct was always Tiffany's approach.

"No, we haven't," Molly confirmed.

"Well, that explains why she's so cranky." Tiffany turned to Mackenzie, who nodded in agreement.

"Like either of you should talk. I don't see either of you guys getting laid," Molly shot back.

"She does have a point there," Mackenzie agreed.

"So we know that you aren't screwing his brains out. Sorry. But are things getting more serious?" Tiffany asked as she swirled the wine in her glass. "This is really delicious, by the way."

"It is, isn't it?" Mackenzie swallowed a large gulp.

Molly rolled her eyes. "I don't know that we are getting serious. You guys know that I'm terrible at relationships."

"Well, do you like the direction that you guys are going?" Mackenzie shrugged.

"No, Molly, you need to be asking yourself if you find yourself in knots and full of butterflies when he is around," Tiffany said.

It didn't take her long to really consider that. Hell, she even got butterflies when he wasn't around. The very thought of Owen caused an uproar inside her. She and her vibrator had worked that out at bedtime on more than one occasion. Her body acted funny when he was around. She was in a constant state of heat and lust at the mere sight of him. It was like she didn't even know herself anymore.

Tiffany gave her a long look. Mackenzie stared at her too.

"I think she's into him," Mackenzie proclaimed.

"No doubt. She's smitten," Tiffany added.

God, smitten? Really? That was definitely not a term she'd use. Molly countered, "I don't know if I'd say that."

"You should, because you are." Tiffany raised her wine glass. "If the shoe fits, lace that bitch up."

Molly wasn't the only one rolling her eyes again, but this time it was with laughter.

* * * *

Her studio was almost too bright that morning, the sun's rays filtering through the large windows, spilling onto the floor and walls. It was the weekend and she shouldn't even be there, but she needed to catch up. After the emotionally exhausting week she'd endured, Molly also felt some much-needed peace being in her favorite place.

She had accomplished a great deal and had actually surprised herself, organizing her schedule for various shoots, tinkering with a few edits and even paying a couple of bills. Now, as the late afternoon sun dipped lower, casting shadows in her studio, she knew she should probably call it a day. Shutting down her computer, she heard her buzzer sound loudly, and she was curious who might be paying her a visit, especially on the weekend. Maybe it was her besties popping in to say hello. She knew that Mackenzie and Tiffany were out shopping, engaging in some cathartic retail therapy, but Molly had been happy to decline. Shopping had never really been her thing. It was definitely more of a sport that Mackenzie and Tiffany were well-trained for and loved.

Slightly jogging, Molly reached the door to greet her visitor. Pulling it back revealed Owen, standing there with an enormous grin on his sexy face, and, of course, holding two coffees.

"Oh, I love you. I love you," Molly squealed.

"Really? Now that's a greeting a man likes to hear." Owen bent down to kiss her, but Molly bobbed out of the way, snatching a coffee from him.

"I was talking to this," Molly said as she raised the large paper cup. "But you're not so bad, either." She lifted up on her toes and planted a kiss on his cheek, his stubble grazing her lips.

"That's what I figured." Owen laughed as he walked inside the studio with Molly, linking their arms together. "Have you been working all day? I tried texting you a little bit ago."

"I stayed off my phone. I had so much crap to catch up on that I didn't need any distractions," she explained before she took a sip, relishing the delicious flavor of the coffee as it entered her mouth.

"What about now? You up for a little distraction?" His eyes looked like coals ashed over, burning with a hint of untamed desire. She swallowed hard.

"I might be. What did you have in mind?" Molly leaned into him. She could smell his spicy aftershave and inhaled deeply, loving the aroma of the cologne and Owen.

He kissed her on top of her head and said, "That's a loaded question there, miss. I could tell you all the ways I'd love to distract you, but I have a feeling just grabbing some dinner and a movie might be more what you had in mind."

"Well, I am starving and a movie does sound like fun. What about a distracting dessert?" Molly couldn't resist teasing him, but she was punishing herself equally.

"You know, we could always order in and rent a movie?" Owen winked at her. His sly, lopsided smirk created a sudden heat in her belly and a dampness was suddenly forming in her jeans. He moved his hands down to her hips, grasping them as he pulled her closer.

This cat and mouse chase had been fun, but Molly was more than ready to take it to the next level. Her body shouted, 'Hell, yes!' But her brain was a little more hesitant, and so was her heart. Of course she was attracted to him. Every single moment spent near him had her in a melted pool of need. That was the only way to explain it.

She wanted him, terribly. But, she also had to take things a little slow, to make sure that she didn't screw anything up by diving in head first and rushing all the fun bits. Even though she'd been angry when he'd stopped her attempted seduction before, she was glad it had happened. *What happens when the mystery is gone? Do those wonderful butterflies in my belly manage to escape?* Molly was scared to find out, so as much as she would love to get tangled up in the sheets with Owen — like yesterday — she wanted to proceed with caution.

Now, she wasn't so sure Owen was on the same page about that. Apparently, Owen hadn't gotten the memo, especially when he was too busy leaving a moist trail of kisses down her neck to her collarbone. Molly moaned. The heat began forming deep inside her. *Is this another one of those moments when I should 'just go with it'?*

* * * *

Owen had made that decision for her. They were now seated at a lively Mexican food place, gorging themselves on an insane number of tacos. Mariachi music played at just the right volume. They were each working on another beer and Molly couldn't keep out of the chips and salsa.

"You're beautiful. Do you know that?" Owen was gazing at her from across the booth.

Molly felt salsa dribble on her chin. *Yeah, real beautiful.* She grabbed a napkin and dabbed the cilantro-infused mix off herself.

"I think it's the taco coma you are about to go into. It's got you hallucinating."

"You can't take a compliment, can you? I find it to be the strangest thing, coming from someone who captures beauty all time," he explained as he added fire-roasted hot sauce to another hard-shell taco.

"Oh, please. Why do you think I'm behind the lens, hmm?"

Owen shook his head as he took a large bite. Shreds of lettuce, cheese and meat escaped onto his plate. He chewed and looked reflective as he ate. "You're wrong," he finally said.

"Um, no, I'm not."

"Yeah, you are. You are so blind when it comes to you."

"No, I own mirrors, Owen, and trust me, I'm not a model." Molly reached for her beer, feeling herself grow agitated and hoping that the cool drink would settle her down before things got out of hand.

"Well, that's the problem right there," he said matter-of-factly, then he took another bite out, spilling out even more of the contents along with sharp shards of corn tortilla shell onto his plate.

Molly cocked her head to the side, wanting him to explain just what the hell he meant. "What's the problem?"

"You."

"More specifically, Owen."

"That you work with these models and it gives you this unrealistic interpretation of what beauty should be." He paused and looked hard at her, holding his stare with hers. "You aren't a model, Molly."

"Well, thanks for pointing that out."

"You're not listening."

"Yes, I am. You think I live in this shallow world where beauty is defined in a way that you don't agree with."

He frowned then replied, "I suppose, but you're missing the point I'm trying to make."

"I don't believe I am," Molly countered, signaling the waitress for another beer.

"You are. Why are you so quick to assume the worst?"

Great, here comes another argument that develops literally out of nothing. Molly exhaled and shot a warning to Owen. "Look, mister. Don't ruin this lovely dinner by starting a fight."

"Babe, I'm not the one fighting." He raised his eyebrows at her then winked.

Seriously? A wink. Now Molly felt her blood pressure rising a tad. She just couldn't help it. Owen had a way of turning her on in an instant and pissing her off just as quickly.

"Why do you do that?" She was growing more flustered by the moment. Molly wasn't sure what she wanted to do more, tell him to go screw off or screw his brains out.

Owen shrugged. "I have no idea what you're talking about, doll." Then he did it again—a sly and sexy grin, accompanied with another wink.

* * * *

"Oh, Moll, come on. You need to quit fighting with him. Quit fighting it." Tiffany was dressed in black leggings, hot pink designer running shoes and an oversized black tank layered with another.

They were running along the shore at one of their favorite little best-kept secrets, Carkeek Beach. It was connected to a fantastic park for families to play with their toddlers or host birthday parties on a sunny afternoon. Very family friendly, but it also was quiet in the early mornings and evenings, which made it perfect for jogging. The serene and simple landscape made the workout almost bearable — almost. Again, not exactly an activity that Molly was fond of, but she could stand to tone up, especially if she did want Owen to see her naked. She wanted that very much. There was no question. Going slowly and cautiously was good, but it was also frustrating.

"Fighting it? Fighting what, exactly?" Molly huffed, trying to catch her breath and keep up with Tiffany.

"You are fighting this whole relationship thing. You keep trying to sabotage it. Knock that shit off." Tiffany stopped suddenly and bent down to tie her shoelace. Molly welcomed the brief pause and stretched. Tiffany looked up at her and said, "Remember your whole mantra, 'just go with it'? Um, you are kinda sucking at it."

"I have been trying," Molly feebly attempted to defend herself, knowing full well she hadn't been really putting in the effort she could be.

Tiffany glared at her. "Seriously?"

"Okay, fine. I was good about Mackenzie bringing her sister's ashes to *Friendship Friday*," Molly pointed out. "You aren't exactly rockin' the dating circuit."

"We were at her house. Besides, I don't think that really counts. This is more about you and Owen — and you and relationships in general." Tiffany pulled her legs behind her one at a time. "This isn't about me."

"I know."

"I thought you were going to try more with him?"

"I am," Molly said, as she adjusted her ponytail that was coming undone. The wind was beginning to pick up, the waves slamming hard onto the sand as a storm started to creep in. Only moments earlier, the evening sun had been out, beating down on them. Now the clouds had snatched it away—typical Seattle weather. "I seem to always mess things up."

"You need to let it go, or let us decide," Tiffany suggested.

"What do you mean?"

"I think we should have Owen over for dinner. We need to get to know this guy a bit. Let's see if he's worth all this trouble." Tiffany set off in a sprint, leaving Molly behind in the sand.

Molly stood there alone with only her thoughts for a second, staring out at the water before setting off to catch up to Tiffany. Could Owen handle her crazy friends? She could only imagine what kind of third degree Mackenzie would put him through. Tiffany, she wasn't so much worried about, though this was her idea. That meant anything was possible to come out of her mouth. That girl lacked a filter when it was most needed. *Crap.* Now Molly felt a little bad for the poor guy. But if he really wanted to be with her, it was best that he get to know her besties. They were a package deal. She couldn't help but smile at the challenge he was about to face.

God help him.

* * * *

"You really up for this?" Molly touched the sleeve of his shirt. It was a little late to be asking him, considering they were standing just outside Mackenzie's door and had already knocked.

"Stop worrying." Owen kissed the top of her head. His hands were full with gifts of pure bribery—flowers, wine and even some gourmet eclairs. *Yeah, he's fully stocked with ammunition.*

"It'll be fun," he assured her.

Famous last words.

Mackenzie opened the door, a cautious and polite smile plastered on her face. "Come on in, you guys."

"Wow, it smells great in here," Owen complimented. He was right. It did smell amazing.

"Thank you." Mackenzie closed the door behind them. There was no turning back.

Owen stood near the opening to the kitchen. Mackenzie came up to him. "I brought some goodies."

"I see that." Mackenzie laughed. Suddenly Tiffany appeared.

"I heard someone brought goodies." Tiffany giggled as she offered her hand to Owen. Mackenzie took the flowers, wine and the pink box that was filled with delicious eclairs. Owen scooped Tiffany up, dismissing her offer of a handshake.

"So, you're a hugger?" Tiffany teased.

"Hey, I feel like I know both of you from all the stories Molly has shared with me."

Owen was good, damn good. Flattery would get him everywhere and Molly watched as he presented Tiffany and Mackenzie with loads of it. *This man and his damn charm.* He even winked at Molly, causing warmth to rush through her.

"Come sit," Mackenzie ordered. "Dinner is just about ready."

"Want some wine, Owen?" Tiffany offered.

"That sounds great." Owen ushered Molly to the table that had been set up quite beautifully. There was a gorgeous arrangement of flowers in the center. Several small candles were lit and flickering a romantic glow on the dishes.

Pulling out a chair for Molly, Owen waited until Mackenzie and Tiffany arrived back to the table. He also pulled out chairs for them and, like the perfect gentleman, he waited until they were seated to finally sit down.

Both Mackenzie and Tiffany threw Molly a look. It pretty

much read, *What's the problem here? Why aren't you jumping all over this?*

"So, Owen, we know a little about you," Mackenzie started.

Tiffany jumped right in and added, "That you clobbered our poor friend with a giant fish. Shame on you."

Owen laughed. "I'd do it all again, but maybe with a smaller fish." He patted Molly's hand.

"Aww," Mackenzie and Tiffany both cooed.

Seriously? Are they falling for Owen that easily? She'd expected them to badger the hell out of him, make him prove his undying love, but no. They were already wrapped around his finger.

Owen's eyes grew stormy as his voice lowered. "Not to dampen this lovely mood, but, Mackenzie, I just wanted to extend my condolences. I am very sorry to hear about your sister."

Crap. Molly looked over to Mackenzie, expecting some kind of reaction — maybe tears, a scowl, something. Instead, Mackenzie smiled gently at him. "Thank you, Owen. I really appreciate that." *Wow, he is really good.*

Dinner carried on beautifully. They laughed as they ate, sharing stories, and finding so many common interests. They realized they knew some of the same people. Even in a big city like Seattle, it was still a small world. Molly couldn't have asked for the evening to turn out better. As they left, Mackenzie loaded Owen up with leftovers and made him promise to come by again.

Once tucked inside Owen's car, Molly released a heavy sigh.

"What was that for?" Owen asked as he started the car.

"Nothing," Molly lied. She couldn't shake the feelings that were breeding inside her.

"You know, you're not a very good liar." Owen backed carefully out of Mackenzie's driveway and cruised slowly out of the quiet neighborhood.

"It's nothing, really."

"Well, it sure didn't sound like nothing."

Molly hated how Owen could read her so easily. No guy she'd ever dated had that ability, and perhaps that was what terrified her about Owen.

"Your friends are lovely." Owen found a freeway on-ramp and started to hit the gas to merge into the light traffic. They were quickly met with a sea of red taillights, causing them to slow to snail's crawl. "Dinner was fantastic. That was really sweet of Mackenzie to give me some leftovers."

"Mac is our mother hen. She's the best," Molly commented as she stared out of the window, thankful for the darkness inside the car. Tears started to pool. *Why am I so emotional? I should be tickled pink that Owen and my friends got along so well.*

"Molly, what's the matter, babe?" Owen's voice was soothing and thick with concern.

What is the matter? Molly really didn't know. The only thought that came into her mind was that Owen might be the *one.* That was something she hadn't expected or really been searching for. She wasn't even sure she wanted it now that she'd found it. A tiny piece of her worried that if he was indeed the guy, the *one,* that it would somehow change everything. Molly didn't handle change well. Would he expect her to give up her friends if they got serious? How could she balance her time with Tiffany and Mackenzie and still have enough time for Owen? Too many questions whirled about in her mind.

The rest of the car ride was quiet. Owen didn't press any further, which Molly appreciated. This was definitely not one of those times when she was ruled by her new mantra. She was caught up in worry, stupid concerns for something that hadn't even happened yet. Nope, she wasn't 'just going with it' like she'd promised herself. She was doing exactly what Tiffany had accused her of, fighting it. Why? She had no idea. Maybe she didn't think she was good enough to land a guy like Owen. He was turning out to be too perfect. And to make matters worse, her friends friggin' adored him. She couldn't wait to get that phone call in the morning.

Chapter Nine

Tiffany and Mackenzie stood just outside her studio door, holding precious coffee and wearing enormous grins. She had been waiting for this all day. Even with the Seattle sun making everything bright, Molly was gloomy. She'd woken up in a sour mood. It had stayed with her all day and wasn't showing any signs of leaving.

"Why are you so cranky?" Tiffany crinkled her nose at Molly as she passed her to come inside.

"I figured you would be all sunshine and roses today, buttercup," Mackenzie added as she placed the coffees on the large glass table.

Molly rolled her eyes and closed the door. She staggered slowly toward them, shuffling her sock-clad feet on the smooth wooden floor.

"Why so not chipper?" Mackenzie asked as she distributed the coffees.

"I don't know." Molly slunk down into the one of the chairs and grabbed a cup.

Mackenzie frowned at her. "The sun is shining. It's beautiful out there."

"You've just got done shopping. I can tell. You're simply glowing." Molly was glad that Mackenzie seemed so upbeat.

"You could have joined us," Tiffany added, raising her eyebrows at Molly.

"No, I'm good. I don't like shopping, even for groceries."

Mackenzie patted Molly's arm. "Tell us what's wrong. You fight with that adorable man?"

"So he won you guys over pretty quickly," Molly snapped.

She hadn't meant for her words to come out so harshly.

"Um, you tasted those eclairs, right?" Tiffany rolled her eyes at Molly. "What happened?"

"Nothing."

"Liar," Mackenzie and Tiffany both said in unison.

"I'm serious...nothing. He dropped me off, I said goodnight, then he went home. End of story."

"Because you wanted it to end that way?" Mackenzie asked slowly, eyeing Molly suspiciously.

Tiffany took a long sip from her coffee. "You know what we need?"

Mackenzie and Molly shook their heads.

Tiffany smiled. "A girls' weekend trip."

Molly felt her mood lift a little. A trip out of the city might be just the cure. "I think that's a fabulous idea."

"Really?" Tiffany looked surprised. "I figured you would throw a fit and I would have to hogtie you."

"Am I that awful?"

"Difficult, yes. Awful, no," Mackenzie pointed out. "I think a girls' trip is a fantastic idea. So, where to?"

"Where did you have in mind?"

Tiffany gazed up at the ceiling, thoughtfully. "Like, how far do we feel like traveling? Where have we not gone together yet?"

Their gears moved collectively, each plotting the perfect destination. It couldn't be too far, but yet had to be far away enough that they felt like they actually weren't anywhere near Seattle.

"Vegas?" Mackenzie finally suggested.

Leave it to Miss Prim and Proper to choose the wildest and most sinful possible place.

"Hell yeah," Tiffany agreed. "What do you think, Molly?"

Molly sat quietly, considering Vegas as an option.

Obviously, in hopes to sway her, Mackenzie added, "Imagine the fun we'd have, sun—lots of sun—and cocktails. Maybe you could use a little of both to perk you up."

"It's sunny now," argued Molly.

"Well, you need more, much more, cranky pants. Then there's the shows, the lights...just the magic of Vegas." Mackenzie sighed. Her eyes seemed so far away, as though she was already exploring The Strip.

"Vegas is kind of yucky."

Tiffany scowled at Molly. "Oh, you stop. There is a lot of fun there—gambling and, like Mackenzie said, shows. Tons of entertainment."

"Yeah, and hookers and strip clubs. Probably tons of homeless people or runaway drug-addicted kids." Molly pouted as she crossed her arms.

"See? Difficult," Mackenzie pointed out again.

"Yeah, just be packed. Mackenzie and I will take care of all the travel stuff."

"Fine. It might actually be fun," Molly admitted. She wondered what Owen would have to say about her leaving on an adventure and she shooed the worry away. She needed this and maybe not telling him would be for the best. What he didn't know wouldn't hurt him.

"Um, that's a given. Us and Vegas... *Boom!*" Tiffany made an explosion sound and they all laughed.

Life had felt like a rollercoaster since she'd met Owen and she longed to have some girl time. A sweet little escape sounded great right now and going with her best friends, even better.

* * * *

Several days later, early morning drizzle covered everything with a cold and slick wetness. Armed with their coffee and rolling luggage, the three friends were standing in the security line at the nearly empty Sea-Tac airport.

"This is going to be so much fun," Tiffany squealed.

"Tone the excitement down. It's a little early." Mackenzie covered her mouth in a yawn. Molly agreed. Her coffee hadn't kicked in enough yet for Tiffany's cheeriness.

"Don't be a party pooper. We're about to storm Vegas!"

"I'm *so* napping on the plane," Molly stated as they moved along in the line, putting their purses into large gray plastic containers to be scanned. Molly was a pro at flying. She knew the routine. She wore sandals to easily remove, if need be. She made sure nothing she wore would set off the machine, unlike Tiffany, who was causing a lot of commotion. Her friend was fussing with her designer mini-boots. Her studded jeans, though fashionably amazing, were making the machine go nuts. Molly winced each time the alarm shrilled. They finally let her through after wanding her, and Molly was more than relieved to be on their way. "Good Lord, woman, next time just wear yoga pants or something. You don't need to be so cute," Molly said as they strolled to their gate.

"Um, what if there is a hot guy that could very well be Mr. Right? He's not going to even look my way if I'm not cute. I don't have people throwing fish at me," Tiffany replied. Mackenzie closed her eyes and huffed.

Molly sighed. She was hoping to avoid any talk of Owen. She had been a doing a good job all week hiding from him. She knew it wasn't fair to him, but she needed some space to wrap her mind around everything.

"You guys suck in the morning, bunch of cranky bitches," Tiffany complained as they got into another line, this one to check in at their gate.

"No, you are just annoying," Mackenzie countered, handing the young woman at the counter her ticket information. The woman smiled and started checking in Mackenzie's ticket.

Molly was next, then Tiffany. Once boarding began, they all started down the carpeted hallway to get on the plane. After stepping inside and finding their row, Mackenzie — being the tall one — stored their suitcases in the overhead compartment.

"You think it's too early for a cocktail?" Mackenzie asked when she took the window seat.

"Not if we're going to survive this trip together," Tiffany whispered.

Molly sat between them to keep them from fighting and was tempted to put her earphones in to drown them out. "Come on, you two. Let's just get there in one piece, please."

Molly didn't like flying. She did it often enough, but she never enjoyed it. Why? One word — *turbulence*. On second thought, it wasn't too early for a cocktail. By the time the flight attendants came around after they were in the air, Molly had made her decision. "Can I get a cranberry and vodka, please?"

The woman raised her eyebrows, but smiled politely. Apparently she thought it was too early to be drinking. Well, she wasn't going to be the one sitting in between Mackenzie and Tiffany for the next two hours.

Mackenzie laughed and ordered a cocktail as well. Tiffany shook her head, but placed her order for one, anyway. She commented sarcastically, "Might as well start this vacation off right."

Or drunk.

Though she never made 'drunk', Molly managed to keep herself buzzed enough to pass the flight time in relative calm. But, as they touched down, the landing was bumpy. The plane bounced onto the runway, causing Molly to grip the arms of her chair tightly. Her stomach jumped around. The welcome relief once the plane taxied around the tarmac filled Molly. *Hooray!* They hadn't died in that tin can.

"Yay, we are here," Tiffany said, unbuckling her seat belt.

Mackenzie opened her eyes. She had napped most of the flight. Molly was eager to get off the plane. Her legs ached and she wanted to stretch. The Nevada heat penetrated the jetway as they exited.

"God, it's hot," Tiffany said, dragging her luggage with her.

"Don't you start. You suggested Vegas," Molly warned her, pulling her trusty suitcase.

"Let's just get to the hotel. I want to get in the pool," said

Tiffany.

"I think I'm ready for some drinks by the pool," Mackenzie added, grabbing the large, dark sunglasses from the top of her head then placing them over her eyes. "It is a tad bright here, though."

"Gosh, so glad you guys convinced me to come." Molly laughed as they emerged into a loud and crowded airport. The ringing of slot machines welcomed them properly to Vegas.

"Let's get our car and get out of here." Mackenzie led the way to the rental counter that had several people already waiting to be helped.

"What's the game plan? You guys want to grab some lunch or something?" Tiffany was staring at her cell phone. "I'm trying to see what they have here. You guys feeling like a burger?"

"Too heavy," Mackenzie answered.

"Pizza?" Tiffany tried again, not looking up from her phone, moving slowly in the line.

"Too hot," Mackenzie replied, taking her wallet out of her large Chanel bag as they neared the counter, inching closer.

"And I'm the difficult one?" Molly teased. "You know what I could go for?"

"Hmm?" Tiffany looked up.

"Greek, like a falafel or something," Molly answered.

"Only one place for that and it's back home — the Grecian Corner by the Needle." Mackenzie smiled as the line moved forward a bit more.

Molly's tummy growled. She hadn't realized how hungry she was. "Good point. I love that place. Their calamari is amazing."

Tiffany turned her attention back to her phone, searching desperately for food options. "Seafood?"

"Not here. You guys keep picking stuff that we could eat back home," Mackenzie complained when they finally reached the counter. Mackenzie gave the clerk her name and started filling out paperwork for the small sedan they would be renting.

They packed their suitcases in the trunk of the fire-engine-red car. It was incredibly compact, but it would do the job.

"Crank the air conditioning, please," Tiffany begged Mackenzie, who was exiting the enormous rental car lot. "It's insane how hot it is here."

Molly sat in the back seat and gazed out of the small window. "What did you expect, Tiffany? We're in the desert."

"I know, but still… I'm not acclimated. I'm a Pacific Northwest girl. I don't really do heat."

"Then why did you drag us to Vegas?" Molly laughed.

"Because it's going to be awesome, so you're welcome for all the thanking you will be doing later." Tiffany smirked and winked at Molly.

* * * *

Okay, so maybe Tiffany was right. The hotel was beyond plush. It was golden and regal. Molly felt like a princess, and that was just checking in at the lobby desk.

"This place is incredible, Tiff," Molly whispered under her breath as they received the key to their suite.

"Oh, babe, you ain't seen nothin' yet." Tiffany sported a wide grin as she spun around with her arms outstretched and led them toward the elevator that would take them to their floor.

Elevators were not Molly's favorite thing, but this one was grand. It had spotless mirrored walls, not a single fingerprint or smudge to be found, glittering tile, and she had to admit it was one of the smoother rides she'd taken.

Molly couldn't believe her eyes as they exited. What she saw was almost too fancy, and it was just a hallway.

"Our castle awaits, my queens." Tiffany slid the thin plastic card into their door until the lock glowed green. They all gasped when Tiffany pushed the door open.

"Oh my God." Mackenzie's eyes went wide as she headed

straight for the giant window that offered a spectacular view of the best bits of Vegas.

Molly peeked into a door off to the side—a bathroom fit for royalty. A shower that was almost the size of her entire bathroom was already calling her name. "I call dibs on the first shower."

Tiffany snaked her head into the bathroom and glanced around. "Wow, this is gorgeous."

"Right," Molly said.

They walked to where Mackenzie was standing and all stared out at the incredible view, linking their arms together.

Molly sighed happily. "This vacation is exactly what we all needed. Thanks for convincing me to come along."

* * * *

Could one really have on too much bronzer? Each of them patted the glittery powder all over their faces and chests, almost to the point of sparkling more than that vampire from the movie that had been filmed near Forks, Washington.

"Oh my God, we are going to have so much fun," Tiffany exclaimed, reaching for the glass containing her pre-drink—rum and Diet Coke, to be exact—for their night out on the town.

They were all lined up in front of the giant mirror with the best lighting Molly had ever seen in a bathroom—the kind where every selfie would come out looking damn near professional. Molly had captured several great pictures of them as they'd gotten ready. It felt so much like old times. The nostalgia was hitting her hard and making her a sentimental mess.

Her cell phone vibrated in the rear pocket of her skinny jeans. Retrieving it would be a little difficult. When she finally did, she noticed that Owen had messaged her, and Molly let out a soft huff.

Shoving her phone back into her pocket, Molly polished

off her drink, feeling the sting of the rum that had settled at the bottom hitting her throat. "Ick, that was rough."

"Stir your cocktail better next time, love," Mackenzie advised as she added more mascara to her already-long lashes.

"I did." Molly carried her glass to the sink and washed her hands.

"Was that Owen?" Tiffany asked, while she applied lip liner, enhancing her perfectly shaped mouth.

"Yeah." Molly didn't want to get into a conversation about Owen, about why she kept ignoring his calls and texts. She didn't want to dig deep into her psyche. No, she wanted to escape, to party like she was in her twenties with her girls. That wasn't asking too much, was it?

"You need to at the very least tell that poor man where you are," Mackenzie insisted, as she dabbed a pale, nearly sheer pink gloss along her lips.

"He knows where I am, Mackenzie." *Well, okay, that isn't entirely true.* He did know that she was busy and out of town. Molly didn't feel like she needed to tell Owen every bit of her business. Guilt started to creep in. Did she owe him that, at the very least? Didn't he deserve to know that she was safe and sound? Wasn't that what real couples did—tell each other where they were, who they were with and what they were doing? She wasn't sure that was even what she wanted.

Molly shooed the feelings away and scrunched her hair, adding some more curl to the wavy locks. As she looked in the mirror at her reflection, she saw a woman who was trying desperately to look young. Squeezing into the tight jeans should be considered a week's worth of cardio in her book. She kept fussing with the cleavage-revealing top that Tiffany had told her would look great on her. It all screamed, *I don't want to grow old! I can still be young and fun.* But the truth of the matter was that as Molly looked at all three of them in the mirror, she saw they were aging. They weren't quite cougars, but they were definitely not the youthful bunch they once had been.

She examined the reflection of the women they had become. Mackenzie wore a slinky black top that exposed one of her thin shoulders. She had on stark white capris with strappy wedge sandals, causing her to tower over them even more. Tiffany was decked out in yet another pair of studded jeans that hugged the curves of her hips. She had paired a mauve silky top with a short leather jacket, one that Mackenzie had warned she would get overheated in, but it looked cute and Tiffany was willing to suffer all in the name of cuteness.

All three looked back at her in this window of vanity. Mackenzie smiled, her smoky eyes still sad from the recent loss of her sister. Tiffany's pouty smirk was the same one she'd always sported, yet the faint but visible, creases around her mouth were evidence that she was no longer that fresh-faced teen Molly had grown up with.

It seemed like only yesterday they had hit up clubs, dancing the night away, out on the prowl for hot guys then getting up the next day like nothing had happened. Now it took her days to recover from a night of partying. She had grown a little wiser and was not rockin' her heels tonight. Instead she was wearing flat boots with her jeans tucked into them. They did nothing for her height, but the black leather that stretched mid-calf was pretty damn sexy.

They put on their final touches and were off for the night, tasting all that Vegas had to offer. They had a great time ducking into lounge after lounge.

Vegas was not like Seattle. It roared with an odd energy, mixed with crazy and sin. Seattle might feel a little weird, but it possessed a whole lot of charm. Perhaps it was the calming effect of the Puget Sound or the laid-back attitude of all the Seattleites. Either way, Molly felt like a fish out of water, a foreigner in this massive, high-wattage city.

"Did you guys just see that?" Tiffany's cocoa-brown eyes were wide, her eyeliner slightly smudged from the heat that was cooking them, even though it was nearly ten at night.

"What did I miss?" Mackenzie spun around, surveying everything in their radius.

Tiffany's mouth was parted in shock. "That was a flippin' hooker, you guys."

"No...seriously?" Molly tried scanning the people that were all about.

"Yep, like right out there in the open." Tiffany pointed and started to wobble. They had just entered a small bar, downed a drink then decided it was a little too seedy for their taste.

"Stop pointing," Mackenzie scolded. "Oh crap, I think I see her, or wait— Is that a guy?"

They all laughed and entered a club that was right off The Strip. It was jam-packed with people. Tiffany was like their leader, seizing control of where they went and not tolerating any belly-aching. She led them to a table that was just being vacated then flagged down a server for drinks.

"Vodka, girls?" Tiffany asked as the server, wearing the shortest skirt that Molly had ever seen, smiled patiently.

Mackenzie held up two fingers and nodded. Molly raised one finger. She was starting to feel a buzz and didn't want to get full-on tipsy. It was early yet. The server returned with record speed and Tiffany lifted her slender glass, a small amount of the clear liquid splashing out as she toasted. "To friendship. I love you guys." She downed a large swig after they all clinked their identical glasses.

The lighting inside the club gave off a purple hue. Not quite like a black light, but it was dark. Loud music poured from enormous speakers stacked on a stage where a DJ wearing large headphones was working what looked to Molly like a spaceship. He masterfully manipulated knobs, lights and buttons galore to please the swarm of people on the dance floor.

Tiffany chugged her drink. "Wanna dance?"

Mackenzie nodded and quickly swallowed both drinks, causing Molly to groan. Mackenzie wasn't a lightweight when it came to holding her liquor. Being of Scottish descent, she always teased that she could drink most men under the table. It was the dancing. Molly didn't want to admit it, but she was already exhausted and so ready to call it a night. *Getting old sucks.*

"Molly?" Tiffany raised one eyebrow and extended her hand to Molly.

"Do I have to?" Molly remained in the comfortable and plush chair.

"Uh, yeah. Woman, we are on vacation. Get your ass up," Tiffany ordered firmly.

Molly whined, "Can't I just rest a little longer? You guys can warm up the dance floor for me."

"Nope, not an option, cupcake. Get your ass up." Mackenzie reached for her and yanked Molly out of her seat.

Damn. For being a tall and skinny thing, Mac sure was strong.

"Fine, bossy-pants." Molly inhaled sharply and readjusted her too-tight jeans that were now feeling like a sticky second skin. She grabbed what vodka was left and downed it in a single motion. After wiping her mouth, she said, "Let's do this."

They danced their butts off for what seemed like an eternity, but Mackenzie assured her it had only been a little over an hour. Somehow, Molly convinced them to head back outside. She desperately needed some air. With the combination of dancing her tail off and chugging a few more drinks, she was burning up.

Molly closed her eyes as the cool late-night air hit her. Relief. Tiffany was starting to giggle and act obnoxiously, not totally out of the norm for her when she'd had a little too much to drink.

"I'm hungry," Tiffany whined, but Molly wasn't so sure that putting food in Tiffany's stomach would be the best idea. She was fairly certain that Tiffany would be getting sick tonight. *Oh joy.*

Mackenzie looked over and shrugged when Molly shook

her head. "I think I saw a hot dog cart back that way." Mackenzie pointed to the right.

"I don't know if eating a hot dog is such a smart idea," Molly countered. How many times had Molly cleaned up puke—in her car, off her floor…heck, even off her?

"I'm hungry too." Mackenzie looped her arm around Tiffany's and they set off in the direction of said mystery hot dog cart. Molly didn't recall seeing one and could only imagine that chunks of hot dog and relish would be splattering the asphalt at some point tonight. Molly trailed behind them as they searched through the array of vendors that lined the street. Molly pulled out her cell phone and snapped various pictures. There were so many lights and people. Tomorrow she would need to venture out and take some decent photos with her camera.

"There he is!" Tiffany and Mackenzie both screamed as they found the small stainless-steel cart with a cleverly painted red and yellow striped umbrella. They each ordered a hot dog with everything—onions, relish, mustard and ketchup. Tiffany even added sauerkraut. Molly begrudgingly ordered one as well, but she added some bottles of water to her purchase.

Tiffany plopped down on the curb, Mackenzie joined her and eventually Molly did, too. Cars cruised by slowly. The foot traffic from the tourists moved all around them. The concrete curb had been cooked all day, and the warmth still radiated so much that Molly felt it heat up her bottom.

Molly glanced over and noticed that Mackenzie and Tiffany had practically scarfed down their food in record time. "I got you guys some water." She tried passing them each a bottle but both refused. "You guys need to hydrate," Molly insisted as she uncapped one and started to guzzle it. *Now who is the mother hen?*

"It'll kill my buzz," Tiffany explained as she crammed the last piece of bun into her mouth. "Besides, we're headed over there next." She pointed to a bar across the street. Patrons were spilling out into a roped-off outdoor beer garden. Rock music could be heard from where they were seated.

More partying? Molly didn't want to ruin their fun, but she would have loved nothing more than to crawl into bed. She yawned and suggested, "Maybe we can check it out tomorrow?"

"Don't be a Debbie Downer or, I guess, in this case, a Moping Molly," Tiffany joked, causing Mackenzie to laugh so hard she snorted and dropped the last bite of her hot dog onto the ground.

"Oh no," Mackenzie cried and stared at the hot dog on the filthy street. Tiffany swooped down and grabbed it.

"Here…five second rule."

"Uh, no. I don't think so." Molly slapped it out of Tiffany's hand.

Tiffany glared at her and whispered something into Mackenzie's ear.

"Seriously, Tiffany?" Molly was starting to get more than a little annoyed.

"What?" Tiffany's voice faked a shocked expression, Tiffany widened her eyes and her voice was high pitched. It started to grate on Molly's nerves.

"You know very well what."

"Moll, just pull the stick outta your ass." Tiffany got off the curb and dusted her butt off, then reached for Mackenzie. They both wobbled for a moment, then steadied themselves by leaning on each other for support.

Tiffany's words stung a little. Molly used to be the fun one, and now she felt boring, and she was keeping them from having a good time. Maybe she should go back to hotel and leave them to their fun.

Mackenzie looked at her, as though she were trying to figure out what Molly was thinking. "Molly, you okay?"

She nodded. She was anything but okay. Molly felt like a third wheel for the first time in their friendship. She felt tired, like everything was changing and that she had no way of stopping it. She even missed Owen, a lot. *What am*

I running from? Why am I so scared of everything that life is throwing at me? Because being an adult is terrifying. Molly was far from okay.

"Then let's go," Mackenzie prodded.

Molly rose off the curb and tried to act happy. *Fake it. Don't ruin this for them, especially Mackenzie.*

Mackenzie grabbed her hand and all three skipped across the street to the bar with the beer garden. They entered the overly crowded venue, and Molly couldn't help but wonder what the fire marshal would think. There were so many people inside. In order to gain access to the garden there was a small fee, then you were rewarded with a bright orange paper wristband and a couple of drink tickets. Tiffany spotted a plastic table that was unoccupied and Molly was relieved they would be sitting.

After they got situated, a waitress wearing short shorts that looked like sparkly undies took their drink order. People were milling around and dancing. The energy was relaxed. Laughter and drunken chit-chat surrounded them. People were having one helluva time. It had that comfortable house party feel, despite being filled to capacity, and Molly wished they could have spent their evening here instead of all the trendy nightclubs they had suffered through, filled with overly expensive drinks and snotty attitudes. No, this was much more Molly's style.

Tiffany pounded down a couple of beers, even though Molly had insisted she stick with the same kind of liquor. Everyone knew that you never mixed beer with hard alcohol. It was like a drinking rule that everyone lived by. Mackenzie and Molly had stuck with vodka. Mackenzie was starting to slur her words, but she seemed to be enjoying herself.

Tiffany begged for them to dance on the makeshift dance floor, where every inch was occupied by people bumping and grinding. Molly didn't want to risk losing their precious spot. "You guys go. I'll hold down the fort." They didn't try to convince her to join them and she was oddly a little sad that they hadn't at least attempted to lure her.

So Molly did what she did best—people-watch. She mentally captured shots of them, studying the angles, their movements, all the characteristics that made them unique. She hadn't been paying any attention to Tiffany and Mackenzie, who had been swallowed up in the sea of dancing bodies, when she heard some wild clapping and turned her to head to see Mackenzie and Tiffany on top of a table. *Oh no.*

Two overly muscular security guys were attempting to remove her friends from it. Tiffany began shouting at them. Darting from her spot, Molly rushed over before things got too out of hand.

"Ma'am, you need to stop yelling," the meatier of the two bouncers said. His black shirt with the bold white letters that read 'Security' clung against his broad chest. Molly couldn't help but realize how hot he was, minus the shiny bald head. Bald was not always beautiful. Some guys could pull it off. This guy? Not so much.

The other bouncer was talking to Mackenzie calmly, offering his hand to help her down, which—thankfully—she accepted without a word. Tiffany was now fighting with the meaty bald one.

"No way. I'm not getting down. It's a free country, Mr. Clean," Tiffany shouted as she continued to move to the music.

Great, so she's noticed he's bald, too. Molly tried not to laugh at Tiffany's remark. She'd have to give it her. It was kind of fitting.

"Come on, Tiff. Get down from there," Molly asked sweetly. She felt like she was talking her friend off the ledge or something, and she felt ridiculous.

"You should come up." Tiffany even tried reaching out to Molly.

The security guard made his move and snatched her off the table. Tiffany started kicking with a stunned look upon her face. He sat her down on the ground and looked over at Molly. "You guys need to leave now before we call law enforcement."

"Yes, sir. I completely understand." Molly smiled and grabbed Tiffany's arm, only for Tiffany to wiggle free.

"No, we paid to be here like everyone else. We're just having fun."

Molly tried to catch a peek at Mackenzie for a little back-up, not that her drunk ass would be much help. She saw her chatting with the bouncer, a wide smile on her face, and he was laughing at something she had just said. Good for her, but she could use her friend's help wrangling Tiffany.

"It's late. We really need to head back to the hotel, Tiff."

The bouncer gave Tiffany a stern look, while she snarled at him. "You suck, Mr. Clean."

Molly grabbed Tiffany again, tightening her grasp so that she couldn't get away. "Enough," Molly quietly growled to her. "You want him to call the cops?"

"Yeah, I bet they're a lot hotter than his stupid ass."

"Please just stop, Tiffany. You are going to get us all in trouble."

Tiffany rolled her eyes and laughed. "He can't do shit. We didn't do anything wrong," Tiffany spouted. Molly could smell the alcohol wafting from her mouth.

Molly offered an apologetic smile to the bouncer. "Again, sir, I'm sorry. We'll be going now."

He nodded but didn't move. Molly knew this wasn't his first run-in with an overly drunk woman, but it was embarrassing.

"I suggest you hurry," he said.

Molly picked up on the irritation in his gruff voice.

Molly dragged Tiffany away. She was growing more heavy and limp. The adrenaline had obviously worn off now. "Mackenzie, we need to go now, dear."

"Boo-hoo. This lovely gentleman is such a riot." Mackenzie was gazing up at him, wearing the brightest smile she'd seen on her friend in a long time.

Molly did have to admit the guy was pretty smokin'.

126

He was clean-shaven and had a strong jawline. His eyes were a hazel tone, from what Molly could make out in the low light. His muscular arms were covered in ink, brightly colored and attention grabbing. He had his hand on the small of Mackenzie's back and seemed intrigued by her. *Too bad*. This very well could have been the start of something quite interesting.

"Here. Let me escort you guys out and make sure you get a cab," he offered. Molly was impressed by his manners. He didn't act like Mr. Clean, who was, in all honesty, just doing his job. But this guy was just more personable and easier on the eyes. Molly was pretty sure all the women were more than happy to listen to him. Too bad he hadn't asked Tiffany off the table. She probably would have happily jumped into his arms, and Molly wouldn't have had to kiss Mr. Clean's ass.

Once outside the bar, he waited with them until a mustard-yellow cab rolled up, the city lights reflecting off the paint. Molly scanned the streets. It was still crowded and it was well into the wee hours of the morning. The bouncer was chatting with Mackenzie to the side, both of them laughing. Tiffany had grown quiet.

Molly opened the cab door. "Go ahead and get in."

Tiffany looked up at her. She appeared a little green around the gills. "I can't."

"Come on. Let's hurry back to the hotel," Molly begged.

Tiffany stared at her, looking as though she were going to speak, then it came. Molly had expected it all night, right after Tiffany had consumed the hot dog. The foul vomit poured like a waterfall from Tiffany. Molly gagged at the stench. She bunched up Tiffany's long hair, keeping it out of her face and was careful to dodge the vomit as it splattered against the black asphalt. Sure enough, there were the chunks of hot dog she'd known she would see again.

Why doesn't anyone ever listen to me?

Chapter Ten

"Ugh, my head," Tiffany whimpered from her bed, nestled in fluffy pillows and piercingly bright comforters and sheets, all a brilliant white.

The room itself was dark. Tiffany had begged them earlier to keep all the blinds and curtains closed. She even wore a washcloth over her eyes, shielding her from any possible light.

"How much did I drink last night?"

"A fair amount," Mackenzie answered. She was sitting at the small table and sipping her coffee. She wasn't the least bit hungover and she nibbled on a cream cheese Danish.

Molly had just gotten out of the shower. She needed to have that shower back home. It was incredible, at the very least. It was relaxing and simply the best thing ever. "Yeah, you were downing a lot of drinks last night, girlie. Where you messed up was mixing that damn beer with all that vodka and rum. You should know better."

"Why'd you guys let me? I don't recall drinking that much," Tiffany muttered.

"Well, I think your aching head and empty stomach will tell you otherwise," Mackenzie said. "So what are you planning to do today, ladies?"

"I was thinking later I'd like to take some pictures around town," Molly answered, towel drying her hair. "Is there more coffee?"

Mackenzie nodded and pointed to the mini pot full of the dark liquid.

"I need coffee, but I don't know if my stomach can handle it quite yet." Tiffany threw the comforter over her head and buried herself farther under.

"You guys want to watch a show or something tonight?" Mackenzie suggested. "Or maybe gamble a little?"

"That might be fun," Molly replied as she poured herself a cup of coffee and joined Mackenzie at the table.

"What do you think, Tiffany?" Mackenzie asked.

"I want to die," was Tiffany's muffled answer. Molly felt awful for her — been there, done that.

"You say that every time," Mackenzie quipped and took a sip from her cup. "You'd think you would realize that we aren't kids anymore."

"She's always been a puker, too," Molly added, plating a berry Danish onto a small saucer.

"You guys suck. You know that?" Tiffany grumbled.

"Some of us better than others," Mackenzie winked to Molly.

"So, Mackenzie, what's up with that bouncer?" Molly steered the conversation. She was curious as to what that whole thing had been about. It appeared that Mackenzie had had an instant connection with the tattooed wonder. Granted, Mackenzie had been a bit intoxicated, but she'd seemed to really like the guy.

"Not much to say, really. I am meeting him later for lunch, though." Mackenzie avoided eye contact and appeared to be waiting for one of them to say something snide or stupid.

Molly shrugged. "That's awesome. Does this bouncer have a name?"

"He might," Mackenzie smiled, savoring her little secret. *Mackenzie deserves to enjoy this, after the craptastic relationships she's been in.* She was owed a fun fling.

"So how long will you be out with Mr. Bouncer?" Molly asked as she brushed crumbs from her chest, plucking a stray piece of pastry from her cleavage. Big boob problems... Snacks tended to land in there a lot.

"Okay, his name is Jason. He's really kind of awesome, to be honest." She squealed with barely contained excitement.

"You got all that from hanging out with him for like...ten

minutes. Love at first sight, then?" Molly teased.

"I can't really explain it, but the connection was instant. I know I was drunk, but I wasn't completely trashed." Mackenzie motioned toward Tiffany, who was silent now, probably sleeping off the hangover.

"Well, you know, sometimes it's like that. It can just hit you that quickly. This is so great, Mac. I totally believe in love at first sight and sharing that crazy connection with someone."

"Like with Owen?" Mackenzie raised her eyebrows, searching Molly with her dark eyes.

"That's different," Molly argued.

"Is it? Because that seemed like a pretty instant connection." Mackenzie slowly took the last bite of her Danish, popping it into her mouth, letting Molly digest the question.

"Oh, Mackenzie, I don't even know where to begin with the whole Owen thing. If I were being completely honest with myself, I do have feelings for him and my body turns to liquid heat whenever I hear his voice or he's around. I'm terrified of screwing it all up, though."

"Molly, what is it that you want out of life?" Mackenzie held her head in her palms, her elbows anchored to the table, while she stared at Molly.

"I'm not sure. I mean, I have you and Tiffany and my work, which is a dream come true. Do I even need more?"

"The simple answer? Yes. The long answer? Yes, you do, because you deserve to have it all, Molly—the career, the friendship, the perfect guy and a happy life, maybe even a couple of kids thrown in for good measure." Mackenzie was fighting back tears.

That caused a swift reaction in Molly, feeling her own salty tears threatening to pour.

"Molly, we all deserve it. But you have always been an amazing friend to me and you, above everyone else, should have that happily ever after. You constantly cut yourself down. You don't see the value that we all see. You are worth so much. You have a heart of pure gold."

"Do you think the casinos here would accept that as payment?" Molly joked. Compliments always made her feel awkward. For some weird reason, Molly couldn't act like a normal person and say 'thank you'. Instead, her mind went into overdrive, crippling self-doubt erupted and she would immediately deflect. She might make fun of herself or turn the sweet gesture into a joke. She wished she were able to break herself of the self-deprecating habit, but Molly had always been that way. She didn't know where it stemmed from. Her parents loved her. Her childhood had been normal and happy enough, so what the heck? She had no clue.

"Moll, please." Mackenzie paused for a moment then asked softly, "Have you considered talking to someone?"

"Um, I talk to you and Tiffany all the time," Molly answered, knowing full well what Mackenzie was suggesting.

A therapist. It had obviously crossed her mind, especially with her fear of relationships. She wanted to be fixed, but it was sort of frightening at the same time. The thought of talking to a professional didn't really bring on those warm and fuzzy feelings — someone getting paid to judge her, to decide just how broken she was? No thanks. Molly would rather buy a bottle of booze and an extra-cheese-covered pizza then hash out her problems with her besties. She trusted their advice, not some guy in an office, probably with a bright yellow notepad jotting down her every word, making her question if she'd slipped up and said something that would make her look crazy.

"Don't you want to know why you are so scared of getting involved with someone? Like why you suck at relationships?"

"Mackenzie, we all suck," Tiffany hollered. She flipped the comforter off herself and sat up. "It's not just Molly or just me. It's all of us."

"Well, maybe you should talk to someone, too," Mackenzie suggested.

"Oh please. I can diagnose all of us. We can spend our money on something much better."

Molly laughed out loud. "I was just thinking booze and pizza."

"Exactly," Tiffany said as she started to remove herself slowly from the bed. She shuffled over to the coffee and poured herself a cup, then joined them. She looked like hell. Her hair was a tangled mess. Remnants of her makeup were streaked all over her face and the whites of her eyes were bloodshot. Yeah, not the least bit cute, but Molly loved her anyway, especially for defending them as all being screw-ups.

"Feeling better?" Molly asked, stroking Tiffany's arm, to which she nodded.

"I just wanted to point out that none of us are married or involved in any kind of serious relationship, so it's not just Molly." She blew at her coffee to cool the steaming liquid and touched her lips carefully to the rim of the white cup.

"I'm not trying to insult her. I was simply advising that she consider seeing someone who might be able to help her resolve her issues," Mackenzie tried to explain, flipping Tiffany an annoyed look.

"Mackenzie, she doesn't need to be fixed. Trust me. Owen is the one. She'll figure that out," Tiffany said, then turned to Molly. "Once she quits overthinking everything, she'll come around and see that everything will be amazing." For a hungover chick, Tiffany was radiating some pretty damn positive energy.

"Thanks. I sure hope you're right." Deep down she wondered if Owen was the right guy for her. She'd find out soon enough.

"I am," Tiffany said confidently.

Mackenzie rolled her eyes. "Okay, lovebirds. I'm not even going to continue this conversation. But, Molly, you should consider seeing a therapist. I'm actually seeing one," she admitted quietly.

"What? Since when?" Molly was shocked. Tiffany looked

equally surprised.

"Oddly enough, since right before my sister died."

Molly and Tiffany exchanged confused looks.

"I needed to see why my relationship with Gideon didn't work out," Mackenzie answered.

Tiffany huffed. "It didn't work out because he was an ass."

"I wish it were that cut and dried, but it's much more complicated. We had a lot of issues, but I loved him."

"He left you. You were engaged. In no way is that cool. There's nothing complicated about that." Tiffany sipped more of her coffee.

"Well, to be fair, I don't think the timing was right. He had just gotten back from one tour and was headed out for another. Sometimes things just don't pan out." Mackenzie looked away from both of them, unable to meet their eyes.

Not too much later, Mackenzie left them to meet up with Jason aka Hot Bouncer. Tiffany was on the mend and decided to join Molly in exploring the city. Molly was eager to snap some great shots that she could tinker with editing once she got home.

Once they'd exited the hotel and set out on foot to check out the more romantic aspects of Vegas, Tiffany pointed at things she felt Molly should capture with her trusty camera. The sun was still beating down on the city, cooking everything. Molly wore a large but fashionable straw sunhat and shorts that exposed her pale legs. She had her camera strapped around her neck and felt more like a tourist than a photographer, but who cared? She was doing what she loved the most. Tiffany was dressed in pale blue jean capris and a simple T-shirt, looking thin and youthful. Molly felt a stab of jealousy. *How is it that even after being so hungover, she still manages to look fabulous?*

"Oh, Moll, get that," Tiffany ordered again. They had walked several miles and Molly's camera was working overtime.

"Do you want the camera?"

"Nah, besides, you won't even let me touch it. You'd think it was your firstborn or something." Tiffany laughed as they stopped near a massive fountain in front of a hotel. The water was springing in synchronized action and was beautifully orchestrated. Only music was missing in this fantastic show. The light mist that hung in the air was refreshing and they both stood soaking in the coolness.

"You hungry yet?"

Snap, click. "I could eat."

"Just no hot dogs, like *ever* again."

"Oh, come on. I thought those were your favorite," Molly teased as she snapped the alternating streams of water blasting up toward the hazy blue sky.

"I will never eat another one again for as long as I live." Tiffany shook her head in disgust.

"I can't say that I blame you." Molly yawned. "You know? I could go for a coffee."

"Me too, actually."

They walked around until they located a coffee shop of sorts. It was hip and trendy, not unlike some of the newer coffee establishments in Seattle, and it did smell wonderful inside. Tiffany ordered a simple iced mocha. Molly ordered the largest cup—unfortunately bucket-size wasn't an option—of a mocha and espresso blend. She hoped the caffeine would revive her. The heat and the partying from the previous night had simply sapped her of any energy. The pick-me-up would rescue her so that she could enjoy the rest of the day without a nap.

"This is really good. Here... Try," Tiffany commented and shoved her cup with the bright pink straw into Molly's face.

She took a sip and had to agree it was pretty darn good. "Here... You try this one."

Tiffany swallowed some of Molly's enormous cardboard cup of pure caffeine crack and her eyes grew wide. "That is strong. How can you drink that stuff?" She crinkled her nose and her mouth turned down in disgust.

"It's survival juice. When one needs caffeine, this is how you get your fix. It goes straight into the bloodstream without needing an IV." Molly took a sip then sighed happily. She could literally live anywhere in the world, just as long as there was good coffee around.

* * * *

Molly changed into a pair of jeans and a fitted top in an apple-red color, feeling a little more attractive than when she'd been out earlier. She was sitting at the table in the hotel room, waiting for Tiffany to get out of the shower. Molly was curious where Mackenzie was. She'd sent her a couple of messages and was hoping she was okay.

She was skimming through some of the shots she had taken that day when she heard the familiar sound of the door unlocking. Mackenzie came in, wearing a magnificent smile.

"Hey, I've been trying to get a hold of you," Molly scolded her as Mackenzie ventured closer to the table where Molly sat.

"Sorry. I meant to call, but I was a little distracted," Mackenzie apologized.

Molly smiled and was happy for Mackenzie, but she knew if she'd been the one to pull the whole not-answering-her-phone stunt, she'd never hear the end of it.

"Sit. I want details, woman." Molly peeked out of the window. They had all the curtains open now that Tiffany felt human again, and the view was stunning, even in the early evening. The sun was beginning to set, giving way to the millions of lights that would soon sparkle and make Vegas magical.

Mackenzie plopped down and looked at Molly. "He's amazing."

"Okay, that's a start. *Why* is he so amazing?" Molly asked with a smirk.

Mackenzie had a faraway look on her face. Her eyes were

filled with delight as she started to explain all the things she'd learned about Jason. Molly would have thought they'd known each other for years from all the information Mackenzie now possessed. Molly would be shocked if her friend didn't know his social security number.

"Really? All this from a lunch date?"

"Crazy, right?" Mackenzie said as Tiffany emerged from the bathroom, wrapped in a white terrycloth robe, billowing steam following her out.

"Mackenzie, how was lunch?" Tiffany asked sweetly.

"I was just telling Molly. It was incredible. He's incredible."

"Hmm, so when are you seeing him again?"

Mackenzie looked up toward the ceiling and replied slowly, "That's the thing. He sort of wants to have dinner a little later."

"Mackenzie, this is a girls' trip," Tiffany complained as she unwrapped the towel from her head. "Can't you see him for breakfast or something?"

"I know. I know. But can you blame me?"

Molly didn't mind the prospect of Mackenzie going out again, but Tiffany did have a point. They would be leaving tomorrow night to go back to their normally scheduled programs — their daily lives.

"It's not like it can go anywhere. I guess I don't see the point." Tiffany's hand was on her hip and her stance was squared.

Molly sighed. She really hoped that the two of them weren't about to battle again. She wasn't in the mood. So what if Mackenzie went out? She deserved to have a good time and maybe even get laid.

"Tiffany, we can still have a great time. We were going to go gamble tonight, and Mackenzie is cheap, so she wouldn't be any fun, anyway."

Tiffany rolled her eyes and started to stomp back to the bathroom. "It's supposed to be a girls' weekend."

"It has been. We're all here, aren't we?" Mackenzie called after her, which was met with the slamming of the bathroom door.

Great, now Tiffany is pissed off.

"Seriously, what the hell is her problem?" Mackenzie turned and said to Molly.

"You gotta see it from her point of view," Molly said calmly, trying to stay neutral.

"She's jealous that it's not her, because if it were, she'd be out and about having a grand ole time and expecting us to just deal with it. But, because it's me, she's all in a huff. This is the crap I can't stand about her."

"You have a valid point. However, just go out and have fun. I've got Tiffany. But maybe tomorrow, let's have a nice brunch and maybe do something together?"

"Fine. I may not be back tonight—just an FYI." There was a sly glint in her eye as she rose from the seat.

"Really?"

"You have no idea how much this guy turns me on."

"And it's probably been ages since—" Molly started to say, when Mackenzie nodded.

"Yes, since Gideon, there hasn't been another," Mackenzie confirmed.

"Oh my, are you serious? Mac, it's been, what?"

Mackenzie raised her hand to stop Molly. "A long time. We don't need to hash over how long. Trust me. I know it's been a very long time."

Molly allowed that to sink in. She'd had no idea that Mackenzie had been celibate for nearly two years. Not that Mackenzie should be out landing as many one-night stands as possible, but it wasn't like she hadn't dated anyone since the breakup two years ago. She was just more than a little surprised that Mackenzie had gone without. Maybe that was why she was so uptight and cranky. The poor dear needed to get laid.

* * * *

"I still think it's kind of annoying that she'd rather go

out with that bouncer guy than hang out with her besties," Tiffany complained as she pulled the lever down on a slot machine. The machine was large and loud, chiming each time she pulled it. It was one of the more old-fashioned ones. Most that surrounded them only required you to press a button.

Where is the fun in that?

"Oh get over it." Molly yanked her lever down, staring as she lost more money. "You should be more annoyed that we aren't winning anything."

"Give it time. Be nice to your machine. Tell it how much you love it. Who is a good lil' machine?" Tiffany cooed to her machine, stroking it gently and patting it. "Who is going to give mama lots of money? You are, that's who."

Molly laughed and, sure enough, as soon as Tiffany pulled the handle down again, it made a different chime, almost a shrill. As though paying the winner actually hurt, coins sputtered out, clinking hard against the metal. Tiffany seized her cup and tried to catch all the dirty silver coins as they flooded out. *Damn, that's a lot of nickels.* Molly snatched her nearly empty cup and tried to assist Tiffany, who wore the largest grin ever.

"I won, Molly. I actually won."

After the machine had quit throwing up a ridiculous amount of nickels and they'd collected the coins, they went to the cashier booth to turn them in. The look of disappointment on Tiffany's face was priceless as she learned she'd only won around forty dollars.

"That's it?" Tiffany asked the lady if she could recount it. The woman nodded and ran the buckets of coins through a large machine. Molly guessed it was a scale of some kind. After being cashed out and paid, Tiffany sulked away. "That kinda sucked."

"You still won forty bucks," Molly tried to point out, hoping to ease the blow.

"Yeah, but I must have put in at least sixty, so where's that money?" Tiffany wore an angry scowl.

"I don't know, but let's grab something to eat. All this winning has made me hungry. And since you're the big jackpot winner, you can treat me," Molly teased as she wrapped her arm around Tiffany's shoulders.

* * * *

It was amazing how fast a trip could go by. There wasn't enough time to see or do everything they wanted, but Molly felt like they'd still had a lot of fun. They'd spent most of Sunday just lounging around the pool and being lazy. Sometimes that was the best. The night before, Mackenzie had come back to the hotel suite around the same time that Tiffany and Molly had. It was nearly time to go. They were reluctantly packing their bags. They had booked a night flight and would touch down in Seattle close to midnight. Overall, the trip had been a success and it had served its purpose. They'd just needed to escape Seattle for a little while.

Molly was filled with some dread as they boarded their plane. As they took off, she peered down through the tiny window at the large square in the desert that was filled with light. The land surrounding Vegas was nothing more than dark and lifeless shadows, nothing shiny and magical about it. The wonder was lost. Vegas almost appeared small. It set in how all of it was an illusion, a magic trick or act, like the ultimate Vegas show. Getting the bird's-eye perspective really drove that home. There was a comfort in knowing that even something that seemed so grand was truly tiny in reality. Molly closed her eyes and instantly saw Owen. Some things in life weren't as minuscule.

Chapter Eleven

Home, sweet home... Molly greatly cherished the forgotten peace and quiet of her beloved space. Her studio... The sunlight filtered in through a mask of gray and white clouds. Molly sighed happily as she worked. The silence in the large space was lovely. Not that she didn't enjoy the constant chatter of her best friends, but some days, solitude could be equally wonderful, and today was that day—no phone calls, messages, models or interruptions. Workdays like this were glorious and rare. She had been equipped with coffee and plenty of editing. The hours of productivity were priceless.

Her cell phone rang. As with everything in life, sometimes things were short-lived. She was reluctant to answer, but curiosity got the better of her. It was Owen. She wasn't the least bit surprised. She had been expecting him to reach out to her at some point.

"Hello," she answered, trying to keep her voice neutral and polite.

Molly had done a lot of thinking while being miles and miles above the ground. She'd come to realize that she needed to focus on work and bettering herself before she could jump into a serious relationship. She owed that to Owen or to anyone else that she might end up with. Maybe it had been the altitude or cabin pressure in the plane, but Molly finally accepted that perhaps Mackenzie was on to something. Molly needed to know why she wasn't any good at being a girlfriend. Was she better off alone, not complicating her life or anyone else's by getting involved, not dragging someone into her emotional abyss?

The thought of getting married or locked into a long-term relationship scared her. Molly was at a crossroads. She needed to get her shit together and learn how to pack away her emotional baggage so she could be able to be in a relationship or accept her fate as a crazy cat lady and start her collection of felines.

"Molly, what are you up to right now?"

Busy avoiding you was the first thought that popped into her mind. She hadn't realized how much she'd missed the sound of his voice.

"Working," she answered coolly, not wanting him to think she was available.

"I figured. You probably have a ton to catch up on since your Vegas trip."

How did he know I was in Vegas? Molly guessed one of her friends must have told him, because she'd kept it vague as to where she was traveling, not wanting to have to explain herself to him.

"Swamped. I haven't left all day — just work, work, work." She emphasized each word.

"Excellent."

Excellent? What the hell? Molly was a tad irritated now. "Well, I'd better go. I have so much to do."

"Great. Well, I'm here. Go ahead and open the door. See ya in a minute."

She could hear him smiling through the phone, which only annoyed her further.

She may have missed the sound of his voice, but now she wanted him to go away. How was she supposed to focus on herself if he was always around? She needed to explain her plan and make a clean break — or, at the very least, get him to understand that they were not a couple. He needed to know she couldn't do the whole relationship thing, not until she got her shit sorted out, then maybe. But only because he always brought good coffee. Molly felt a laugh attempt to escape her.

She answered the door, trying hard not to smile. She

didn't want to encourage him in any shape or form. She repeated to herself, *Act cool and calm. Be nonchalant.* "Hey, Owen."

"Hey, Molly," he mocked her in his usual silly, but adorable, fashion. He held up two white plastic sacks with red Chinese lettering on the outside from her favorite restaurant.

Damn him.

"Did you get extra fortune cookies?" Molly couldn't believe the words had just slipped out of her mouth. She was mad at herself for being so easily won over by coffee and food.

He nodded and kissed her on top of her head. "How could I forget?"

Why does he have to be so perfect? There had to be flaws somewhere. Maybe he hid bodies in his basement — or something truly awful — because no one was that awesome all the time. And she certainly didn't deserve such a thoughtful guy.

"Oh, just get on in here with that," she ordered and closed the door.

Owen was already at the table, emptying the bag. Various sizes of white cartons were lined up when Molly stood next to him, watching him work. He dumped out packets of soy sauce, chopsticks and at least a dozen fortune cookies he'd thoughtfully brought.

Molly was wrong. There were close to two dozen fortune cookies. "How were you able to score so many of these?" She couldn't resist and snatched one. *Do I dare read the fortune? Nah.* Molly savored the toasty sweet flavor of the hard golden cookie, crumbling up the tiny paper message in her palm. *Screw Confucius.*

"Oh, they love me there. Ming is the sweetest lady," Owen explained.

"You even know her name?" The old Asian woman who ran the best takeout place in all of Seattle wasn't Molly's biggest fan — or at least that was what she figured, since it was like pulling teeth getting extra fortune cookies.

Owen nodded and asked, "You eat there all the time and you don't know her name?"

"She's usually stingy with the cookies."

"It's probably because you haven't asked her name." Owen pulled out chopsticks for both of them. "Sit and eat."

Molly sat and he started to serve her. "I can get it."

"No," he said quickly and shoveled chow mein onto a paper plate.

Instead of arguing, Molly began to eat and was enjoying every bite that she managed sloppily to put into her mouth. She'd not mastered the art of using chopsticks, even with all the times she'd ordered takeout Chinese. She just wasn't coordinated enough. Owen joined her. They ate in comfortable silence, then he stared at her for a moment.

"You have a little something right here." He pointed to the corner of his mouth, but quickly took a napkin and gently dabbed her mouth with it. "Got it."

"Thanks," Molly said awkwardly.

Owen sighed. "So, what's going on, Molly?"

She'd been expecting this. He had every right to question her, but couldn't a girl finish her Chinese food first?

"What do you mean?" *When in doubt, play dumb.*

Owen rolled those gorgeous eyes toward the ceiling. Molly could see the frustration brewing behind them. "Come on. You know exactly what I mean. You take off. You don't tell me to where. You hardly answer my texts. What happened with us?"

Like a bandage, sometimes just ripping it off quickly was for the best. "There is no *us*, Owen."

"Well, you could have fooled me."

"You said we were a couple. I never did. I told you I was horrible at relationships. You were warned." *Great.* Now she was losing her appetite and everything had been so delicious, especially her favorite orange chicken.

"Is this because of the way dinner ended that one night?"

"It's much more than that." Molly had begun to feel guilty

as she watched the array of emotions pelt his handsome face. "Owen, I like you. I really do."

"But?"

"But, I need to figure out why I suck at this." There. She'd said it. She had been honest.

"You don't. You just don't want to give us a shot, and I don't get it. I mean, what are the odds of us meeting the way we did?"

"I know," Molly answered softly. He was right about that. It wasn't every day you got a fish thrown at you by a hot guy.

Owen was quiet and Molly could see he was thinking and pondering a solution. "I have an idea."

"Hmm, okay, let's hear it." She was open to hearing him out, but she had no intention of going along with whatever solution he had in mind.

He reached across the table, cupping her hand. "Give me a week."

"A week for what?"

"To make you realize that this could work between us. Think of it like a fun challenge, to see why we are good together and that you don't suck at relationships." He winked. It was like the fatal blow. His wink always got to her.

Molly huffed. A week wasn't going to prove much — or would it?

* * * *

Day one of the week-long challenge that Owen had issued started the very next day. She wasn't quite sure what he had up his sleeve, but, knowing Owen, it was going to be good. He was going to pull out all the stops just to prove a point. Molly had even called Mackenzie and Tiffany to ask them their take on the whole thing. Of course, they had both sided with Owen, who had naturally won them over. Big surprise there. *What did he do? Show up with Chinese food or coffee? How does he have this great power over my best friends?* They were supposed to have her back, not his.

Since there was no one to convince her that she was right, Molly decided stick with her original game plan, 'just go with it'. She was going to enjoy the week with Owen for what it was, knowing in her mind that there was no way one week was going to change a lifetime of her being flawed in the relationship department. In the back of her mind, she prayed that maybe she was wrong, but a leopard didn't change its spots.

He'd called her earlier that day, telling her to be ready by six for dinner. She spent the afternoon prepping for the date, everything from shaving to plucking, blow-drying then straightening. She then skillfully applied the mask she could hide behind — eyeliner, mascara, shadow, blush...the works. Debating what outfit to wear took up a good chunk of time. Too much effort was required to look halfway decent and not like some troll under a bridge. If men only knew the struggles women faced getting ready to go out. When it was finally all said and done, she'd rather call the whole thing off and stay in.

She was starting to pace in her apartment. That was where he wanted to meet her for the first official date of their week-long experiment. He was running a little late. Prickly self-doubt emerged. Maybe he had come to his senses and realized it wasn't going to work out after all. Molly starting fluffing pillows and tidying up things she had already straightened only minutes ago.

Then he was officially late and, at that point, a borderline no-show. Molly would wait a little longer, then off would come the makeup and bra and into the jammies she'd go. She was pissed. This was so unlike him. Then her mind started to unleash a flurry of images, a storm of worry. What if something had happened to him? She grabbed her phone and messaged him. Molly saw that he had read her message, so he wasn't dead. Too bad, because now she'd have to kill him for putting her through this hell.

That's it, she finally decided after more time had passed. She'd waited long enough and went into her bedroom and got undressed. She wiped off the makeup. As she scrubbed it off gently, she felt herself grow angrier. All this effort for nothing and now she had to figure out what to do with herself for the rest of the evening.

Her stomach growled out of hunger and boredom. Molly peeked inside her fridge. She hadn't bothered going to the grocery store since she'd come back a few days ago. There was a head of lettuce. It was mildly yellowed and wilted, nothing that a little salad dressing couldn't remedy. Her hair was now up in a loose bun. She was incredibly annoyed that she had worked so hard on making it sleek and sexy earlier, only to have it up and looking like a sloppy mess now. She padded barefoot toward her cupboards to see if there was an alternative to the less-than-appetizing lettuce. Sadly, her cupboards weren't offering a lot of choices either. She heard her cell ring. It was probably Owen.

Molly hastily grabbed it from her counter and was a little surprised to see it was Mackenzie calling. "Hey, Mac."

"Hey, yourself. How's it going?"

"Well, he's a no-show. I'm just glad it wasn't me this time that screwed it up."

"That's so strange. I'm a little shocked that he would pull a stunt like this."

Molly could have sworn she detected something in Mackenzie's voice that was a little off.

"You certain about that?" Molly was hoping that maybe she could get Mackenzie to slip up.

"Molly, give me a break."

Molly was about to make a nasty comment — her mood was ripe for it — when she heard her doorbell chime. "I'll have to let you go. Someone's here."

She took a deep breath and tried to cool down. As she opened the door, she saw Owen standing there with a lopsided, sexy grin, his arms loaded with all sorts of things. She realized right then that this had been part of his plan.

Damn it. He'd even got her friends to go in on it.

"You look beautiful," he said. Molly was anything but amused or wanting to hear compliments fall out of his mouth.

"Owen, please don't."

"You're ready, I see." His gaze traveled up and down Molly's body.

She suddenly felt self-conscious in her pajama bottoms and Seattle Mariners T-shirt.

"I love the Mariners."

"Nope, you can go home. I'm not playing games with you."

"This wasn't a game. Yes, I'm a little late, but that's because the pizzeria took a while for our order."

"A little late?" Molly could feel the anger rising in her voice.

"You have neighbors, don't you?" At her nod he said, "We should probably take this inside."

He had a point, even when she had all the right in the world to be upset with him. She didn't want to cause a scene in her building's hallway. He'd had the sense to nip that in the bud and keep them from getting into any kind of trouble.

Once inside, she followed him as he went into her kitchen. He placed all the items he had been loaded with onto the counter. She could see pizza, a movie rental, and he was now removing some items from a grocery bag. Ice cream and a bottle of wine. She hated him because he could do no wrong. Even playing her like this, he'd still managed to be incredibly romantic and thoughtful. *Damn him.*

He spun around and said, "You still wanna discuss this?"

"Well…"

"Where's your bathroom?" He had a small plastic grocery sack wadded up in his hand. Molly had no clue what he was up to.

"Over there." She pointed at a door that was visible from the kitchen and living room. He brushed past her, leaving a kiss on top of her head as he disappeared inside.

She took this opportunity to peek at the goodies he'd brought. She lifted the cardboard box of the pizza. It was half extra cheese and pepperoni on the other side. She'd probably only mentioned it in passing, but he had remembered she loved extra-cheesy pizza. Molly grabbed the ice cream, a fancy blend of everything scrumptious — ribbons of caramel, peanuts and fudge — and placed it in the freezer. She chilled the wine next. He really had thought of it all. Too bad she felt like a complete miserable slob. Where had he been when only about an hour ago she had been dressed cute, with amazing makeup and her hair on point? Now her face was scrubbed free of all the makeup, not even a trace of mascara was left on her lashes and she was wearing pale-blue flannel pajama bottoms and her well-worn and beloved Seattle Mariners shirt. And she didn't want to start on her hair. So yes, she had every right to be upset. She'd gone to a lot of trouble to look good for him. Molly kept herself from giggling. He deserved her looking like this. It served him right. The problem was he didn't seem to mind it one bit.

Owen emerged from the bathroom wearing navy blue flannel pajama bottoms, a nearly identical Seattle Mariner shirt and a smug smile. *Seriously? What are the odds?* It had to be a sign, not just some coincidence. Maybe she needed to listen to what the universe was trying to tell her.

"You've got to be kidding me." Molly slapped her forehead and laughed.

"Right?" He moved closer to her, wrapping his arms around her, pulling her gently against his chest.

Molly could feel the strong muscle carved from hard work. He smelled of fabric softener and sunshine. She melted into his chest, letting her head rest on him. She could hear the beating of his heart.

"Told you it was fate," he said.

Even Molly was starting to think he might be right.

"Come on, you sexy thing. Let's eat that pizza." Owen

released her, and she instantly missed the feeling of him, the absence of his strong arms and his scent.

Molly reached for some plates on the tips of her toes. Short girl problems—kitchen cabinets were not designed for vertically challenged people. Owen came from behind her and grabbed two plates with ease. The sensation of him behind her and the roughness of his hands as they skimmed across hers to retrieve the plates caused her to sigh. She hadn't even realized she'd done that until he commented.

"What was that for?"

"I don't know what you mean." Molly watched as he placed a large slice on each plate. He looked so comfortable in her kitchen, her space, her home and in her life.

"The sigh, beautiful."

"Oh, that."

"Yes, that." He held the two plates and was turning to go to her small table in what was hardly a dining room. Owen stopped and kissed her forehead. He had already kissed her several times, none of which were on the lips. Was this part of his plan, to drive her crazy? If so, it was working brilliantly.

"Table or couch?"

"Um, wherever," Molly sputtered, her mind was not focused on the pizza, but on the gorgeous man in his pajamas. She couldn't help but wonder if this night might turn into a sleepover. *Fingers crossed*.

"Well, we could sit on the couch and pop the movie in. Sound good?"

"Sure."

"Let me pour us some wine, too," Owen said, as soon as he'd dropped off the plates on her tiny coffee table. He hurried back to her kitchen.

Molly got up to get the glasses, but he beat her to it. *How did he even know where I keep them?* Well, to be honest, there weren't that many cabinets to choose from, so the odds were kind of in his favor.

He poured the wine and held a glass for her to take.

"Cheers," he said and winked as he clinked their glasses together.

Owen ushered her back to the couch, his hand on the small of her back. Molly had to admit this was all very nice.

Tucking her leg under her, she grabbed her plate then bit into the slice. Her taste buds went wild with the burst of perfectly blended flavors. The sauce was the best ever. "This pizza is amazing," Molly said as she tried to catch the gooey cheese with her mouth.

"I've been going to this place since I was a kid. It still tastes the same after all these years."

"How did I not know about this place?"

"Well, you do now. You're welcome." Owen winked at her and bit off more pizza.

They chatted easily, discussing random things, everyday life stuff. They ate another slice of the best pizza Molly had encountered, and Owen poured them more wine. Molly was enjoying his company. She felt horribly guilty and was kicking herself for being such a bitch to him the last couple of weeks. He was total boyfriend material, if not hubby. He looked incredibly sexy in their near-matching pajamas. To think he'd done this on purpose, bringing everything for — quite honestly — the perfect date night. It was quite clever on his part to be intentionally late, knowing full well that she'd wipe the makeup off, be in her jammies and in her rawest, most comfortable, form. That was how he'd wanted her. She'd listened on as he explained why he'd done it, and she had to give the guy credit. He'd explained that they'd already done the get-dressed-up-and-go-out thing, but now he'd wanted them to experience what being a couple really could be like. She had to admit that it was kind of awesome, just hanging out like this. Molly could get used to it, and she realized that had been his plan. She was now curious as to what the next six days of this challenge would feature.

Happily stuffed, Owen started the DVD. As the movie played, Molly wasn't really paying much attention. He had wrapped his arms around her and they snuggled on the couch like they had been doing this for years. Owen would stroke her arm and sometimes run his fingers through her hair. She noticed he didn't talk during the movie — nothing more than an occasional laugh — but he appeared to be fully engrossed in this comedy that he'd chosen for them. Molly wished she knew what the story was about, but her mind kept wandering. She felt herself relax and grow sleepy.

The credits were rolling and Owen whispered, "Molly, wake up."

She'd fallen asleep — and not dainty, pretty sleep. She had slept hard and there was enough drool to prove it. She was horrified. She'd probably even snored, because no doubt the universe hated her. "I'm sorry. I didn't mean to fall asleep."

"It's okay. You're probably exhausted from your trip. I didn't mind." Owen was running his hand gently up and down her shoulder and side. She was nestled against him and never wanted to leave.

Looking up at him, she took in the dark stubble covering his jawline and his dark-gray eyes. Simply put, this man was desirable. She slowly eased out of her position, slinking her way up toward him. Her hands splayed on his chest. She could feel the hard muscles right below the thin material of the cotton shirt, and instantly she wished it was off him. The next thing she knew, Molly had straddled Owen's lap, her hands still flat against his chest. His hardness was growing between his muscled thighs. It was really turning her on. Her own arousal grew, deep in her core. He finally moved his hands to her hips, then up her ribs, brushing the sides of her breasts as he secured her to him. Molly looped her arms around his neck, desperate for contact, then she crushed her mouth down on his and pushed her breasts with their pebbled nipples against him. Mind-blowing was an understatement. *Am I really supposed to see stars or feel like electricity is burning through me?* Molly had never experienced anything quite like it, and she'd kissed enough frogs to know.

She wanted more. She ground against him and drove the kiss deeper. He nipped at her lip gingerly, causing Molly to moan. God, she wanted him — needed him was more like it.

Then he pulled away. When Owen gazed into her eyes, she could tell that he was holding back.

At first she was mildly confused, dazed by the lust that was singeing her on the inside, her passion begging to be sated, but to see his restraint? It was beyond impressive. Molly was slightly jealous that he had the remarkably quick ability to spark such a flame in her, even if it was threatening to burn her alive with sexual wanting. She couldn't help but feel a little glad as she watched him battle the same desire. She could feel the evidence that he wanted her the same way she wanted him. She knew that it was not part of his plan to lure her into this relationship. She guessed he knew that if he spooked her by moving too fast, he'd risk failing the week-long challenge. *Did I turn the tables on him?* The thought made Molly a little giddy.

Molly almost laughed out loud when she saw him so conflicted. It was obvious he wanted nothing more than to scoop her up and show her how much more amazing their relationship could be. His eyes betrayed the level of lust he was feeling. She almost wanted to scream, 'Just go with it!' Wasn't that the motto she'd been trying to live by? Apparently, that wasn't his.

"I'd better head home. It's late." He kissed her softly this time, teasing her as he tugged on her bottom lip with his teeth, driving her mad. He had regained his cool. *Damn him.*

It was time for her final attempt at seducing him, time to step up her game. "I don't know if I can let you leave," Molly cooed in his ear, licking his neck and nibbling on his ear.

"Hey, you gotta buy the cow. No free milk here, sweetheart."

Molly pressed her forehead against his and smiled. Her desire diminished and the heat in her belly cooled, but she wasn't upset. He was going to make her work for something that they both wanted. He was definitely not like any guy she'd ever dated. *Bring on day two of this challenge!*

Chapter Twelve

"So, how was it?" Mackenzie asked. She was sitting across from Molly and Tiffany at one of their favorite coffee shops.

It was late afternoon, middle of the week, and Molly was telling her friends about the night before—day one of Owen's week-long challenge.

"Well, it really went great, actually, even though I was initially upset. Mackenzie, you knew, and I could kill you, by the way." Molly laughed and took a sip of her coffee.

"He told me not to say anything," Mackenzie defended herself.

"Uh, I'm your best friend. Owen isn't."

Mackenzie shrugged. "I don't know. He's pretty nice and not nearly as cranky as you."

"Stop, you two, I want to know what's next," Tiffany added. "You guys got plans for tonight?" Tiffany's eyes grew large with excitement.

Molly was curious, too. After last night, she wasn't certain what he had up his sleeve, but she knew now that she couldn't figure him out. Never would she have thought he'd pull the stunt he had last night. First, pissing her off to a whole different level, only to have her wrapped around his sexy little finger hours later. This man had her world all mixed up and she was starting to enjoy the crazy ride.

"I'm not sure, but maybe Mackenzie knows," Molly teased and winked at her. Winked? Really? That was a total Owen move. *Oh dear.* He was really starting to rub off on her.

"I promise. I have no clue this time. But you have to admit, it was pretty cool."

"I was cute before he showed up. I had done my hair and makeup. All that hassle for nothing," Molly complained with a smile on her face, one that had been there since she'd woken up that morning.

"I love how happy you look," Tiffany commented. Mackenzie nodded in agreement.

"Gosh, what if this actually works out, guys?"

"Molly, quit having doubts. I already told you that he's the *one*." Tiffany rolled her eyes in frustration. "I need a guy like Owen. Hell, we all do."

"He is pretty special," she admitted. Day one of the challenge had been more than successful. She wouldn't dare admit that to him yet. She wondered if he was also buzzing around like a joyful honeybee, just as she was. Molly was probably in one of the best moods she'd been in for a quite some time. She knew it wasn't the delicious cold leftover pizza she'd just devoured for lunch, but the guy who'd brought it over.

* * * *

Owen smiled at her across the table—not just any table but an air hockey table. He'd picked her up from her studio and brought her to an old teenage hangout of his. The arcade was the last place she'd expected him to take her. The loud noise made it nearly impossible to talk. Instead, they expressed their competitive sides, battling each other at various games. First, it was shooting basketballs into a moving hoop, not a fine moment for Molly, but that wasn't going to stop her from trying to kick his ass at another game. That didn't happen at the next one either, but when they stood in front of the skee-ball machine, she knew she had it in the bag. He groaned as her machine spewed out dozens of bright red tickets that could be turned in later for some goofy prize.

But even with her success, Owen looked at her across the air hockey table and said, "Now, I don't want to brag, but—"

Molly held up her hand and stopped him. "But you're going to, right? Well, sir, I'll have you know that much like that little ole skee-ball game I just beat you at over there" — Molly tilted her head in the direction of the line of skee-ball machines — "I'm really good at air hockey."

"Woman, I used to own this table. I beat every kid that challenged me. I got this, sweetheart."

"Do you now?" She sent the plastic orange puck sailing across and made a goal. "Looks like I just scored. And, babe, I'm not one of those kids." Molly stuck her tongue out at him. "You sure it was this very table you owned?"

He gave her a sexy grin and pushed the plastic puck past her as she tried to block it. "Goal."

They kept it up, back and forth, each trying to outwit the other, and even using flirtation as their ammunition and tool of distraction. Molly hadn't had so much fun in a long time.

"You ready to give up yet?" Owen asked as he hit the puck back to her.

"Not on your life, buddy," she answered, biting her bottom lip and concentrating hard on how to get it past him. Something must have worked because the next thing she knew, it slid into his goal. She'd won.

He groaned, but not the way it sounded when someone lost. It had a more hungry and primal tone. "Why'd you have to do that?"

"What?" Molly asked innocently. In all actuality, she had no idea what he was talking about.

He came around from his side of the table to hers. He snatched her, bringing her to him. "This." Owen bit her bottom lip softly.

Oh, that.

"I think I like it a lot better when you bite my lip than when I do."

"Me too." Owen wasn't in a hurry to let her go and Molly didn't mind one bit.

* * * *

Day three of his silly challenge was taking them on an adventure. On the way home after their date the night before, he'd told her to take the day off but to bring her camera.

The entire morning she'd felt as if she were floating on air. The sun had been shining brightly, not only on the gorgeous city of Seattle but on Molly as well. When the time came for Owen to pick her up, she almost couldn't contain her excitement any longer.

He drove them to the harbor. Rows of boats of different sizes and varieties bobbed on the dark water. Now she wasn't so thrilled. As much as Molly adored the ocean, the waves of the open sea didn't agree with her tummy and the very thought made her clench her mouth shut.

"You don't like boats?" Owen asked as he held her hand and led Molly along the wooden dock.

"It's not the boats so much as it's the water."

"You get seasick?"

She nodded and began to grow queasy when they stopped by an enormous boat.

"She's the smoothest float on the water," he tried to reassure Molly.

"It's not her I'm worried about," Molly laughed nervously, begging her stomach to settle down.

"I have some motion sickness pills aboard. We'll get you taken care of."

Molly didn't move as he tried tugging her hand.

"I promise, sweetheart. You won't get sick—not on my watch." His gray eyes were light today. Mischief twinkled in them, and, somehow, Molly believed him and they cast off.

Dang if he isn't right again. His boat seemed to be gently cruising along the ocean waves that curled with whiteness and pounded brutally against the sides. She looked back. Seattle had disappeared, and only ripples of dark blue surrounded them. As they ventured farther out, Owen pointed out the shadowy glimpse of the fins of several killer whales that were swimming in the distance.

Owen even let her steer the large wooden wheel, but she was much more comfortable watching him look incredibly sexy as a captain. Molly snuck a few shots of him with her camera when she was fairly certain he was busy navigating or making sense of all the dials, compasses and knobs that were in front of him. At one point on their voyage, she begged for him to wear a cap so she could see him fully in the role. He obliged her, doing several silly poses, and she almost regretted asking him, because now she wanted nothing more than to see him with only the captain's hat on and nothing else. Her mind had been in the gutter all day. They'd exchanged sexual innuendos the entire trip, only fueling the brewing tension and the heat she was getting desperate to quench. All the sweetness had been fine and dandy, but she needed more. Again, she couldn't help but think that it was all part of his plan.

He sailed them to a small island, anchoring them and preparing a smaller boat to take them to the shore. Molly watched him work. He was a seaman through and through. He knotted and untied ropes with a speed she hadn't known was possible. He was skilled, moved quickly and was light on his feet. This man was a sailor. The ocean was his. Somehow, Molly couldn't escape the thought that she was his also.

He'd packed a scrumptious dinner of cheeses, fruits, crackers and, of course, wine. Molly was more than content with the idea of having him for dessert, but instead he had brought a mini cheesecake. After lounging on a blanket that was spread over the soft, warm sand, digesting the lovely food and one another's company, Owen grabbed her hand and instructed her to bring her camera.

They hiked along the shore. She snapped seagulls pecking at mussels, leaving the broken bits of purple shells scattered everywhere. The cliffs, covered with algae and salt-stained, demanded to be shot. Molly trained her camera on the simplicity of their astounding strength. These walls of stone had been beaten by ocean storms, carved by wind and rain and yet still managed to stand like ancient stoic giants.

There was no one else around them. It was as though this was their island. The solitude and feeling of complete privacy was not lost on her. Owen scooped her up in arms, and in complete Tarzan style, threw her over his shoulder, causing Molly to squeal with delight. She liked this primal side of him, purely male, especially when he lowered her onto the sand and hovered over her, exploring her neck and collarbone with his mouth. She wanted his kisses to venture farther. She hungered for him to just take her right there, but that didn't seem to be Owen's style. Instead, he pushed her to limits that drove her to the brink of insanity and left her trembling with want. Somehow she knew that when he did finally give in and let her have him, it was going to be explosive and probably the best sex ever.

After several more impromptu make-out sessions, a few where she was up against the stone walls with him grinding his impressive — and hard — length against her, having her mouth ravaged in ways that made her fiercely crave him, she was left breathless and wet with desire. Other times, he would pause in their path and kiss her right where they stood. Even just holding his hand and walking back to where they'd eaten earlier was romantic. Everything — every moment they shared that day — felt so completely right, like this man was meant to be hers.

The wind was light and carrying the salty scent of the sea with it. The sound of the waves lapping against the shore was hypnotizing, and having Owen's arms wrapped tightly around her was heaven. She couldn't have planned a more romantic date. Owen had once again pulled out all the stops. But it was the way he'd done it that had made it so wonderful. He was anything but traditional, yet he was a complete gentleman. He'd shown her the natural untamed beauty of this island, shared in the serenity that it offered, and given her a glimpse of what they could have together. She didn't need to complete the rest of the week to tell that being with him would be something special.

* * * *

"Okay, if you don't want him, I do," Tiffany exclaimed on Friday night as they all snuggled on Molly's couch.

"Did he say when the next date was? We obviously got you tonight." Mackenzie smirked and took a long swig from her beer bottle.

Molly held her bottle loosely between her fingers, enjoying the coolness of the glass against her skin. She wasn't quite ready to admit to them that she was pretty certain she was in love with him. It was as though Molly wanted to savor that morsel, her own cherished secret.

"Well, we are halfway through his little challenge. I'm sure we'll probably see each other tomorrow." A sliver of Molly wished she were with Owen right then instead of with her besties. She'd never in all of her relationships felt that. She'd always picked Mackenzie and Tiffany over any guy, but Owen had somehow weaseled his way into her heart, occupying a large chunk of space. She actually missed him and it hadn't even been twenty-four hours.

"Gosh, what do you think he'll do next? That last date is going to be hard to top," Tiffany commented.

"I can think of a few ways he can top it." Molly grinned and swallowed some of the bitter ale.

"I think it may even have to do with him being on top of her," Mackenzie joked, slapping Molly on her pajama-clad leg.

"I'm not picky. I'll ride," Molly countered with a shrug.

They all started to laugh, but Molly was dead serious. She needed Owen with such intensity that she wasn't sure how much more she could take. Him and his damn 'not getting the milk for free' crap. Granted, at this point she'd buy the whole damn cow.

Her girls teased Molly all night while they enjoyed their drinks, carbs and movie. Thoughts of Owen and what would be next on his agenda kept creeping into her mind, even as they had their fun evening.

Then the night was over and Mackenzie and Tiffany left. It was a little after midnight, another well-spent *Friendship Friday*. She was brushing her teeth and getting ready for bed when she heard the doorbell ring. *Maybe one of the girls has forgotten something.* Molly jogged lightly to answer it, her toothbrush dangling in her mouth with minty toothpaste threatening to drip out. She decided at the last minute to run to the kitchen sink and spit.

"I'm coming," she called out as another knock sounded from the other side of the door. "Gosh, what did you guys forget?" Molly asked when she opened the door, expecting to see Mackenzie or Tiffany, definitely not Owen.

His hands were shoved in his jean pockets and he leaned against the door frame. "I know it's late, but I couldn't not see you today."

"Growing a little attached, are we?" Molly crossed her arms.

He straightened up and moved closer, evaporating any space in between them. "Very attached." The thickness of his voice, heavy and lust-laden, instantly turned her on. But that was nothing compared to the rush of sensation and instant swell of need that surged through her when he grabbed her by the nape and took possession of her mouth — hot, wet and demanding.

Molly pressed her body hard against his. She could feel heat emitting from Owen. The doorknob was jabbing her in the small of her back but that didn't bother her. She'd suffer to keep his lips on her. He stole her breath. Molly's heart was beating a fast rhythm. It felt like a hummingbird was lodged inside her chest. Her heartbeats were matched by the throbbing in her clit. Only this man could make that happen.

When they broke away, she asked in an airy voice, "Is this

date four?"

"Nope. This is just me showing you how much I missed you," Owen sighed and took her in his arms, swallowing her up. "Oh, Molly, you have no idea what you do to me, babe."

"If it's anything like the hell you are putting me through, then yes, I do." She peered up at him.

He lowered his gaze. "Please don't look at me like that — not now, anyway."

"Why not?" She couldn't help but push her pelvis a little harder into his. She hoped he wouldn't be able to feel the wetness he'd caused in her jammies — or did she?

"Because otherwise I won't be able to stop, and we need to make it through this week, Molly," he said, nearly groaning, but returning the pressure she held on him, grinding his hardness against her.

"Who is to say that this can't be part of the week-long challenge?" she asked hopefully, wandering her hand across his flat stomach. She needed to see him naked. She needed to feel his skin on hers. She needed to feel his hands all over her. She wanted to feel him inside her.

"Because this week is to prove to you that we should be together." Owen exhaled loudly and continued. "Besides, I want all of you, not just this, as amazing as that would be." He ran his hands down her arms. "I need to know that you want there to be an *us*. Remember, you were the one that didn't think we should be a couple?"

Does he really need to point that out right now? Yes, it had been her that said that, but she'd also said a lot of other stupid stuff. Hopefully, he'd learn that soon. Mackenzie and Tiffany were used to it. He could always ask them for notes.

With her body raging for fulfillment, she made one last attempt. She knew he'd probably say no, but it was worth a shot. "Do you want to come in?"

"You're the devil. I swear." He shook his head and quietly muttered, "I'd better not. I just needed to see you. Hearing your voice wouldn't have been enough."

Molly couldn't help but feel disappointed. Knowing full well she'd see him tomorrow wasn't enough to douse the sadness that was filling her and the emptiness that was still left inside.

He stroked her cheek, moving his thumb slowly over her lips. "Good night, Molly."

He didn't kiss her again because they both knew that if he did, there would be no turning back. They'd come to a fork in the road. They both knew there was something there between them. She couldn't deny that any longer. Owen had never bothered fighting it. Owen had set out to prove to her that they were supposed to be together. That had worked fairly quickly, probably far sooner than he'd even realized. Molly knew deep down that no matter how much she'd tried to shove away her feelings for him in the beginning, they had always been there, and now, if she listened to her heart, it told her that they always would be. She'd thought that maybe she'd loved someone before, but as she watched Owen leave, turning back for one last look, she knew that this was truly her first experience at being completely in love. It scared and thrilled her, all at the same time.

Chapter Thirteen

Coffee. That would be the only solution for how absolutely miserable Molly felt. She'd slept like crap, tossing and turning all night. She hated nights like that. She knew that seeing Owen just moments before she'd gone to bed had been the main culprit. He'd once again taken her to the edge of fulfillment and left her hanging. This sexual frustration was the pits, and here she was, wanting him and not at all as relaxed as she should be, as a result. It was still dark and way earlier than Molly wanted to be up, but what was the point of just lying there?

She stared at the coffee pot with complete disgust. "Hurry up," Molly shouted angrily at it. It sputtered and spat steamy dark liquid into the glass pot. It would have been quicker to just eat the beans and cut out the middleman — water.

Molly wondered when Owen planned on calling her. She just needed to survive until Tuesday, the day when this dumb challenge would end. She had no idea that a week could both fly by and crawl at a snail's pace. The one thing she was proud about was that she wasn't questioning things like she had been. By letting herself truly 'just go with it', she'd found she had little doubt and she wasn't overthinking things or creating worries out of nothing. Granted, Owen had made the last several days some of the best she'd ever had. He was special. There was no question. She even felt like she matched him pretty well. That realization was a first for her. She never had thought she was good enough for anyone, but they complemented each other nicely.

But him leaving her last night? That had nearly shattered her heart. The want and pent-up desire was making her crack. It was why she hadn't been able to sleep. She'd gone from being single in Seattle to being sleepless in Seattle. Molly sighed. Neither was good, and she was both.

Turning her attention back to the coffee pot that had been slower than molasses at creating drinkable magic, she saw that her coffee was nearly ready. Her bright yellow mug with the tiny chip was her favorite. It was large and held just the right volume of coffee, which was a lot. The freshly brewed pot had filled her apartment with its strong aroma. She doctored it with her favorite creamer, a spicy cinnamon and vanilla blend. Molly grabbed her mug and went to sit near the window to see what the Seattle weather was doing today. The first sip kissed her soul, warming her to her very core. Only coffee had that power — that first swallow that traveled down her throat, possessing her like the caffeinated demon that it was. Coffee owned her. It was that simple.

She was finally beginning to perk up when her cell phone let out a piercing cry, destroying the calm and peaceful love affair she was engaged in with her coffee and newspaper.

It was Mackenzie. Molly was curious what she wanted. Mackenzie was well known for sleeping in on the weekends, and after a week of dealing with kindergartners, Molly couldn't blame her.

"Hey," Molly answered.

"Hey, yourself." Mackenzie laughed on the other end.

"A little early for you, isn't it?"

Mackenzie was quiet for a moment. "It kinda is, isn't it?"

Detecting something strange about her voice, she asked, "What's wrong, Mac?" Molly grew nervous and took another sip of coffee in hopes of calming herself. Was more caffeine really a wise solution?

"Nothing really. Have you talked to Owen yet?"

"No, why?" Now Mackenzie had Molly's undivided attention.

"Well, it's about his plans with you tonight."

"Mackenzie, spit it out," Molly commanded.

"Okay, okay. He thought it would awesome to have you both come over to my place for dinner."

"That's it?" Molly wasn't upset but maybe a little disappointed. She didn't feel like sharing him with her friends, but, then again, it was important that they all got along. But these special dates were exactly that—special—and it was nice spending that time with him alone.

"You're not upset?" Mackenzie asked softly.

"Why would I be?"

"Because, if you recall, last time you and he came over, you quit talking to him and sort of freaked out, babe," Mackenzie reminded her, not that she needed it.

"It's fine. I mean, it's a little strange that he wants to spend our date with you guys. I guess it's cool, right?" The thought was now starting to sink in.

"See? There it is. I knew you weren't going to be all right with this."

"I am okay with it, just a tad thrown off is all," Molly lied and prayed that Mackenzie couldn't see through her bullshit.

"Moll, you do realize the purpose of each of these dates, right?"

"Yes, Mackenzie, I'm not stupid. He's trying to prove to me that he was right and we should be dating," Molly said confidently.

"Well, I think it's a little more complex than that. Think about it. He has shown you several different types of dates so far, truly giving you a glimpse of what being in a relationship with him would be like. It's kind of genius on his part."

"Yeah, that's what I meant," Molly replied. Actually, she had taken it more at face value, not really diving into some deep philosophical meaning behind each date. Sure, she realized he was showing her all the fun aspects of them spending time together, but had each date really had some hidden motive? Maybe she was sort of stupid, because

Molly hadn't seen it that way at all.

Molly spent the next several hours after she'd hung up with Mackenzie, stewing about everything. Now she was doing exactly what she'd been so proud of not doing earlier. Her brain was fully engrossed in overthinking and playing up different scenarios and ridiculous reasons for why Owen had gone to all this trouble. Sometimes Molly wished there was an off switch she could use to just shut it all down for a while.

With the combination of crappy sleep and having a female case of 'blue balls', Molly almost didn't want to go to dinner at Mackenzie's. But when Owen called, she'd caved and said yes. He had asked her what was wrong, being the perceptive little shit that he was. Couldn't he just let things go and not ask? She had done what came naturally and lied. She had said everything was fine. That should get him off her back, right?

Now he would be showing up soon and here she was in her bedroom, severely lacking motivation. She'd gotten partially dressed, slipping into a comfortable pair of jeans and wearing only her bra. Deciding which top to wear had been a half-hour-long struggle so far — one that she was not winning — and she ultimately surrendered by plopping on her bed and staring up at the stucco ceiling, contemplating canceling dinner. When the better half of Molly really got to thinking, though... In reality, why was she even upset? Owen just wanted to show her that they could maintain a relationship and a friendship with her friends. Somewhere in her mind, she'd never thought to really join the two. Her girls were an important part of her life and Owen was another new, important part. She'd accepted that it did make a little sense to merge those relationships, but now? Wasn't it a little soon? She hadn't even met any of his friends yet.

Molly's eyes fluttered open when she heard a noise, then realized it was a knock at her front door. She was confused and a little dazed. She must have fallen asleep. Her brain had finally shut down. Even if she had only slept for a little while, she was thankful.

Still just in her jeans and bra, she slowly removed herself from the bed as the knocking increased. She looked at the piles of discarded shirts that were strewn all over. She considered just grabbing one and throwing it on. The rebel inside her begged to differ. *Screw it.*

Answering the door in only her bra and jeans was probably one of the dumber things she'd done in a long time, but why not? She had been on a roll lately.

She didn't feel like herself at all. Who was *this* Molly? It was a bitchy, slightly horny, under-caffeinated and exhausted version of herself, that was who.

Yanking the door open, she prayed for a split second that it was Owen and not the apartment building manager. Or maybe she'd get a reduction in rent if she flashed a little skin.

It was Owen, wearing a shocked expression. "Um, wow."

"Just come inside." Molly led the way in and continued toward her bedroom. She had to find a top to wear so they wouldn't be late. Owen trailed after her.

"You okay, Molly?"

Why does he have to keep asking that? "I'm fine."

"Molly." He grabbed her by the waist and she could feel his warm fingertips on her skin.

She looked up at him and said, "What?"

"Even when you're upset, you're beautiful. You know that? That's one of the things I love about you."

"You love that I'm upset? Because I'm not," Molly argued. She started to feel awkward standing there in her bra. She suddenly felt vulnerable. Where did that rebel attitude run away to?

"Yes, you are. But you're gorgeous, especially now," Owen whispered, his voice rougher this time. "Want to just stay in?"

"Oh, but remember, that's not part of your master plan?" Molly shot back with more sass than she'd intended.

"It's not, but plans change." He dragged his index finger up her spine, running it along her shoulder, then neck, and finally over the swell of the flesh that was bulging out of her hot pink bra.

Her chest heaved, her feeble attempt at slowing her breathing as she tried to gain control of what was happening. A wave of heat flooded her. She was still on lust's edge from the night before. On one hand, she wanted nothing more than to strip them both and finally explore this waiting passion. On the other she was angry — not really at him, but at herself again. She'd fallen into the same trap or rabbit hole, the one that always took her mind and filled it with doubt. She felt lost and needy but, most of all, upset with herself because she didn't have a handle on this situation.

And she was bitter, because why was Owen making all the calls in this relationship of sorts, and would this be another decision he would make for them? How was it fair for him to decide when they could finally sleep together? Was this how it would always be? Would she ever be the one calling the shots? Or was she resolved to 'just go with it' for however long this lasted?

"Molly," he whispered in her ear. He flicked his tongue against her earlobe, then again on the tender and ticklish part of her neck. He moved his hands from her back, slowly up her ribs then finally to her breasts. He cupped her mounds, applying gentle pressure with each squeeze. He traced his thumbs over her nipples, bringing them to life when he swiped against the fabric barrier.

She moaned when his teeth grazed her skin, sending a sharp shiver through her. She could feel the dampness in her panties. She could feel the hardness in his jeans. Molly held on tightly to him and ran her hands under his shirt, roaming the flat, tight muscles of his stomach. *Damn.*

"Owen, this isn't part of that stupid challenge, is it?" Molly managed to get the words out.

"No, babe, the challenge is over."

For a split second she was almost sad to hear that, but

she was also thankful that they could now investigate the relationship's physical side, and she had a lot of ideas as to how that exploration should go. Just to be sure, she asked, "So that means—"

"You're mine." He removed her bra and stood looking at her. Molly saw the wave of emotions in his eyes—hunger, appreciation, happiness and…love? But she didn't have time to dwell on that last one when he bent to take her erect nipple in his mouth, lavishing it with attention, pausing for only a moment to pull back, look at her and say, "And I'm yours."

Molly looped her arms around his neck and she kissed him, hard. She opened her mouth to invite him in, and they locked into the hottest, most passionate kiss that Molly had ever had.

But she wanted more. She broke the kiss to quickly remove his shirt. *Skin… I want to feel him.* She found a tan chest with a spray of fine dark hair. A sexy trail led her eyes past his sculpted pecs and dipped into the waist of his pants, teasing her with hidden promises. She spied his abs and almost died. She knew well-defined abs and that precious V all too well. She took pictures of nearly naked men all the time. But Owen was naturally a beautifully designed and sculpted man, and she wanted more than ever to have him naked on her bed. *Now.* She was on fire, and the heat was all for him.

But she would only get to do this for the first time once. She took a deep breath to calm the raging lust inside her and decided to make it more of a show. Molly gave him her best sex-kitten look as she let her jeans fall from her hips. She stepped out of them and sashayed closer to him. Once her hands were on his belt, she decided to speed things up a bit. She was not going to have him change his mind now. When he said her name under his breath that only spurred her on, giving her the confidence to shuck his pants off his hips. She heard his sharp intake of breath. It thrilled her and made her even braver and more ready for their shared pleasure. She knelt in front of him. She looked up and smiled. His stormy gray eyes were darker, almost black, with anticipation of what would happen next. Molly couldn't help but think, *Now who's calling the shots?*

Owen had his fingers knotted in her hair, and he moaned. She was delighted with the knowledge that it was all her doing. She was the one providing that pleasure to him, making him lose control. Besides, it gave her a first look at what she was going to be working with a little later. She considered it a test drive of sorts. It also turned her on more than anything. She pushed down his briefs and there it was…the most beautiful cock she'd ever seen. She nuzzled it lovingly. This was hers, and she was going to enjoy it. She wrapped her hand around it, pleased to see that her fingers didn't completely meet. This man—her man—was very well endowed. She began to alternately lick and suck it, then took the velvety, leaking head into her mouth to finally taste the very essence of Owen. When she deep-throated him, Owen uttered a groan from somewhere very deep inside, then he pulled her off and lifted her away before he pushed her onto the bed.

He quickly divested himself of his shoes, briefs and jeans to stand completely naked before her.

Then he dove. It was the only way to describe the vehemence with which he spread her legs and thrust his face and hands between them. He began to ravage her dripping pussy and her clit with his teeth, tongue and fingers.

Molly grabbed the sheets, bunching them tightly in her hands as a spasm rocked her body, but Owen wasn't finished. He had just caused one of the most intense orgasms she'd ever experienced. The sinister smile on his face told her he was nowhere near done. He hid once again between her legs, doing things with his tongue that she didn't know were possible.

The tension within her began to grow once more. He sucked her fevered clit then rammed two fingers into her wet depths, pumping them fast.

"Owen!" Molly screamed as another hard orgasm racked her body. She had been right. She had known that the first time they had sex it was going to be incredible, but maybe that was because they weren't just screwing, but it actually meant something much deeper. Or maybe it was the explosive chemistry that had been brewing from the start? Either way, Molly knew that she was in for what would probably be the best experience of her life. And they hadn't even gotten around to the making love part yet.

Owen moved from between her legs, running his tongue up her stomach until he was only inches away from her face. He looked at her with a mix of desire and something else. It was genuine and almost shy. It would be the first time that they would be connected in such an intimate way and it was as though he wanted to savor each second.

This was it. His velvety cockhead nudged at her pussy's entrance. Molly opened her legs farther and pulled her knees up to give him welcome.

"You're beautiful, Molly," Owen said as he sank into her.

Molly took in a sharp breath as he filled her. The sensation was incredible when her body accommodated him. He entered her slowly, and each inch only made her yearn for more. Finally, he bottomed out and rested there. Molly had never felt so full, so complete, so in love.

Then he began pumping his hips, thrusting into her, and she matched him. They moved in rhythm, each challenging the other—harder, deeper. Molly circled her legs around him to pull him closer. Molly could hear the sounds of Owen's breathing, grunting as he worked to bring her to climax again. She whimpered. He grabbed her legs and rested them on his shoulders to find new depths when he plunged in again. Molly called out in ecstasy.

Owen showed no signs of tiring and continued to drive Molly to the edge. She saw light splinter from behind her eyelids and felt another rippling spasm take her over. Then Owen rolled away from her to tug her on top of him. Molly grinned down and ground hard against him. She gripped the headboard as she rode the wave of yet another orgasm. Owen clutched her tightly to him and arched deep inside her until he came.

Her heart was thumping a mile a minute as she collapsed on top of Owen. He rested his hands on her hips, still inside her. They were both too sensitive to move quickly. No gymnastic dismount points would be given for this performance.

* * * *

"God, that was amazing," Molly finally said. Her skin was sticky with sweat. So was Owen's. They hadn't left her bedroom for several hours now. Her body tingled to the point of being almost numb.

She had managed to text Mackenzie at one point when she'd slipped away to the restroom for more condoms. Mackenzie had replied with a thumbs-up icon and a smiley face. Tiffany had quickly messaged her with a ridiculous series of icons and a joke about cobwebs being cleaned out. Only her friends would cheer her on with a thumbs-up and tease her during a brief pause from the throes of passion.

Good job on getting laid!

Yay, you did it!

Can you still walk?

Take a picture for us!

These had been among the messages they had kept sending to Molly. After laughing in the bathroom, she'd finally shut off her phone and returned to Owen. They'd gone right back at it, making up for all the lost time.

"It was pretty damn incredible, but I'm starving." Owen grabbed Molly's hair in his hand, pulling it back and away from her face. He rose slightly and kissed her.

"I thought you had enough," Molly teased but felt her own body react once again to his kiss.

"Sweetheart, I won't ever be able to get enough of you."

Owen was apparently bound to prove it to her. *Guess we'll just eat a little later.*

Chapter Fourteen

Breakfast in bed—she could live with this. But she didn't remember there being any eggs, much less anything else edible in her fridge. *Who cares?* She had food and a delicious man in her bed. Life was good.

Owen was shirtless, and Molly had spent all night trying to convince him that he didn't need to own shirts anymore. He'd said only if she promised to do the same. *Well, crap.*

"This is wonderful. Thank you," Molly said around a mouthful of fluffy scrambled eggs.

"You're welcome." Owen bent over from his side of the bed and kissed her on the head.

Content, that was how she felt. *Is this what it can be like? Lazy Sundays in bed, eating breakfast after our sexual appetites have been fed?*

"What do you feel like doing today?" Owen asked, stabbing several pieces of egg onto his fork.

"This," Molly answered.

"I have an idea. How about a change of scenery?"

"Sure, where?"

"My place." Owen smiled as her.

She still hadn't been to his home, and the idea of seeing where he lived appealed to her. She could really get a sense of someone by being in their personal space, to see their personality by their choice of décor. Molly was excited now.

"That would be awesome. Dinner?"

"Sure. I'll take of everything."

"Oh, let me bring something or help you cook. It'll be fun," Molly begged.

"You can be the entertainment and dessert." He winked

at her and she felt her body react instantly. *God, what is it about this man?*

Molly touched her hair. She had the worst case of bed hair, a complete tangled mess. "I need to shower."

"Sounds good to me." Owen gave her a sexy grin.

Molly had a feeling that this shower wouldn't be for the purpose of getting them clean, but she quickly scurried off to her bathroom with Owen hot on her trail.

Molly thought of the song *Jungle Love* that had a line about things being better when wet. She couldn't agree more. Suds covered both of them. The slick soap ran down their bodies. Molly rinsed the shampoo out of her hair, Owen helping her. Well, not really. He was busy cupping her breasts, tweaking her nipples and licking her neck. She needed a bigger shower, like the one back in Vegas. Hers was cramped. The tight space made it nearly impossible to move around much without touching, which Owen seemed quite happy about. He hadn't taken his hands off her since they'd entered the steamy shower. Molly couldn't deny it was incredibly erotic. 'Wet and wild' barely began to describe it.

"Ouch. God, that burns," Owen cried out.

Molly saw him trying to flush his eyes with the water from the shower head.

"Sorry," she apologized and kissed his collarbone. The water beat down on her back and head. "Here... Let me make it better." She kissed him again, running her tongue along the flat muscles of his chest as she traveled lower.

He moaned loudly and braced himself against the tile wall. Molly crouched in front of him. They stared at each other, neither speaking. Then Molly leaned forward and reached his groin, using her tongue to lick up the water that was dripping off him. She gripped his thighs as she tried to balance. He was rock-hard again and his cock bounced in front of her, tempting her, asking for her attention. She tasted the warm water from the shower and Owen when she opened her mouth wider, taking in her new favorite plaything, all the way to the root. She was beyond turned on. She felt his body react when she licked up then back down his heavy shaft, when she nipped around the mushroom head and she hollowed out her cheeks, sucking him hard. Molly wanted to drive him crazy. Teasing him was part of the thrill. She wanted to see just how far she could push him before he could take no more.

He tangled his hands in her hair as he battled for control. "God, Molly, you're killing me."

She pulled off him, looked him straight in the eye and winked. "Good."

Payback was a bitch, and for all the weeks he'd made her suffer, Owen deserved a little torture. Molly ran her tongue along his inner thighs, nipping gently. Owen tried to steer her back to what he wanted. Looking up at him with a devious smile on her lips, Molly reminded him that right now she was in the driver's seat.

* * * *

"Wow, I love your place," Molly said as she started to remove her sweater. Owen came up behind her and helped her out of it, but not without kissing her neck.

"I'm glad."

His home was incredible. There were windows everywhere that gave a view of Elliott Bay. The exposed, dark wooden beams and rich tones were masculine. It was open—all the rooms connected. The living and dining room merged right off the kitchen. There were no walls, just lots of space. There was no hint of femininity anywhere. This was a man's home, from the large, bulky furniture to the enormous television that was perfect for watching a Seahawks game with his buddies. The kitchen—cherry cabinets, stainless steel and granite countertops—was neat and orderly. Molly didn't notice any food on the stove and everything was spotless. They were eating, right? Her stomach growled and she was kicking herself for not having eaten all day.

His lips were still on her neck as she took in all the details, the little touches that were Owen — picture frames containing photos of an older couple, some with him. A lot of the frames held shots of fish or the ocean.

Owen was behind her, his arms around her waist. "I can't get enough of you," he whispered into her hair.

Her body began to hum. It was becoming his instrument, begging for his touch, for him to play music all over it with his fingers and his tongue.

Molly spun around. She didn't even have to search for his mouth. He captured her the moment she'd faced him. She loved the way he tasted, the soft way he kissed her, but there was a searing passion that she knew burned behind it.

"Okay, we'd better eat before I haul you off to my bedroom." Owen released her, but snatched her hand and pulled her to follow him. He led her through the home, telling her about each room, but he paused at one that had double doors, not saying anything. He ushered them in a different direction. Now she was curious and hoped that they would visit that room later.

"I thought we could eat outside," he said as they wandered out to an expansive redwood deck. A small patio table with four chairs was off to one side. There were several loungers and an obnoxiously giant barbecue, again incredibly male. She saw smoke coming out of it and smelled the delicious char of cooking meat.

The salty air mingled with the scent of steaks that were nearly ready to take off the grill. Owen threw on an adorable apron and peeked inside something wrapped in foil — salmon. Molly stood next to him, holding a beer and feeling very *wifey*. This whole scene was domestication at its best.

She wanted to assist in making the salad, even though he playfully scolded her for helping, explaining she was his guest. They bickered like a real couple, but Molly won that battle quickly after flashing him by the kitchen sink, telling him she'd brought dessert. Granted, it was in the form of a red lacy bra and panties. He threatened to take her right then and there. She egged him on, daring him, only to run away when he went to grab her.

The flirty cat and mouse game had them both smiling all through dinner and even after she'd finished washing their dirty dishes. They worked well as a team. Both helped clean up and put away any leftovers, working in sync. They finally wound up on the deck loungers, quiet all around them as the sun ducked lower into the horizon, casting a sherbet-colored sky over the bay. They drank their beers, laughing at several seagulls that visited them on the deck, looking for a handout. The peacefulness and overwhelming sensation of how right this all felt flowed through Molly. She was happy — truly happy — more than she'd ever felt with someone else.

"So, about that dessert..." Owen's eyes turned bright with lust. Molly brought her leg up over his stomach, securing herself to him. He ran his hand up and down her bare calf. They were sharing a lounger, snuggled close together, watching the world around them change colors as the shadows of night emerged.

Feeling daring and confident, Molly unbuttoned her turquoise-colored blouse slowly, giving him a peek-a-boo glimpse of her red bra. She couldn't explain why this man brought out the brazen wildcat in her, but she liked watching the desire burn in his eyes and it stoked a seemingly unquenchable fire of need in her. She'd never felt so wanted in all her life. Owen made her feel special, like she was the most sexy and beautiful woman in the world. Molly wasn't stupid. She knew things weren't as tight or toned on her body as they'd used to be — she wasn't in her twenties anymore. But to have a man treat her like the rarest and most precious of treasures was welcomed and appreciated — and about the hottest thing she could imagine. "You love torturing me, don't you?"

"Maybe just a little." Molly moved in to kiss him. It was as though her mouth was magnetically drawn to him.

In a quick maneuver, Owen pulled Molly and, suddenly, she found herself on top of him, comfortably pressed against something very big, very hard and very Owen. This was one of her new favorite positions. Owen undid the rest of her blouse then traced the outline of the bra. He ran his tongue through the smooth valley of her soft mounds.

Molly sighed, then it dawned on her they were outside. "What about your neighbors?"

"What about them?" His voice was muffled, he continued to nuzzle her chest. Owen held her hips and was too busy to exploring her breasts to pay attention to her concern.

It was difficult for her to stay focused, too, when he took a nipple into his mouth through the lace, biting it gently. It sent a spike of lust straight to her sex. "Owen, I'm serious. What if they see us?"

"Then they're a bunch of lucky bastards, if you ask me."

She slapped him lightly and tried to pull away. "I mean it." Molly saw the sky growing a deeper purple as night swallowed up the last remnants of the day. Stars were already playfully twinkling above them.

"Okay, okay." In a fluid motion, Owen gently moved Molly off him as he rose from the lounger. He stared at her briefly then hoisted her up. With a sexy grin on his handsome face, he tossed her over his broad shoulder.

"Put me down," she squealed.

"Nope." Owen carried her through the sliding glass door, past the living room then down the hallway he'd shown her earlier. The inside of the house was dark, but she could make out the outline of the double doors as they approached. It was the one room he'd not shown Molly yet. Owen used his free hand to open the door. The next thing Molly knew she was in the air for a brief moment, then landed on a soft surface. He flicked on the light and she saw the gorgeous room. The bed was massive, with carved wood posts at all four corners. The room was decorated with the sea in mind. A captain's wheel was hung above the headboard, and there were framed prints of driftwood-covered beaches, raging ocean waters and his boat.

"Who took those?" She pointed to the pictures that were hanging on the wall.

"Some guy."

"Come on. Who?" As a photographer, she was drawn to the composition of the edits and the simplicity of each shot. Sometimes nature was the best model, but whoever had taken these had some skill.

He exhaled loudly as he joined her on the bed. Their legs were intertwined as they both stared at the wall. "Me."

Molly let out a gasp. "No way. Really? They're beautiful, Owen."

"Thanks. But I see something far more beautiful." He began to kiss her exposed, bra-clad breasts, her blouse nearly completely unbuttoned. He began to roam his hands over her body, but Molly was more focused on the fact that Owen had failed to share that he was also a photographer.

"So, how long have you been taking pictures?"

"Those are old." He pulled her nipple out and sucked gently.

Molly moaned then gathered her thoughts. "So you stopped?"

Owen huffed and looked up at her. "Yes. Now, are we having dessert or discussing those old pictures?"

"Can't we do both?" Molly grinned. *Come on. I'm a photographer. What does he expect?* After finding out those were his shots, she wanted to know more.

"I can't multitask, so it's one or the other, babe," Owen said as he returned to exposed nipple.

Fine. They would definitely be returning to this conversation. Molly wove her fingers through his hair as she wrapped her legs around him, locking him to her. She had so many questions, but right now she had a hungry man that needed his dessert.

* * * *

"That's friggin' hot, Molly," Tiffany said in short breaths. They were jogging, the sand heavy under their running shoes. Carkeek Park was quiet this evening.

The tide was pulling away from the shore, exposing a raw ocean dinner for the seabirds that were pecking at the sand.

"Damn, Tiffany's right. How in the hell did you get so lucky?" Mackenzie huffed as she ran.

Molly could feel her legs burning, but now that she was going to be naked a lot more, she figured she'd better step up her fitness game. "You guys have no idea. But now I need to make myself sexy."

Mackenzie winced. "Ah, the pressures of being perfect for men. Sucks being a woman sometimes, doesn't it?"

"I don't get it. You guys already screwed. He saw you naked and didn't run away screaming. Trust me. You're good, girl," Tiffany confirmed as they kept in sync.

"True. But it wouldn't hurt to slim down a wee bit to try to see if I can keep these puppies from dropping down any lower—at least for a while." Molly clutched her chest as they continued to run.

"I wish I had boobs," Mackenzie complained. Her figure was lean and athletic. She still looked like a teenager. But she was right. She was more than a little flat-chested. Mackenzie wore a bright neon blue sports bra, baring her midsection and black leggings that made her long legs seem even longer. They all envied her abs. They weren't the ugly, over-defined type but were trim, flat and smooth. Mackenzie looked incredible when swimsuit season rolled around.

"You are welcome to have some of mine," Molly offered playfully.

"I have too much ass. You want some, Mackenzie?" Tiffany laughed. She was wearing animal-print-style leggings that were cropped mid-calf, and her usual black layered tank. Tiffany could pull off pretty much any swimsuit as well, but she did have a large butt. Molly was completely and utterly jealous of it. Any jeans, yoga pants—literally anything—

looked great on her figure.

"Look at us, such pathetic examples of women. Here… I want what you have and you want what I've got. There's just no pleasing us, is there?" Molly said when she considered her body for a moment. Her middle was soft. It needed some work for sure. Looking down at her gray and pink shorts, she saw that her pasty legs needed more sun and they could be longer. She wore a faded pink Seattle Mariners baseball shirt. Under it she had doubled up on her sports bra in hopes of not getting a black eye during this jog, one of the many reasons why she loathed running.

"Nope. We are constantly on the hunt for perfection. It's nowhere to be found. I swear, it'd be a whole lot easier if I quit searching for it," Tiffany replied.

They paused for a moment by a log that had washed up on the shore, catching their breath and stretching as the sun sank below the horizon. The sky was a smeared lilac hue with traces of gray clouds. The wind was beginning to pick up and they needed to get back to their cars before it started raining. The workout had felt great. Molly knew she'd be sore tomorrow, but it would be worth it. Knowing how much Owen loved her assortment of bras, she'd come up with a goal for herself. She wanted to lose around fifteen pounds, then she was going to splurge on some sexy new undies, just for him. Granted, she wasn't sure how that was a reward for herself, but somehow her mind was made up that it was a good plan.

"So, you guys are like a thing now, right?" Tiffany asked as they set back off in the direction they had come from.

"Yeah, I guess you could say I'm Owen's girlfriend now." She liked the way it sounded as the words exited her mouth.

"Gotta admit, it has a nice ring to it," Mackenzie commented with a genuine smile.

"That reminds me. Did you ever hear from Jason, that bouncer guy?" Molly asked, her lungs beginning to beg for mercy. She hated running, but Tiffany had insisted that this was how she would lose weight.

"Actually, he called me last night." Mackenzie laughed nervously in between gasping for air.

"Oh really? Do tell," Tiffany pleaded as she increased the pace they were running.

"Just one thing, why did we decide to go jogging? This sucks," Molly blurted out. "We could be drinking wine and talking about men right now. Just sayin'."

"Yeah, but there will be no men to talk about if we're fat," Tiffany countered.

"I'm fat now and I'm getting laid," Molly pointed out smugly.

"True, but remember... This was your idea."

"What? I don't recall that," Molly lied.

"As I recall, you said, *'Tiff, please help me. I'm a fat cow. I'm one pint of ice cream away from mooing'* or something along those lines," Tiffany said as she reenacted their conversation.

"Yeah, I kinda remember saying it, now that you mention it."

"So see? I'm keeping you from being a cow. You're welcome."

"Who wants to grab some froyo after this?" Mackenzie asked.

"Mackenzie, jeesh, didn't you just hear us talking about Molly becoming a cow?"

"Yeah, but they have dairy free. Besides, I didn't offer to help her. I offered froyo, so really... Who here is the better friend?"

"I kinda like Mac a little more right now," Molly teased.

"Fine. We're all going to end up as fat cows anyway. So how about this... Last one to the car has to pay?" Tiffany suggested.

"Moo!" Molly shouted as she sprinted for the car with all the energy she had left.

They all laughed as they picked up their speed and started to race along the shore.

And even after they'd made it to their cars and gotten to

the frozen yogurt place, they were still smiling and laughing when one of them would offer a spirited 'moo'.

The brightly colored shop was family-friendly with a trendy and hip flare. They were seated in a booth enjoying their treats. Molly had lost the race and had to pay, but it was so worth it.

"This was fun," Mackenzie said as she licked her spoon. "But I better get home. I have grades to do. Anyone wanna help?"

"You have to grade kindergartners? Like what do you grade them on, who doesn't eat crayons or paste?" Tiffany asked as she scraped the last bit of froyo out of her bowl.

Mackenzie shook her head. "Actually, you'd be shocked on what we have to grade them on. Don't get me started on what the state wants them to know by now."

"I can't believe summer is almost here," Molly added.

"This school year flew by, yet was kind of agonizing. I'm so looking forward to summer." Mackenzie looked at them seriously and asked, "We going on vacation anywhere awesome this summer, ladies?"

Over the last decade summer had consisted of multiple trips, usually down to the Oregon Coast, but they always tried to escape somewhere different and unexplored. Not being tied down in a marriage or with kids did have its advantages. It allowed them to go practically anywhere they wanted. Mackenzie became a different person during the summer. Something about her changed. She would become more carefree, easygoing and just up for anything. Once September hit, she was back to early bedtimes and creating little geniuses. Tiffany had a Monday through Friday, nine-to-five kind of job, but she hoarded all her sick days and vacation time to use during summer, so they made the most of it. Molly could go anywhere, any time. That was the beauty of her career. She'd even dragged Mackenzie and Tiffany along to some of her location shoots as a part of their vacation getaways.

"Gosh, somewhere incredible... A place we've never been

to—Ireland, maybe?" Tiffany suggested. "I have always dreamed about going there. It seems so romantic."

"It can't be too far," Mackenzie added. "Besides, what is so romantic about leprechauns?"

Molly agreed. "Leprechauns aren't romantic. They are super creepy."

Tiffany rolled her eyes as she quietly slipped a spoonful of froyo into her mouth.

"Anywhere is fine with me," Molly said.

"You sure about that?" Mackenzie gave her a confused look.

"Yeah, why?"

They both stared at her for a moment, causing her to shift nervously in her seat. *Why are they looking at me like that?* Then she realized, *Owen.*

"Well, you know, this whole thing you've got going on does sort of change things a little," Mackenzie explained.

"Does it? I mean, I'm not his wife. We aren't married. Even if we were, I could still travel."

"Yeah, Mackenzie is right. You're in a relationship now, doll. You can't just go jet-setting around the globe without talking about it with Owen first," said Tiffany, and she frowned slightly.

Molly still didn't see how that had to stop her from having fun with her best friends, or was that the reason why none of her relationships had ever worked out? Maybe it was because she'd never given it a second thought. Molly had never asked permission. She'd just gone and done what she'd pleased. For the first time ever, she knew that her carefree, do-whatever-she-wanted life just might be changing for good.

Am I okay with that?

Chapter Fifteen

"Nope, you gotta take it off. Those are the rules," Owen said with an evil smirk on his lips as he raised his beer bottle to his mouth.

He was enjoying things a little too much as he watched her like a hungry wolf. She had been scammed, played and now was nearly naked. Strip poker was obviously not her game, after all.

"You suck," Molly spat as she peeled off yet another article of clothing. This time it was her jeans that had to go. She slowly pushed them over her hips. Her shoes, socks and soon jeans, in a neat pile on the floor, were proof she was terrible at the game.

"I could totally make an inappropriate remark, but I won't." He took another swig from his bottle as his eyes stayed trained on her.

"You lied and I demand a rematch." Molly made a point of wiggling a little more than necessary. She might as well make this fun and torture Owen a bit while she was at it.

"You said you were good at poker, so I guess you lied, too," Owen pointed out casually, raising his eyebrows as he saw the sheer black panties that Molly revealed when she stepped out of the jeans and added them to the rest of her lost garments. "Damn. I'm so glad you're terrible at this game, babe."

Molly shuffled the cards, cut the deck then started to deal the next hand. She grabbed her bottle of beer and swallowed. *Get your game face on, girl. You got this.*

It had been almost a week since Molly had been to his home. Here she was, nearly naked...again. It had been a week since they'd first slept together. The magic of the weekend before had lingered all week long, but real life had resumed. Work for Owen meant early to bed and early to rise. Molly had completed a couple more book covers and had landed a couple of huge clients who she was scheduling within the next couple weeks.

But real life hadn't endangered this new relationship so far. They had managed to call and text, and Owen had continued his ritual of bringing coffee to Molly's studio in the afternoon. They had gone out to dinner once during the week and had ordered takeout at her apartment one night. Molly found herself thinking about him all the time, checking her phone more than ever, seeing if he'd messaged her. He had even started to invade her dreams at night. They varied from over-the-top hot and sexy, all the way to downright boring, mundane stuff. Either way, Owen was constantly in her thoughts.

It was now Saturday night and they were sitting at his dining room table, an assortment of snack food surrounding them — nothing healthy, so much for her diet. She'd been fairly good all week. Even the previous night at Tiffany's house she hadn't over-eaten, which was hard as it had been all about fish 'n chips, one of her favorites. French fries were the devil — granted, a greasy, delicious devil.

"You really need to work on that gorgeous poker face, babe," Owen said as he won again.

"Ugh, this game would be a lot more fun if you lost a couple hands." Molly pouted. Off came her T-shirt, a snug V-neck that showed her figure in a flattering way, which meant it was slimming. Into the pile it went.

"I can't help it that I'm so good. But for you, I'll lose the shirt." He lifted his ancient Seattle Supersonics basketball team shirt over his head.

Damn, that man shouldn't ever wear a shirt. She loved his chest. It was muscular, but just the right amount. His abs were one of her favorite features. They were etched under a fine layer of dark hair.

They sat there, both topless. Well, she still had her matching black bra on, but she knew it wouldn't be for much longer.

"Isn't this better? It feels a bit fairer, doesn't it?" Molly asked, grabbing a corn chip.

"Yeah, a little. But you know what would be even more fun?"

"Hmm?" Molly eyed the cards he was dealing to her. *Great, another crap hand.* Okay, so maybe she didn't have any clue how to really play this dumb game after all.

"If we take this game into my bedroom," Owen suggested, licking his lips again, like a hungry wolf. They hadn't made love since the middle of the week, and he was acting like it had been months.

"Nope. I plan on winning this one." Molly bluffed, trying to make an overly happy face as she stared at her cards.

"Really? You must finally have some good cards."

"Maybe." She winked at him and silently prayed that she had fooled him.

It wasn't that she didn't want to play her favorite indoor sport, but this had become more of an ego thing now. She'd practically lost every hand and was now only in her bra and panties. This was not how she planned to go out. He'd only lost his socks and now his shirt, which was a mercy removal and didn't actually count.

He folded, and just like that, his pants were off. "Now can we go?"

"Just when I'm on a roll?"

"You fooled me. My hand was better," Owen said when he looked at her cards.

"Isn't that the point of this game? Bluffing?" Molly asked in her sweetest voice.

"Okay, next hand, let's up the ante."

Molly eyed him suspiciously. "Like, add money?"

"Nope, all clothing."

"I'm game." She flicked her bra strap at him and watched as he bit his lip.

The cards were dealt and before she knew it, Owen folded.

"What the hell?" Molly cried. He hadn't even tried to win. He'd played her yet again.

Owen moved to her side of the table in all his nude glory. "Look. We both win. Come here, you."

He was her jackpot, and she was going to enjoy her winnings.

* * * *

Molly was flipping through the Sunday morning paper. Her mind wasn't focused on the black and white print in front of her. She'd had to reread an article a few times to try to comprehend what was even written. Molly's brain was foggy. It matched the weather perfectly.

Last night had been a lot of fun. Every time she was with Owen, that was how it was. But she hadn't spent the night, nor had she the previous time she'd been there. *Two for two.* The way she saw things, it was that Owen hadn't asked for her to stay. If he had, maybe then she'd sleep over. *Is there a reason why?* Doubt tried creeping in and Molly almost invited it to come inside.

The relationship was new. Even as comfortable as they felt with each other, they had not been together very long. What exactly was she expecting, a marriage proposal? No, but maybe some guidelines as to how the whole slumber party thing was supposed to work. She didn't want to just show up with her toothbrush in her hand and ask which drawer was now hers.

Communication. It was so important and vital for a relationship to work. Maybe she should just ask. *Ugh.* She worried that if she didn't express her concerns or thoughts now, she never would. *Been there, done that, broke up.* It was as though, if she didn't speak up in the beginning, it would suddenly be too late. He'd have already stamped *Welcome* on her and she would be a doormat. All these thoughts over whether or not she should have asked about spending the night shouldn't even be crossing her mind. Molly's worries were probably fueled by her having had a lovely breakfast in bed following him sleeping over at her place. Somehow, she'd expected a similar turnout at his home. The bar had been set, and she was even thinking he would raise it. Instead, he'd told her to drive safely and had let her leave.

Molly hated this part of a relationship—the drawing of lines in the sand, figuring out boundaries. What were hers? She hadn't even really considered what she wanted or expected to get out of it. It literally had come out of nowhere, much like that fish. It had been unexpected and she was not at all prepared for something so wonderful. Molly had dated nearly half of Seattle. Not actually, but it felt like that sometimes. Finding a good cup of joe was a whole lot easier than finding a good man.

She sipped her coffee. She'd just folded up the paper, giving up on trying to read, which she'd always enjoyed doing on Sundays. Molly exhaled loudly. *What now?* She had no plans for the day. There were things that needed to be done around her place, like laundry. The overflowing hamper and lack of clean jeans kept reminding her that it was long overdue. Her apartment could use a good cleaning, too. She could scrub the shower, maybe even mop the floors or dust. She'd had a life before Owen, so why was she trying to find random tasks to keep herself occupied? Molly should just laze about and soak up the quiet time.

Her cell phone buzzed and she noticed it was Owen. She was half-tempted not to answer, as though she needed to prove something to herself. God only knew what. Because what would be the point of not answering his call? What would that really solve, anyway? She wanted to talk to him. The devil on her shoulder tried to convince her that maybe she should make him suffer a little for not asking her to spend the night. They could be eating breakfast and staying in bed all day right now. The weather was perfect for it, foggy and cold. That sounded like all the makings of a snuggle fest to her. But Molly missed him. It hadn't even been twelve hours since she'd seen him. Her body wanted him, but her heart needed him. She picked up the phone to answer.

She was hopelessly in love.

* * * *

The rest of the week was more of the same, except that the weather was better, a lot better. Everywhere was being doused in ample sunshine. The overload of vitamin D had people acting more cheerful and friendlier than usual. The coffee shop and her 'dealer' barista that supplied her addiction every day had even thrown in a free cookie with her order today. Yeah, everyone was all sorts of happy, even Molly.

Tomorrow was Friday. She had plans to hang out at Mackenzie's place. It was *Friendship Friday,* after all. Despite their tradition, which had only been broken when Tiffany and Mackenzie fought or if one of them was sick, Mackenzie asked Molly earlier if she should clear it with Owen first. Her answer was simple—no. After being so conflicted on Sunday morning, Molly had decided to sort of slow things down a bit—not drastically by any means, but enough to keep from going all in so fast. She was hardly pumping the brakes on their romance. That much was evident when she'd gone over to Owen's for dinner the previous night and had ended up as dessert again, but this time with actual chocolate syrup and whipped cream. Owen had gone as far as to toss a few sprinkles and a cherry on her. His own lil' sundae and he'd licked every bit of sweetness off. Sticky and still a little horny, she'd gotten to discover just how much better his shower was than hers, too. It still didn't compare to the Vegas one, though but his had more room to play in and a giant shower head that reminded her of a stainless steel sunflower.

She'd explained it to Mackenzie over late afternoon coffee, that she was her own woman, that Owen didn't own her.

Molly had felt like she really had to sell it to her friend, like neither of them had totally bought what she was saying. Regardless, *Friendship Friday* was happening. If anything, it would be so she could brag about her new and improved sex life.

She was proud of herself for taking her stand, so she shocked herself a bit later.

"Yeah, we always do this little get-together on Fridays. You don't mind, do you?" Molly found herself explaining to Owen. He'd stopped by, bringing some fish with him from Pike Place and wanting to cook her dinner.

"It's not that I mind. I just thought since I had tomorrow off, we could go out on the boat."

The disappointment in his voice made her cringe. *Shit.* Mackenzie had been right, per usual.

"I can cancel, I guess." The moment the words left her lips she regretted it. *Am I really going to choose Owen over my girls?*

Owen gave her a weak smile, but it was obvious he was thrilled. "Only if you don't mind."

But she did. Her resolve had collapsed. Her promise to her friends had been completely dismissed, and her argument to Mackenzie that she was her own woman was now gone.

Her appetite had also vanished. She picked at the fish and felt Owen watching her.

"You don't like it?"

"I'm just not super hungry," Molly replied, grabbing her wine glass and swirling the pale liquid absentmindedly.

"What's wrong?" Owen's face was filled with concern. He set down his fork and waited for her to answer.

"Nothing. I'm just tired," she lied.

"God, I hear that." Owen yawned. He did look tired. The man worked hard, and now Molly felt guilty. He'd just wanted to make her dinner, when, in reality, he probably should be the one being cooked for.

Molly recalled her mother always having dinner ready for her father by the time he walked in from work. She used to tell Molly that it was what a good wife did for her hardworking husband. Granted, Owen wasn't her husband, but he was out there busting his ass. God knew her mother had tried to instill the values of being the perfect domestic goddess. What had happened? Molly wasn't the domestic type. She didn't own an apron or a cookbook. She didn't even own a houseplant in fear of killing it. That was why she wasn't married and didn't have any children.

The mood continued to shift to a quieter and more uncomfortable tension until Owen said goodnight. Molly ended up crawling into bed right after Owen left. She wrapped her blanket tightly around her, almost swaddling herself like a newborn. Tomorrow she would need to call Mackenzie and admit defeat. She felt tears starting to stream down her face. Her friends had explained to her that now that she was involved with someone, things would change. Molly had denied that it would. She'd refused to believe it or allow it. So these tears stemmed from the frustration she felt for failing her friends and for not having a backbone. That was how she saw it, anyway, and she didn't like it one bit.

* * * *

"Oh, Molly, it's okay."

"It's not. I told you that I would be there." Molly wiped away some leftover tears that decided to surface after she'd stayed up most of the night crying. She was an emotional train wreck. She was either crying or on the verge of it. *God, am I already hitting menopause?*

"It's not like you're missing out on something important. You were there for me when I needed you."

Her sister's death. They hadn't discussed it since their Vegas trip that now seemed like a distant memory, and it hadn't even been two months ago.

Tiffany jutted out her bottom lip. "I don't get why you're so sad. I feel a little lost here. Wanna clue me in?"

They were eating breakfast at a tiny diner close to Tiffany's place. A hole-in-the-wall place that served the best waffles in all of Seattle.

Mackenzie sighed and stirred her coffee. The cream she'd just added colored the dark brown into a light beige, much too light for Molly's taste. It was like murdering coffee's true personality — watering it down and changing its very purpose. Okay, perhaps she was being a little extreme and sentimental, but this was coffee she was talking about.

"Molly seems to think that somehow by her not hanging out with us tonight, she's becoming subservient or some nonsense. She's concerned she will lose our friendship."

Tiffany still wore a confused expression on her face. "I don't see how you going out with Owen tonight changes our friendship. Even if we never did another *Friendship Friday*, we're your besties forever, Molly. We aren't going anywhere just because you've got Owen now."

"She's right. We're like sisters. I'm thrilled you are finally happy, Molly. You know how much I wanted you to meet the right guy." Mackenzie started to tear up. "And you did."

"And I told you that Owen was the one, didn't I?" Tiffany asked as she popped a small square bite of pure golden and fluffy syrup-drenched perfection.

"You did. But I don't want us to lose this," Molly said, her voice uneven, as she reached across the table and grabbed each of their hands. "You guys are my everything."

"We always will be, but Owen is something special, too." Mackenzie looked away, wiping a stray tear that had fallen.

"He is," Molly said softly.

"Oh, knock it off, you two. Good grief, this isn't anything to be sad about. It's the beginning of something absolutely amazing." Tiffany radiated complete optimism. That was why Molly adored her. She was their little ray of sunshine. "I just want to know which one of us gets to be the maid of honor and to be in the delivery room with you. I also think you should name your firstborn after me — just putting that out there. I'm going to be the cool aunt."

Nothing dried up sad tears quicker than laughter. Molly was relieved to know that her friends were not going to be left behind, not by a long shot. They weren't going to allow it and they would always be her best friends. No relationship, marriage, or anything would change that. They were excited about the future – more than she was. They were already making plans for a nonexistent wedding and children that hadn't even been conceived yet.

They both might be pretty sure of everything, but Molly still had her doubts, even if Tiffany had said Owen was the *one*. How would she really know if she'd met Mr. Right and not Mr. Right Now? But who was she kidding? Of course Owen was Mr. Right. It was the idea of marriage and babies that terrified her. That damn self-doubt was trying to sneak in again.

* * * *

She dug her toes into the sand. Owen was sitting behind her with his arms wrapped around her. Molly had leaned back and was soaking up the moment. He kissed her neck, tenderly whispering some of the loveliest words that Molly had ever heard, and they were all for her.

But nothing had made her smile more that day than when Owen pointed to a large piece of driftwood that looked familiar. Yet all the weathered and sun-stained logs all looked alike to Molly. "There, that one."

"Yeah, it's lovely," Molly replied. She had no idea where he was going with this.

"Yes, it is, but it's the first one that I took a picture of."

Ah, they were discussing photography. She was all ears now.

"Is that the one from your bedroom?"

He nodded, running his hand nervously through his black hair. The sunset was casting a romantic halo above him.

"I love that shot, and the edit you did on it was incredible,

Owen."

"Thanks. Yeah, I took a lot from here. You can't help but want to capture all this beauty."

"Exactly. That's why anywhere I go, I have a camera. It's how I remember everything. I can recall how something tasted or smelled by looking at an old shot I took of it," Molly explained, hoping he would understand that her love for photography ran deep. "It's like this scrapbook of my memories of my life. Without taking them, I think I'd be lost."

He looked away from her and stared at the log. "I get that. Once upon a time, I loved taking pictures."

"Why don't you do it now? I couldn't imagine not having my camera on me. I swear that I'd die if I stopped taking pictures," Molly rambled.

"Yeah, I used to feel like that way, too. But you don't die. You survive." He stood, pulling her up, then turned around and grabbed her hand, leading her away.

She had more questions than answers, but somehow knowing that he'd loved photography as much as she did made her happy.

They got back on the boat. Owen's mood was somber. Molly didn't want to pry even more than she had, but there had to be a reason why he'd stopped taking pictures – a major one.

Once they docked they stayed on the boat for a while longer. The lights from the harbor cast an eerie glow on the murky water.

"What are you doing tomorrow?" Owen asked.

"Um, I'm not sure. Maybe some much-needed grocery shopping."

"That's true. You have nothing in your fridge. I don't know how you survive." Laughter came from him, but it was awkward.

"Takeout." So cooking wasn't one of her finer skills.

"So, no plans then?"

"Hey, I'll have you know that when I go grocery shopping

that also means I'm shopping for coffee. That is a staple I cannot and will not live without," she said playfully.

"So you're free after you pick up some magic beans?"

Molly giggled. "I guess you could say that. Why?"

Owen grabbed her hand, rubbing his thumb in small circles. He seemed to be stalling, but he finally said, "I wanted to take you to meet my parents."

Molly swallowed. *Meet his parents?* She hadn't even told hers about him yet. Only Mackenzie and Tiffany knew about Owen. She had wanted to see where this relationship was headed before Molly told her parents or brother. They had seen her go through enough relationships to know that they usually never worked out. They knew her pattern, and she'd long since decided not to bother them with anymore crummy attempts at a happily ever after. Her family looked at all of her prospective relationships like a joke — that she'd never taken any of her romances seriously and that she was simply playing a game.

Oh crap, Owen and I just leveled up, didn't we?

Chapter Sixteen

"He wants you to meet his parents? Wow, shit just got real, didn't it?" Tiffany said.

Molly nodded. "I think so."

They were sitting on Mackenzie's living room floor. It was still Friday. Granted, it was late, but better late than never to celebrate *Friendship Friday* with her girls.

"I know. I'm a little surprised that he's ready to have you meet his folks." Mackenzie nibbled on a slice of pizza. "But it's a good thing, right?"

Earlier Mackenzie and Tiffany had ordered one with every topping possible and were already hanging out at Mackenzie's place, having their own *Friendship Friday* night together. Molly couldn't help but feel a small stab of jealousy. Molly was sitting cross-legged and reached for a slice, then started picking off the bell peppers and onions. "I'm terrible at meeting parents. I get all nervous and act like an idiot."

"No, you don't," Mackenzie tried to assure her.

"No, I do. Remember Kevin's parents. His mom hated me. Or what about Nick? I think his mom wanted to murder me. Then there was David's dad. He was more interested in me than his son was, and that pissed off his wife." Molly laughed, even though it really hurt knowing that these mothers hadn't liked her. She worked on removing the mushrooms from her pizza and continued, "It's usually the moms that can't stand the thought of me not cooking or being little Miss Betty Crocker for their baby boys."

"So what if you don't cook or act like a fifties housewife. Who the hell cares? As long as you love the guy and are good to him, isn't that enough?" Tiffany asked.

"Nope, I don't think so. That's why we are all single," Molly pointed out, flicking more onion off her pizza slice and onto her paper plate.

"We're single. You aren't," Mackenzie countered playfully. "But I get what you mean. Gideon's mom loved me, so I totally thought she'd be an awesome mother-in-law. Then when we broke off our engagement, I never heard from her again. It's like that was it. She was done with me."

"Well, it would kind of make sense, right? You weren't with her son anymore," Tiffany said.

"I don't know, but I thought we were closer. I even ran into her at the grocery store one time. She was polite, but it felt so weird." Mackenzie frowned.

"Why does he even want me to meet his parents? I mean, I can understand why you met Gideon's. You guys were going to get married, but…"

Mackenzie and Tiffany gave Molly a knowing look.

"He's obviously serious about you, Moll," Mackenzie stated as she stretched her long, pajama-covered legs.

"It's only been a few weeks that we've been dating."

"Yeah, but you got hit with that fish months ago and that's really when all this started," Tiffany explained.

"I suppose you're right."

"Of course we are," Tiffany laughed.

"But gosh, meeting his parents… I'm just not ready yet," Molly whined, pushing her pizza away. She'd lost her appetite. Her stomach had been in knots ever since Owen had asked her to meet his parents at the end of their date.

"Suck it up, cupcake. This is part of it." Mackenzie winked at her and offered to refill her wine.

Molly sighed. "Do you think they drink?"

"Why?" Mackenzie asked as she filled Tiffany's glass.

"Because I have a feeling that's the only way I'm going to survive dinner."

"Oh, stop. You'll be fine. Just be you." Mackenzie smiled

gently at her. "They'll fall in love with you just like Owen did."

"Or offer for them to throw a fish at you," Tiffany teased. "That might be a good ice breaker."

"God, I wonder what they must think. Some clumsy fool that gets clobbered by a flying fish." Molly rolled her eyes, recalling how dumb she must have looked.

"It was his fault, not yours, so they can blame their son, if anything," Tiffany explained. "He could have hit anyone."

"But he hit you," Mackenzie added. "It was fate."

"That's what he said that day."

"Because he knew how rare and odd a thing it was to happen," Mackenzie continued to say. "It was all meant to be, Molly. He knows it and that's why you are meeting his parents. You're the one."

Tiffany reached over and hugged Molly. "Hey, you were the catch of the day. He finally reeled in the best fish in the sea."

* * * *

Her stomach thrashed about. Her nerves were a jumbled mess, and Molly was quiet as Owen drove them to his parents' home.

"It'll be fine. Why are you so nervous?" Owen asked as he steered the car through the narrow streets of a quiet neighborhood far from downtown.

"Because they are your *parents*." *Really? Do I need to explain why?* Meeting anyone's family for the first time was nerve-racking, but it was far worse if you were meeting those of a boyfriend. There was more judgment involved than with just a friend. Scrutiny at its best, there was nothing like being pinned under a microscope for the parents to look for any flaw, any red flags.

"My parents are the nicest people. You'll love them," Owen tried to convince her.

"Of course you think they're nice. They're *your* parents.

I'm not worried about not loving them. It's more about them not liking me," Molly admitted.

"Babe, they know how happy you make me. I've told them. That's all a parent wants for their kid — for them to find happiness."

"I know, but moms want their boys to marry perfect women that can cook, clean and raise perfect little children. I'm not perfect, not in the least."

"That's why I love you. You're *you*. You're talented, beautiful, sexier than hell and, above all else, you make me happy." He looked at her as he parked the car. His eyes spoke volumes. They were filled with love and honesty. Her heart melted a little, if nothing else she'd endure meeting his parents just for him. Molly had a feeling she'd do just about anything he asked if he kept looking at her like that.

But Owen being Owen, he kept up small talk and told her funny stories all the way there, just to keep her from being so scared. As it turned out, though, once she'd entered Owen's parents' home, all her preconceived notions were squashed immediately.

* * * *

She hated being wrong, but in this case she didn't mind it. Molly's sides actually hurt from laughing so hard. They looked through several thick photo albums in his parents' living room. Decades of family celebrations — birthdays, Christmas, Halloween and more — were glued to the yellowing sheets in the books. Molly sat next to his mother as she pointed out the many phases of Owen's life. Owen had inherited his mother's beautiful gray eyes, but he was the spitting image of his father. Sharing memories like that helped Molly feel even more connected to Owen, seeing him as an infant, toddler, a little boy covered in mud, then as an awkward teenager. As a photographer, Molly appreciated his mother giving her the inside glimpse into their family, and she could tell that his mother cherished the photos with all of her heart and was proud to show off her son. Though it was obvious that the woman adored Owen, she seemed quite happy and pleased to meet Molly.

Dinner hadn't been awkward at all. It had been wonderful and delicious and, much to Molly's surprise, it hadn't been his mother who had prepared the dinner but his father. Somehow that made Molly love his mother that much more, especially when she'd admitted to not being very good in the kitchen and that the only reason she hadn't starved to death yet was because of her husband.

Molly could honestly say she'd never been more comfortable or felt more at home in all her life. Owen was right. They were nice people. All her fears were gone and she looked forward to the next dinner.

Saying goodbye was almost difficult. Molly would have gladly spent more time with them, especially going through the family pictures, and his mother assured her there were tons more to look at. Molly couldn't wait.

"See? That wasn't so bad, was it?" Owen opened the passenger side door for her to get in.

Molly stood on the tips of her toes and kissed him. "Nope, it was great."

"I think they really liked you."

"Well, yeah, what is there not to love?" Molly teased as Owen wrapped his arms around her.

"My thoughts exactly."

* * * *

"God, babe," Owen whimpered.

Molly was straddling him, firmly gripping the headboard of her bed. She rocked back and forth, swallowing his thick length entirely inside her and it still wasn't deep enough to satisfy her. She'd already come a few times, and she was inching toward another threshold where an orgasm waited on the other side. She was nearly there, but Owen kept talking. Not that she minded a little communication during sex, but right now she was focused.

"Shh," Molly ordered him as she picked up speed. He was hard and she was wet — the perfect combination. *Almost there.*

Owen's hands tightened on her hips. There was a sheen of light sweat on his bare chest. In actuality, the poor guy had to be spent. They'd lazed around in bed nearly all day, kissing and snuggling, which, of course, always led to Molly needing more.

Molly looked down. Owen's eyes were closed and he almost looked like he was in agony. *Am I hurting him?*

"You okay, babe?" Molly asked.

"I'm close," he managed to say in ragged breaths.

Thank you, God. Me too. Molly picked up her pace and trained her efforts on meeting her goal. The finish line was just ahead, and she could feel the pressure building inside her. She changed her angle just a bit, enough to apply more pressure to her hungry clit. Finally, the wave crashed over her at the same time as Owen groaned and arched up farther into her. She could feel the heat of him coming deep inside her. When they'd both finished, she collapsed onto Owen's chest. The room was quiet except for the pounding in her ears as her heart rate tried resuming a normal beat.

"Should we order a pizza?" Owen finally asked.

"You need more energy for another round?"

"Babe, the gas tank is empty, and I think I'm out of service now," Owen admitted.

As Molly rolled off him, she grabbed his quickly deflating manhood. "I see that. How's your tongue feeling?"

"Fine. Why?" Owen threw her a confused look.

Molly kissed him hard and pulled away with a wink. "Then you're hardly out of service."

They both laughed as Owen brought her back, closer to him.

* * * *

Summer had officially arrived in the Pacific Northwest. The gloomy and rainy days took a vacation during this time of the year. People were out and about everywhere. Seattle came alive in the summer. Everyone was making the most of the short window and that included tons of visitors. The days were longer and felt endless. The sun was staying up far past its winter bedtime now. Molly took advantage of it, scheduling all-day shoots because the lighting was perfect for hours.

Work was going great. Her relationship with Owen was amazing and life was good. They had settled into a nice routine, even including Mackenzie and Tiffany. Mackenzie was now out of school and had invited them all over for game night and dinner and she'd met up with Owen and Molly for lunch. Tiffany had recently invited them over for fondue and they'd all eaten far more cheese than the average human should ever consume. Mackenzie and Tiffany adored Owen, treating him almost like a big brother. Things felt natural, which had been a huge concern of Molly's in the beginning. She was able to put those worries to bed and focus on the happiness that was in front of her.

Owen and Molly had hung out with his parents a few more times, including a day trip on Owen's boat. She found herself growing more attached to them, and she had even met his siblings when they'd come to Seattle to visit. He had a younger brother who looked nothing like him, and a sister, a sweet girl who was just starting her second year in college. Owen and his siblings bickered and teased each other, but anyone could see that they loved each other immensely.

After seeing him with his family and spending time with them herself, Molly had decided it was the right time to have him meet hers. Even that had gone well. Her father and brother were convinced that Owen was the coolest guy ever, and her mother was beyond impressed with him. No real surprise there, though. Owen had the best manners of any guy she'd ever dated or brought home. He'd also come equipped just as he had when he'd met her friends for the first time — flowers, baked goods and his charm, of course.

Molly couldn't believe how smoothly everything was going. She couldn't help but feel like it was going too well, and she kept waiting for the other shoe to drop. *Or could this be how life will go now?* None of her past relationships had been so easy. And the old saying that '*Anything worth having doesn't come easy*' kept taking root in her mind. *Shouldn't this be harder?*

But then Owen had hit her with that one question over dinner had that left her filled with anxiety. She'd kind of been waiting for it to come up, but not this soon. She didn't think they were anywhere near crossing over that weird threshold where one asks the other to move in then the other has to decide if they are willing to leave the security of their home. Apparently, Owen felt that they were ready to cross that bridge and he wanted her to be the one to give up her place.

She'd lived in her apartment for years, since right after she'd started to make a name in the photography business. Sure, it was over-priced, much like her studio, but it was her space. Was she really ready to move into another person's domain? Follow their rules? She'd lived with someone before. Moving in had not been an easy adjustment. Merging her stuff with his had been a disaster. Then she'd tried again with another guy but, this time, she'd had him move in with her. It had ended up feeling more like an invasion than a shared residence. Molly wasn't so sure if moving in together was the right call.

Owen seemed pretty confident that it was the next step for them to take. Molly was barely starting to spend overnights, but moving more than her toothbrush and an extra pair of underwear? Well, that was commitment. It was one thing to be asked to stay the night, but to share their lives under one roof? That was *big*. Would things change between them if she did take the leap of faith?

Mackenzie and Tiffany said she could always keep her

apartment for a couple of months, just in case it didn't work out. They were right. It was a good option, but Owen said it made him feel like she was only one foot in, and he wanted both. *Easy for him to say*. He wasn't having to give up his home, put stuff in storage and try to fit into a space that wasn't his.

Molly sipped her first cup of coffee of the day as her mind toiled with all those thoughts. Things were going so well. Why did Owen have to complicate things? In the back of her mind, she knew it was because it was the next logical step. They were getting serious. She did want that *eventually*, and by now she was pretty sure she loved him more than anything in the world, but they hadn't even discussed marriage at all. Was that part of the game plan? Molly hadn't even told him that she loved him. She hadn't heard him say those three little words either, so she had been waiting to say it. She didn't want to risk being the foolish one. What if he didn't actually *love* her? What if she was only his Mrs. Right Now?

The one thing she knew for certain was that she enjoyed drinking coffee out of her yellow mug with its stupid little chip, and if she decided to move in, it was coming with her. When it came down to it, Molly was a simple woman about some things. Just as long as she had her coffee and her camera, she was good. She closed her eyes and took another sip of her coffee, and told herself, 'just go with it'.

* * * *

Molly sat on the floor of her now-empty apartment. Owen was outside trying to cram more of her stuff into the rented moving truck. Mackenzie and Tiffany had helped her box up her life, and Molly had realized she had way too much stuff. *Who owns that much crap in an apartment that isn't even seven hundred square feet?* The boxes that had just been loaded into the truck would prove that Molly was indeed that person — a hoarder. Not like the 'newspaper towers up to the ceiling' kind of hoarder, but she was just someone who owned far too many trinkets and random things that had no use or real purpose but held sentimental value. They were all packed up now. Mackenzie had helped her throw out and donate a lot of it, too, which made the madness much more bearable.

She was grateful that her friends had stepped in to help. She had been overwhelmed the last several weeks. Moving was stressful. She'd tried to sell a lot of her furniture, but there were things that she couldn't part with. In the back of her mind she kept thinking, *just in case*… Owen was tickled pink and practically humming as he filled the moving truck. He didn't complain once. Owen had even brought help, and Tiffany kept whispering to Molly and Mackenzie about how hot his friends were and why in the hell had Molly been holding out this entire time. Molly hadn't even met those guys until then, but Tiffany was right. These were Owen's strong fisherman buddies, and they were extremely hot. But Molly only had eyes for one, and, to her, he was the sexiest fisherman ever and he was all hers.

Eventually they'd gotten the job done and everyone had dispersed, leaving Molly and Owen to begin the new phase of their life together.

"Home, sweet home," Owen teased as they entered his home after stuffing a storage unit full with her life.

Molly was worn out and more than a little emotional. Even though she'd been bringing some of the more essential stuff over the last couple of weeks, there was something about closing that metal door and putting on padlock on it, kind of like the final nail in the coffin. God, she was overly dramatic.

Owen had made more than enough room for her. He'd practically given up his closet, moving most of his things into the spare room. It had made her feel a little guilty, but he'd sworn he was happy to do it.

He hugged Molly as they stood in the open space that was now also hers. It was home now. Maybe once she added more of her own personality, it would feel more like it. Right now, it felt like she just staying over at Owen's. Then she turned her head and caught sight of a beautiful floral arrangement. Like a burst of summer, cheerful sunflowers of different yellows and oranges were in a vase on the kitchen island. It was thoughtful of him and it warmed her heart.

"Those are beautiful," she said.

"Not nearly as beautiful as what I now have in my house — our house." Owen kissed her and Molly started to feel all the doubts about moving in erase from her mind. There would be perks to living with Owen, this being one of her favorites.

* * * *

Molly woke up a little confused. *Where in the hell am I? This isn't my bed? Oh yeah, it is now.* Owen's arm was draped over her, and Molly snuggled closer to him. The disorientation passed. This did feel wonderful, and she couldn't deny that. It would just take some getting used to but, ultimately, it was the right decision. She could feel it deep down.

"Good morning," Owen whispered. His voice was rough and thick with sleep. He pulled her even closer to him. "That's better."

"It is, isn't it?" She purposely wiggled her bottom against his hard erection.

He moved his hand to cup her breast, squeezing it softly, then running it down her side. It made her shiver and started the heat building deep inside her. They'd slept naked, only because they had been too exhausted to get up and put pajamas on after they had celebrated her moving in with some of the best love-making they'd enjoyed to date. Molly hadn't even realized she'd fallen asleep, but it had been the best kind — deep, coma-like slumber, the type where you don't move or switch positions all night. It had been one of the best sleeps she'd had in a very long time. Waking up in

Owen's arms had been just the icing on the cake.

"How did you sleep?" he asked, as he started to explore more of her body. *Like I can hold a conversation with him touching me like this?*

"Great. You?" she managed when the sudden urge to pee hit her.

"Great, because you were next to me." His hand ventured lower but she had to stop him.

"I gotta pee." Molly bolted out of bed, heading to the adjoining master bathroom.

"Way to kill the mood, babe," he called out.

"Hey, you wanted a live-in girlfriend. Get used to it, buddy."

He laughed.

Yes, this is going to work.

Chapter Seventeen

"I think we got it," Molly said confidently as she snapped another shot. "You know, though... Let's do one more." She wasn't satisfied with the image she'd just peeked at on the tiny screen of her camera. This one had to be perfect. There was no room for error.

It was by far the biggest deal Molly had landed, and in front of her was one the most famous and sought-after models in the industry—Diane Sinclair. She was nearly six feet tall, all legs, and she probably had the best ass Molly had ever seen. Was she jealous of how gorgeous this creature was? Hell, yes. Did she love her attitude? Hell, no. The woman was by far the bitchiest model she'd ever worked with. She was snotty, rude and knew she could get away with just about anything. That made working with her even worse. Molly had to play nice and be on her best behavior. If either Mackenzie or Tiffany had had to deal with this model, they wouldn't have lasted five minutes without telling her off. To say Molly's tongue hurt from biting it was an understatement. She would survive just a few more shots.

The doorbell rang. The model rolled her eyes in annoyance.

"I'm so sorry. Let me just see who that is." Molly scurried quickly to the door, not even putting her camera down, as another ring shot out. *Oh dear Lord, really?*

"I'm coming," Molly yelled as she reached the large double doors. When she opened one, she saw Owen standing there with their usual afternoon coffee. *Crap.* She would have to send him away. Hadn't she told him about this insanely important shoot?

"Hey, babe," Owen said right before he kissed her forehead.

"I'm working. Remember that really, really important client and model I am working with?"

"Was that today?" He shrugged and moved past her. "I'm sorry. I just knew you probably needed coffee and I missed you like crazy." Owen paused to kiss her on top of her head, then headed for the large glass table.

As sweet as it was for him to stop by and to be missing her so badly, she was too irritated with this model to appreciate it. Molly huffed as she shut the door then followed him inside the studio.

Suddenly everything changed. She saw Owen's back grow rigid and he turned around to look at Molly. Confusion, mixed with something else, swirled in his eyes — maybe shock, or was it fear? Molly wasn't quite able to make it out.

"You okay?" Molly asked. Then Owen looked back at the model. The color had drained from his handsome face. Okay, now she was worried. He looked like he'd just seen a ghost.

"Owen?" Diane's aristocratic voice sounded in the studio, loud and arrogant.

They know each other? How is that possible? Now Molly was even more confused.

Owen stood there like a frozen statue. He was still holding the coffee. Molly carefully grabbed her precious caffeine from him. "Babe, you okay?" she whispered as she pried the cardboard drink holder from his hands.

"Um..." Owen tried to speak.

Diane strolled up to them. She towered over Molly, making her feel like an ugly Oompa Loompa. Her professionally manicured hands were on her bony hips. Her head was cocked to the side and she was biting her bottom lip. She looked every bit the cover model posing for an editorial shoot. "It *is* you, Owen. Funny, running into you here."

"Yeah, I could say the same," Owen's voice was deep and it didn't sound happy one bit.

Molly looked at both of them, watching the stand-off and wondering what in the hell she was missing. She was lost.

"Owen, you know Diane?" Molly asked sweetly, being sure not to ruffle the model's feathers.

"Yep, I sure do, but it was a long time ago." His gaze was fixed on Diane. Neither of them moved and Molly started to feel uneasy.

"It was a *very* long time ago. Almost ancient history, right?" Diane laughed. It was more of a cackle and her lips bared her flawless teeth, stark white against the cherry-red-stained lips.

Owen's eyebrows furrowed and he glared at Diane. Molly could feel the anger and hate coming from him. This was not the Owen she knew and loved. *Who is this guy?*

Finally, Molly had enough of feeling out of the loop and asked, "Sorry, but how do you guys know each other?"

Diane whipped around to look at Molly, her blonde waves sweeping across her thin, tan shoulders as she said, "He's my husband."

* * * *

Molly's eyes hurt. They were red, swollen and raw, just like she felt inside. Well, gutted was a more accurate description. She was in Mackenzie's arms. Tiffany was patting her back and whispering that everything would be okay. *How can it be?* Owen had failed to mention that he'd been married — or, rather, that he was still married. That was one of those major topics that should have come up, at least after the first date and most definitely before he'd invited her to meet his parents or have her move in. *How could he not tell me?*

"Wow," Mackenzie kept repeating. She was in shock. Hell, they all were.

"I can't believe he didn't say anything about her." More tears poured from her. It was heartbreaking.

This was the other shoe, the thing she'd been waiting

for. She had known everything was too good to be true. Of course, some sort of shady shit had to go down, because that was Molly's luck. The universe hated her. It was that simple. She'd finally been happy. Living with Owen had proved to be far better than she could have imagined. Stupid things like sitting and watching television were better with him—cooking together, cleaning the house together and sleeping together. The thoughts of marriage had been circulating through her mind the last few days. Even Owen had joked and called her *wifey*. Thinking about that now made her furious.

It was very clear to Molly. They had been playing house. That was all it had been.

Molly's heart squeezed. She was so broken.

But it appeared her friends weren't going to allow her to stay that way.

"Get up. We're going out," Mackenzie announced as she pulled the comforter off Molly. Molly tried to yank it back. She wanted to hide back inside her cocoon. The outside world had no appeal.

"Tiffany, a little help, please," Mackenzie yelled.

Molly had taken residence up in Mackenzie's guest room for the past two days. Tiffany had come over that afternoon. *Is it afternoon?* Molly didn't know or care.

She could hear Tiffany enter the room. "Molly, come on, love. You gotta get up."

"Nope, I actually don't. Thanks," Molly argued.

"We are going out. We need alcohol, and you need a shower," Mackenzie stated firmly.

"Can't we just get drunk here?" Molly offered.

"No," Tiffany and Mackenzie said in unison.

"I don't want to go anywhere. Please don't make me," Molly begged, but knew it fell on deaf ears.

A telephone was ringing in the other room and Mackenzie set off to answer it, but she gave Molly a look, telling her to get her ass up now.

Moments later Mackenzie returned, wearing a sour

expression on her face.

"What's wrong?"

"Nothing. It was Owen, calling for you *again*. Moll, before I say anything else, did you talk to him at all after you found out?"

"She didn't have to, Mackenzie. Owen lied to her," Tiffany quickly defended her.

Lied was a strong word, but saying he'd withheld information seemed far too nice. It had been, and still was, easier to go with *liar*.

"Well, according to him, you didn't even let him explain," Mackenzie said.

"Screw him, Mackenzie. Do *not* defend his ass. He broke her heart. There's nothing more to discuss. He didn't tell her he was married. I'm sorry, but that's not okay with me," Tiffany spat. She'd joined Molly on the bed and was prepared to face off with Mackenzie, who stood inside the room with her arms across her chest.

"Molly, do you love Owen? Yes or no?"

Molly still did, but she was furious with him. She didn't answer Mackenzie because they all knew the truth. She hadn't just fallen out of love with Owen, even when it felt like he'd chopped her heart in half, leaving it splintered and ruined.

"You know the answer. Forget it." She threw her hands up in the air and stomped out of the room, leaving Molly and Tiffany.

Tiffany exhaled loudly. "I support you, no matter what. You know that. But did Owen explain what the hell was the deal?"

Molly shook her head.

"Why the hell not?"

"Because I didn't give him a chance," Molly admitted softly.

Tiffany hugged her. "Eeww. Mackenzie's right. You do need to shower," Tiffany teased, causing Molly to laugh through the steady stream of tears that were now falling.

She was still crying when she threw back the comforter and headed to the bathroom, resigned to her watery fate. She'd managed to stop by the time she got back. Fortunately — or unfortunately, Molly wasn't sure — her friends were both waiting for her.

Mackenzie brushed Molly's clean and partially wet hair while she sat like a bump on a log. Tiffany insisted they should go out, and she was applying an ample amount of concealer and eye makeup on Molly to hide the puffy and gross result of crying for two days. Molly was not the least bit interested in venturing outside. The thought of interacting with people held little appeal, but she would happily consume more adult beverages.

Molly lifted her glass. The contents were simple vodka and orange juice. The screwdriver was helping her mood considerably. She downed the last little bit and was sad it was gone. Who was she kidding? She was just plain sad in general. Everything was shit. Alcohol was only making that clearer.

"You know, I really thought about marrying him, and to think I couldn't, even if I'd wanted to," Molly commented as Tiffany took her empty cup.

"No more discussing Owen."

"She needs to, Tiffany. Well, what she really needs to do is to call him," Mackenzie said as she ran the hot hair straightener through Molly's now-dry brown locks.

"There's time for that later. Right now she needs to forget her troubles."

Molly didn't think all the drinks in the world could make her forget. That was all she'd been doing — thinking, lots and lots of it. And as sick of it as she was, she knew she was going to continue to think about Owen until she did speak to him.

"Can you make me another screwdriver, Tiffany?" Molly asked. She knew she wouldn't be able to dull her thinking, but she might as well numb the hurt.

She didn't know how many drinks that would take, but

as they went out of the door, she vowed to find out. Several bars later, she knew it was impossible.

"God, I miss him," Molly slurred. The alcohol hadn't helped. It had only made things worse. Now she was crooning about her true love. Mackenzie looked annoyed and Tiffany only pretended to listen.

They had made the bar crawl and were now sitting in one that was about to close. They'd called a cab and when it arrived, they would soon be home.

"I know you do. I hate to admit it, but Mackenzie's right."

Mackenzie perked up at the sound of her voice. "Really? Tell us more about this incredible creature known as Mackenzie."

They all laughed.

"Molly needs to call Owen. How else is she going to finally stop talking about him? I don't know about you, but I'm kinda over it." Tiffany sucked more rum through her straw and winked at Molly.

"I'm sorry that I'm so annoying."

"Yeah, you are a little," Tiffany agreed. Mackenzie playfully slapped her to hush.

"Molly, babe, you're hurting. You finally found the right guy and you feel betrayed. But you need to call him. Trust this old girl, okay?"

Molly nodded. Mackenzie never steered her wrong. She only wanted to the best for her. Tiffany had her back, no matter if Molly was in the right or wrong. She was the ride and die kind of friend. Molly was lucky to have these women in her corner. No matter what happened with Owen, she'd always have them.

* * * *

Molly tried to peel her eyes open when she heard people talking in the other room. The light noise had woken her up. She tried burrowing farther into her comforter, but she knew there was no escape. Then she heard his distinct laugh. *What the hell is Owen doing here?*

She waited and listened. Sure enough, it was him. Molly tried to gather her wits, despite having a killer hangover, and she got out of bed. She didn't care if she looked like death warmed over. She wanted to know why he was there and why Mackenzie hadn't gotten rid of him yet.

Mackenzie's eyes grew wide when Molly shuffled into the living room. There on the couch sat Owen and another guy, the bouncer from Vegas. Molly froze. *Crap.* Then she spun around fast and darted off into the bathroom.

Mackenzie followed her and tapped on the door. "Molly, can I come in?" Molly opened the door and Mackenzie slipped through.

Molly sat on the edge of the tub, running her fingers like mad through her tangled hair. "Why didn't you wake me up or tell me people were here?" Molly was seething mad. "I look like hell, Mackenzie."

"You don't look that awful. They just showed up—both of them at the same time. What was I supposed to do?" Mackenzie grabbed a washcloth, ran it under warm water then handed it to Molly.

"I don't know. Friggin' warn me before I came out looking like this? Especially that it wasn't just Owen."

Mackenzie sighed.

"What does he want?"

"Owen's here for you," Mackenzie started to answer.

"Not him, the bouncer dude."

Mackenzie blushed. "Well, he and I have been texting and he wanted to surprise me, I guess. He had some business in Seattle and decided to stop by."

"Well, isn't that sweet?" Molly stuck her finger down her throat.

"Stop. Just because you are having love troubles doesn't mean I can't enjoy a little romance."

"Whatever. So what does Owen want? Did he say anything?"

"Not too much, because Jason came around the same

time. But Owen looks terrible. You guys really do make quite the pair," Mackenzie teased.

"We aren't a pair anymore. Good. I'm glad he looks like a wreck." Molly had lied. She wasn't happy that he was suffering. She wanted nothing more than to run out there, hug him and beg him to tell her it was all some dumb mistake.

"Moll, it's going to be okay, but you need to talk to Owen."

"Please, not now. I feel like shit and look it." She felt queasy. The night's beverages were ready to pay her a visit.

"Seriously? You don't want me to send him in?"

"Please, no. I just can't right now."

Mackenzie nodded. She understood. She might not agree with Molly, but she clearly understood. Mackenzie left the bathroom and Molly purged the night's entertainment until she was empty.

* * * *

"Do you think I should sell my studio?" Molly asked as she and Mackenzie drank coffee in the sunny dining room the next morning.

"Why in God's name would you do that?" Mackenzie held up a green jumbo-sized mug. That woman loved her coffee almost as much as she did—at least, in terms of quantity. She still butchered it with too much cream and sugar.

"Because it's like I can't even go back in there."

"Oh, stop. I could understand if he was screwing someone in there. This is not the same thing and that is your special place, so knock it off."

"You don't see how the environment is now tainted?" Molly lifted a mug that was most certainly not her favorite yellow one, but it had Van Gogh's painting, Starry Night, covering every inch of it, so that made it kind of cool. Her poor mug was being held captive in the fortress where she had no intention of ever returning.

"It's not. You still need to talk to him."

"There's nothing to discuss," Molly argued softly.

"Okay, that's it. Yesterday morning when he showed up here, you were too sick and scared to deal with it. Today, you will. I am tired of you moping around here and belly-aching about him. Thinking about selling your studio... Have you lost your shit? Because you are about to make me lose mine," Mackenzie nearly shouted in frustration. "This is why we are not roommates. You drive me crazy."

"Oh, and you're a peach to live with?" Molly rolled her eyes. Maybe she was overreacting a tad. Mackenzie was right on so many levels and Molly hated that. Now she understood why Tiffany always got upset. It sucked having someone always giving advice and it always being right. "Fine," she relented. "I'll call him."

"Thank God." Mackenzie got up, put her mug in the sink then went into her bedroom.

Wow, is Mackenzie really that upset with me? Molly finished her coffee then sulked in the room she had deemed as hers. It had nothing of hers in it. All that she owned was either at Owen's or in some stupid storage unit.

She gazed at her cell phone. She procrastinated, fiddling with some images in the photo gallery. *Why am I stalling? Won't it be better to just get it over with?*

Molly swallowed back the lump that was forming, along with torrent of nausea, that swam in her belly. She dialed his number.

"Molly," Owen answered on the third ring. "Please don't hang up, babe."

The sound of his voice was torture. God, she missed him, but she couldn't bring herself to speak. No words wanted to come out of her mouth.

"Before you hang up, please, just let me explain. Can we grab dinner or can I come over? Please, sweetheart, please," Owen begged.

"Okay," was all she could manage.

"Okay? Like come over or go out — or just talk right now?"

When she finally found her voice, she said, "I don't know,

Owen."

"Babe, I know you're upset and you have every right to be, but I can explain everything."

"Can you? Because it seems pretty cut and dried. You're married." Molly felt herself grow angry.

"Babe, I'm not. I *was* married — past tense. I'm divorced," Owen explained.

"But Diane said you were her husband." Molly was confused. *Is he or isn't he married?*

"Yeah, she loves to say that to get under my skin. Trust me. We can't stand one another, and I think once she realized you were my girlfriend, she wanted to hurt not only me, but you, too."

"So, wait. You were married, but you still never told me about it. Why?"

"I don't know. I guess I never thought about it. It was so long ago, and it is something I try to block out of my memory, to be honest."

She could tell he wasn't lying. There had been no malicious intent on his part. "I still wish you had said something."

"You're right. I should have. It never crossed my mind. I was only focused on us, Molly. You bring so much happiness into my life. That's all I could see. It's like I didn't even have a past before I met you, that I could only see our future and nothing else mattered."

"But marriage is a big effing deal. How could you just forget that you were married, once upon a time?" Molly's voice cracked, strained under the pressures of the volume of hurt she'd been holding in.

She heard him release a heavy sigh. "It was a long time ago, way before she was some big-time model and back when I thought that I wanted to be a big deal, too. I had my moment in the spotlight and I didn't like it, but she did. We were so young and stupid. I thought I knew what love was, but I never experienced the real thing until I met you, sweetheart."

Tears started to run down Molly's cheeks. "Oh, Owen,"

she whimpered.

"I'm sorry. I never meant to hurt you. It kills me knowing I caused you any kind of pain." He paused and there was silence. "I love you, Molly."

Just like that, once he said them, those three little words mended her broken and savagely torn heart. It made mountains move and birds sing. It was what she'd longed to hear but, more importantly, what she'd needed to hear.

* * * *

Molly had agreed Owen could pick her up from Mackenzie's house. She was pacing the living room waiting for him. Mackenzie sat on the couch, watching her go back and forth.

"Stop pacing. You're making me dizzy," Mackenzie ordered.

Molly stopped for a moment. "Do you think he's telling the truth? I didn't get suckered again, right?"

Mackenzie gave her a closed-lipped smile. "Molly, he told me when he called here, but it wasn't my place to tell you. I kept telling you to talk to him. You know how women can be vicious bitches. That stupid model saw that he'd moved on, and she wanted to hurt both of you. If she knew how much pain she caused you guys, she'd probably be thrilled."

"God, how evil is that, though? Who in the hell does that?"

Mackenzie shook her head and said, "Bitter bitches like that. You can't let her have that victory. Owen is *your* man now, and you need to fight for your happiness."

"You're right. He *is* mine. I love him so much, Mackenzie," Molly exclaimed as she collapsed on the couch next to her best friend.

"I know you do. That's why you can't just give up so easily. Should he have mentioned that he was divorced? Yes, he should have. Do I think he avoided telling you on purpose? No, not at all."

"God, Mac, why didn't I let him explain? I have been in agony for days."

"Not just you," Mackenzie joked and made a wide-eyed expression.

"You loved having me stay with you. Don't even try to deny it."

Mackenzie shrugged. "I like you better when you're in your own home."

"Whatever."

There was a knock at the door, and Molly felt fluttering inside her. She took a deep breath, trying to tame it.

Mackenzie eyed curiously. "Butterflies?" she asked.

Molly nodded.

"Good. Once you quit having those, it's over. You should be with a man that makes you feel like that. Gid used to give me the butterflies, sometimes just by the way he would look at me or smile." Mackenzie had the faraway look she often got when she talked about Gideon. Molly wished things would have gone differently for them.

"So, what about Jason? Any butterflies there?" Molly asked as Mackenzie went to answer the door.

Mackenzie smiled and replied, "There might be a few."

Mackenzie opened the door, moving to the side to let Owen in. The moment Owen saw Molly, he gathered her in his arms and hugged her. There was no proceeding with caution or walking on eggshells in case she was still upset. Molly melted against him. She was back where she belonged, in the arms of a man she loved with all of her flawed, over-caffeinated and quirky self.

He finally let her go long enough for them to bid a hasty farewell to Mackenzie. She was with Owen, where she belonged. But now that they were driving, the car ride was quiet. Owen held Molly's hand. Molly sat and reflected on everything they had been through. She watched the sun, a red ball floating above the Puget Sound. The sky was a swirl of sherbet colors, raspberry and orange. Violet clouds looked like cotton candy that was stretched across the open air. God, it was a beautiful evening.

She hadn't even been paying attention to where Owen was driving them. Molly was just happy to be sharing the same oxygen with him, being in close quarters, knowing that he was next to her. She had missed him terribly and, even in the silence, she was content.

They parked near Pike Place. The smell of the raw ocean water floated on the gentle summer evening breeze. The waterfront was mildly crowded. People were taking pictures of the gorgeous sunset. Molly had forgotten her camera but was mentally snapping pictures.

"It's lovely, isn't it?" she asked Owen, as he held her hand and led her toward the market.

"Not nearly as lovely as you, but it's pretty nice."

"I wish I had my camera." Molly absorbed all the elements that surrounded her—the cries of hungry seagulls, the laughter and chatter of people just living and the warmth of the air as it kissed her bare shoulders. The light wind whispered in her ear and played with her hair that was swinging loosely. Summer evenings in Seattle were spectacular. She loved her city and, seeing the stunning view of the sun reflecting off the boats and water, she knew that there was no way she could have ever sold her studio.

Molly felt Owen tugging her along, but she was filled with so much peace and delight that she hadn't noticed they were already entering the market. Not as many people were there. Molly cringed as Owen led her past the nasty rainbow of the famed gum wall—gross, just plain gross. *And Portland thinks they're the weirdos.*

Owen stopped. They now stood by the fish market. It was closed for the day, and no one was around. Molly knew the significance of them being there. It was where fate had stepped in and gifted them each other. Molly's chest heaved with emotion. Everything hit her all at once. Her body shook and tears burned her eyes. Owen scooped her up, bringing her to him. She felt secure in his arms and was surprised when he released her suddenly. She heard Owen inhale deeply and watched as he got down on one knee.

Oh God.

He took her hands in his and never broke eye contact. They were a soft sweater gray in the light of the shadowy evening. She could swim in those soul-baring eyes forever.

"Molly, you know why we're here. This is where fate threw us together," he started to explain.

"No, it's where you threw a fish at me—but same difference," Molly interrupted, causing them both to laugh.

Owen wiped a stray tear from the corner of his eye as he continued. "Molly, you are nothing I expected but everything I wanted. I couldn't have dreamed up a better person I'd want to spend the rest of my life with." He withdrew one hand from her and reached into his pocket. "I have been carrying this around for a while now, waiting for just the right time." He exposed a small fish-shaped velvet box. "I knew the moment that I had you in my arms that I never wanted to let you go. That was the day I first met you."

Molly's chest tightened. The words that were coming from his soul entered her like a ray of light, shooting beams of brightness, illuminating every dark corner where doubt had lived. Indecision fled as he opened the box and revealed the most gorgeous ring, a soft pink pearl in a crown of diamonds. But it was more than just the ring that he offered. "I can't live another moment without knowing you will be in my life forever. Please say you'll marry me?" Owen asked, his gray eyes shiny with tears.

"Or what, you'll hit me with another fish?"

"You and those damn jokes." Owen wiped the soft creases of his eyes again. "That's why I love you, Molly. Even during the most serious of times, you manage to make me laugh. It's like your superpower or something."

The truth was Molly didn't know how to act when she was nervous and she tended to get a little goofy.

Molly reached for Owen's hands and yanked him up.

He wrapped his arms around her, clutching the ring in his palm. "So whaddya say. Wanna marry this smelly ole fisherman?"

"You mean sail off into the sunset with the man I love with all my heart, even though he's been known to throw a fish at me?"

"One fish, one time, but yeah, that guy."

"Then yes, I do."

Owen stared at her as if he didn't believe she was real, that she was a figment of his imagination or a siren from the sea. He grabbed her hand and slipped on the ring, then kissed her more tenderly than she had ever been kissed before. It formed a bond that had been there since their first meeting, but today it burned through to her core. She could feel it searing her soul, marking her as his forever.

Not to be outdone, Molly hooked her arms around his neck, deepening the kiss. Now she had marked him as hers. They were one now and Molly couldn't be happier.

Well, she could be, if only she had her camera to capture the moment.

More books from
Totally Bound Publishing

667 WAYS TO F*CK
UP MY Life

Lucy Woodhull

Sometimes, there's nowhere to go but f*ck up

*Sometimes, there's nowhere to go but f*ck up…*

STACEY SOLOMON

BEST THINGS IN LIFE

Walk on By

Parties...check
Gay best friend...check
Happiness...?

Book one in the Best Things in Life series by Stacey Solomon

Ever since Charlotte Taylor was a little girl she's wanted fame and fortune. She sings with the voice of an angel and is soon plucked out of obscurity and launched into the limelight as the overnight sensation 'Lola'.

Experience has shown Paige Wilder that relationships end badly, so she's not looking for another. That is, until she meets Jude Martin.

If you must look back, only look at the best!

About the Author

Gloria Herrmann

Gloria Herrmann is a contemporary romance author living in beautiful eastern Washington. All of her books have been set in Washington and she is proud to show readers how gorgeous her state is.

An avid reader and lover of words, becoming an author has been a dream come true for her. She still pinches herself all the time and wonders how she got so lucky.

Gloria remembers her mom giving her a paperback romance novel when she was a teenager. It was a pretty exciting book, filled with suspense, love, and an overall excellent storyline. That was it. She was hooked. Gloria began to devour these romance stories that varied over the years from sweet to sultry, consuming thousands of books and stories. Each time she finished reading a novel, the desire to write her own grew stronger. As ideas for books were born, her go to genre was contemporary romance. Why romance? She simply loves it. That's why she writes it. What is there not to love about falling in love and finding that special person to share your life with? Who doesn't wish for a little passion, butterflies fluttering in your stomach, and that happily ever after? In Gloria's eyes, that's what it's all about.

Gloria Herrmann loves to hear from readers. You can find contact information, website details and an author profile page at https://www.totallybound.com/

Home of Erotic Romance